In 1982 Grace McIntyre is living an isolated existence as a reluctant expatriate in Western Kenya with her tea planter husband and their young son. She has made no attempt to integrate with the Africans around her. Her horizons begin to widen when she employs a new gardener, Isaac, who has had to leave the university in Nairobi in unexplained circumstances, which Grace learns of over time. Through Isaac, Grace is introduced to a Kenya, and its people, she hadn't met before, and comes to appreciate their embedded values and ways of life. Through learning about them, she learns much about herself.

Over the course of three months the relationship between Grace and Isaac grows closer, but it is set against growing political unrest in the country, and, when Grace learns that Isaac is at the very heart of the subversion, she becomes unwittingly drawn into it. Things reach a climax in an abortive attempt to overthrow the government in a coup, and Grace is witness to the increasingly random violence that follows. She then has to decide between helping a desperate Isaac escape these reprisals, or abandoning him to take his own chances. Resolving this conflict is the biggest decision of her life.

2

The Charcoal Burners

A novel by

Kate Cooper

4

Chapter One

Grace wakes to an unmistakeable drumming. The frantic beating of thousands of tiny wings as the beetles in the roof rafters above her head struggle to escape the relentless onslaught of safari ants. They'll be swarming through the bore holes that have been chewed out, devouring everything that crosses their path. The beetles make such a noise in their panic to escape that they may as well be screaming. Grace was terribly upset the first time she heard them. She could picture them up there, fat bodies squashed together in the holes while the ants surged over them, biting and stinging. Used only to the gentle drone of bees on a summer's day at home, Grace didn't know before she came to Kenya that insects could make such a sound, broadcasting their terror by their thrashing and squirming. There were a lot of things she hadn't known six months ago.

She fishes around in the drawer by the bed for a pair of thick socks, and pulls them onto her feet before she gets up and pads across the concrete floor to check on Tom. He is still asleep, flat on his stomach, Postman Pat covered limbs sprawled wide on top of the covers, in the complete abandon only small children can achieve. One arm flops over the side of his bed, fingers grazing the floor, and Grace tucks it safely back under his pillow. She's already learnt to her cost that soft skin like his is a magnet for the ants if they get into his room. She makes sure his bed legs are firmly anchored in their saucers of Doom powder, then carries on down the corridor to the kitchen.

George is already up, making tea. He is always up early here. He says he likes to catch that brief moment when night turns to dawn at the equator, but Grace thinks he just can't wait to get on with his day, he is so happy here.

'Ants,' she says unnecessarily.

'Don't think they'll come into the house this time. Think we've got away with it.'

He nods towards the window as he speaks, and when Grace crosses the floor to stand next to him, she can see the thick black trail of ants crawling out from under the eaves and marching down the trunk of the yellow poinsettia just beside it. The trail ploughs through the flower beds and patch of grass in front of the house on its way towards the field beyond their compound. The ants' unswerving determination to follow their chosen route never fails to amaze her.

'I've been over to the village,' George tells her. 'Got fresh *mandazi* for breakfast.'

She moves over to the table and fishes in the brown paper bag lying on it, debates for a few seconds, and finally picks out the smallest pastry, still warm. She didn't think she'd regularly be eating fatty doughnuts for breakfast a few months ago either. George pours tea and pushes a cup to her across the table.

'Any plans for today?' he asks. Grace eyes him, suspicious of any touch of irony, but it seems a genuine enquiry. Does he really have no idea how mind-numbingly boring and uneventful her days in this godforsaken place are? How the six months might have been six years for all she knew? Apparently not.

'Esther's bringing a boy in to see if he'll do as a *shamba* boy, to help with the garden. Probably one of the extended family, someone they can't afford to send to school. How much are we going to pay him? We don't need someone every day, do we?'

'Depends on what you want him to do. See what he'll do for a hundred bob a month. Couple of days a week probably, I'll trust your judgement.' George stands up and brushes crumbs off the front of his shirt. He goes through to the back of the house and re-emerges with his briefcase and a pile of marked homework. 'Got to dash, staff meeting this morning. Tom's not awake yet, say goodbye from me.' He leans to kiss her and she feels his breath brush her cheek.

'Well,' thinks Grace, 'Another exciting day to get through. Lucky me.' She puts the dirty dishes in the sink, ready for Esther to see to when she starts work at eight o'clock.

She is relieved to find there is water flowing from the taps when she goes into the bathroom. She turns them on full, to clear the brown residue out the pipes, and when the water runs as clear as it is ever likely to, puts the too-small plug in the basin and tries to wash before the water seeps slowly down the drain. Back in her bedroom, she pulls on a cotton dress, takes off the thick socks and replaces them with rubber flip-flops. She knows the African teachers at the school disapprove of her wearing them, 'bathroom shoes' they call them, but she doesn't care. She pulls back the thin curtains and opens the window wide. In the Chebeles' garden next door the jacaranda is just bursting into life, fragrant flowers opening along the branches, that in a week or two will form a vast purple canopy. Everything else is just the same as it was the day before. Then she goes to wake up Tom, if only for the company.

'Come on, lazybones. Time to wake up.' She strokes his back gently and he makes little snuffling noises. She swaps the stroking for tickling the back of his neck and the downy skin below his ears, and the sleepy snuffles are replaces by giggles of delight. She doesn't understand how he can wake up so happy every day. Are all children like that, she wonders, or has he inherited his father's sunny disposition? Rudimentary washing and careful tooth brushing seen to, she helps him dress quickly. She peals the Postman Pat pyjama top over his head and lets him choose his favourite T-shirt, so Jess the cat is replaced by Mr. Tickle's long orange arms winding themselves around his little body. It is a good choice.

The sound of the outside door being opened signals the arrival of Esther, prompt as usual. Like every white or Asian family here, and the African ones who can afford it, Grace and George employ a servant to help in the house. Help, in this case, means doing everything except the cooking. Grace has to have something to do. Esther is their housegirl, but Grace can never bring herself to call her that, it sounds so demeaning. If nothing else, the woman is at least fifteen years older than she, if not more. Esther speaks a little English, knows how to cope with the odd ways of expatriates, doesn't steal and works hard. And she loves Tom. Grace and George pay her twice the normal rate, and are soundly criticised for it. After all, it wouldn't do to set a precedent. Grace remembers the would-be garden boy will be with her this morning, so she gathers Tom up in her arms and hurries back to the kitchen.

Esther is already busy with their breakfast things, but stops what she is doing and wipes her hands on the tea towel when she hears Grace come in.

'The boy outside. Isaac. For the *shamba*. I breakfast Tom.'

Grace hands him over and opens the door. A little way off, observing the rows of pitiful maize plants she and George are trying to grow, the *shamba* boy stands with his back to her. She guesses from his height that he is a Kalenjin, a local. Some of the boys in the school are taller than George; it is no wonder they are such good runners.

'Isaac?' she calls.

He turns and comes loping back to the house with easy strides, relaxed and confident. He smiles broadly and holds out his hand, sure she will take it.

'Mrs. McIntyre. I am Isaac Kithu.' His voice is deep and barely accented. Grace notices he is wearing good shoes and a clean shirt, not usual for house and garden boys. She is perplexed. He isn't what she has been expecting at all. She doesn't think he'll be happy with a hundred shillings a month. She isn't sure he looks as if he's ever mowed a lawn in his life, or hoed weeds, and the hand he holds out is certainly not roughened and calloused. Where on earth has Esther found him? All Grace knows for sure is, he is not a boy.

Chapter Two

Grace is right. Isaac is not a gardener. She finds out from Esther that he is – was – a student at the university in Nairobi. She cannot exactly interpret from Esther's fractured sentences why he is here, but gathers it's something to do with the university being closed. It seems a strange state of affairs, but she can believe anything of Kenya.

Despite her misgivings, he certainly knows how to work. He arrives at the house before Esther, a *panga* held loosely in his hand, and works steadily throughout the morning, barely stopping for the chai Esther makes when Grace has her coffee. Grace, watching him now from the front porch, sees the *panga* moving back and forth in long sweeping arcs as Isaac attacks the overgrown grass. Whenever his arm scythes up to the right, the *panga* glints in the glare of the sun, reflecting sparkling light, and Grace sees bright golden patches dancing over the surrounding bushes until the down stroke snuffs them out.

Isaac has been working steadily on clearing the large area in front of the bungalow for two days, and Grace thinks he'll finish it today. Then she might ask him what to do about the maize. George stops and speaks to him on his way out every day, but Grace has barely exchanged a word with him so far. There is something about him that unnerves her. Looking at the piles of cut grass turning to hay in front of her, Grace goes down the steps and gets as close as she dares. She is careful to stay well away from the sharp blade.

'We've got a rake, when you've finished cutting.' She has to wait for him to complete the row he is working on before he stands up. 'Are there any other tools you need, or do you have your own?' She knows it sounds stupid as she says it.

'I just need the *panga* and a *jembe.* Have you got one?' He bends and carries on, moving steadily, making his own rhythm.

'If I knew what it was, I might have.' Grace has to raise her voice for him to hear her. She doesn't like talking to his back.

'For hoeing.' He doesn't stop what he is doing to answer her.

Grace has seen the Chebeles' *shamba* boy using a tool with a heavy, broad blade on a short handle when he digs their bean patch. That must be what he means.

'We can do better than that,' she calls. 'The shop in Eldoret sells proper long handled hoes. Much better. No bending.'

'Not strong enough. The ground gets too hard; too many stones.' Isaac finishes the last row and stands up. 'You Europeans always think you know best. Believe me, a *jembe* will be fine. I'll bring one with me next time.' Grace thinks he is laughing at her.

He pulls a rag from his pocket and wipes the blade clean.

'But the rake will be very useful, thank you. Show me where you keep it, and I'll do that before I go home. I can stay later today.'

Grace turns her back on him and strides round the house, assuming he is following. In the corner of their compound is an old brick building, a sort of hut, that Grace and George have stored their boxes in, along with a few bits they've brought out with them. Grace unlocks the flimsy padlock. The rake is hanging on a nail.

'We've got this storeroom,' she tells Isaac. 'I can let you have a key.'

'You know this is a house, don't you, Mrs. McIntyre, not a storeroom? Servants' quarters. You're lucky no-one's broken the lock and moved in. You need a much stronger lock than this.'

'No-one could live here.' Grace is shocked at the thought. 'There's no light or water. It's filthy. Don't be ridiculous.'

'I'm not ridiculous, Mrs. McIntyre. I'm perfectly serious. Do you think the people in the village have water and electricity? No, trust me. A building like this would be a godsend. A whole family would be happy here; five, six people. I can't imagine how many would fit in your house.'

Isaac reaches past her and takes down the rake, testing its tines with his thumb and rubbing at some rust that is discolouring the metal.

'Don't forget about the lock, Mrs. McIntyre.'

Grace feels colour flushing up from her neck to her cheeks. He isn't laughing at her, he is practically telling her off; patronising her. Who does he think he is talking to? He might have been at university once, but he should remember he is no more than a servant now.

'If it's servants' quarters, it'll suit you then. You move in if you think it's so wonderful,' she snaps.

13

She leaves him standing there and rushes back indoors. She doesn't see the look he gives her.

Chapter Three

The afternoons are long for Grace. George dashes in at midday and eats whatever she puts in front of him. He has a rough and tumble with Tom and reads him a story, Burglar Bill is the current favourite, and then he's gone again in no time. Esther goes home after she's washed up the lunch things, and, if Tom has a nap, as he still does sometimes, the house is silent. There's no television, and the radio they brought out is useless. They hadn't thought about what they needed when they bought it, just took the word of the man in Curry's, a big mistake. They can't pick up the World Service clearly, the signal fades in and out, and the radio merely crackles most of the time. Sometimes she puts the stereo on, as loud as she dares, Led Zeppelin or Blondie, and dances round the living room like a mad woman, but thinking about clubs and parties and friends only makes her feel more isolated.

'If we hadn't come to Kenya,' Grace thinks, 'I'd be back at work by now, in the library, cataloguing reference books.' There was always someone to talk to and laugh with, staff or customers. That's where she met George, when he was a research student. Grace hasn't met anyone here to have a joke with. Nobody to share her secrets.

She sighs. She is feeling sorry for herself. To cheer herself up, she decides that she'll go shopping. Eldoret is about forty minutes away and every so often they drive in to stock up in one of the supermarkets. Well, they are called supermarkets, but Grace thinks they are more like upmarket corner shops. If she says that to George, of course, he gives her that look of his, that 'what are you on about?' look and reminds her she is in Africa, for goodness sake, not Canterbury. As if she needed telling.

Approaching the outskirts of Eldoret she has to slow down for the road check. Policemen, armed with rifles slung casually over their shoulders, wave them through with the most cursory of glances, and Tom cheerfully waves back. Once, Grace was quite intimidated to see armed police on the streets, but now she doesn't bat an eyelid. After all, they have them in lots of places these days, she reasons with herself. For all she knows, they'll be patrolling the streets of Kent when they get home.

Awar's is on the first corner of the main street, and Grace can see an empty parking space right outside. She pulls in, opposite Kip Keino's sports store and the stationery shop, and anchors Tom in one of Awar's small trolleys, to stop him running amok among the tins and jars.

Mr. Awar is hovering just inside his door, his customary position. He wears a spotless white shirt and has turned its cuffs back in neat and exact folds so Grace can see the beautiful gold watch on his wrist. She can't decide if it is the genuine article or a cheap Nairobi copy. He smiles and pushes his round glasses on top of his head, where they perch like a second pair of eyes.

'Good day, Madam. Welcome, welcome. We are pleased to see you this afternoon.' He holds up a finger and moves to the counter, lifting the flap and sliding behind it smoothly. 'Wait, what do I have here? I think it might be a sweet for my favourite boy.'

Mr. Awar chooses a lolly from the tin under the counter and presents it to Tom. It is the same every time they come; is the same for all the children that are brought in, Grace suspects. Mr. Awar is charm itself to his European customers, but Grace notices he is distinctly less welcoming to the poorly dressed Africans who hang around outside his shop, hoping for some sort of charity.

'Go away from the door,' he snaps. 'I don't want any stealing. Leave here.' He shrugs his shoulders, looking back at Grace.

'They will take anything,' he says, 'Anything.'

Grace thinks he looks at her as if he's found an ally and it infuriates her. What gives Mr. Awar the right to assume she wants to be complicit in his nastiness? The Africans that drift about begging do annoy her, sure enough, but she isn't convinced they are necessarily prone to shoplifting. She'll make sure that when she leaves she'll give Jacob, the old African who works for Mr. Awar, packing groceries, two shillings when he carries the brown paper bags to the boot, not just one.

The inside of the shop is dark and cool. A large fan whirrs overhead, and to one side stands a large cabinet freezer where Mr. Awar keeps not only meat and fish and bags of ice, but butter and milk and cream. The heat would turn them to greasy pools in seconds otherwise. The locals, who don't have fridges and freezers at home, buy their Blue Boy margarine and Kimbo lard in tins. All the shoppers that come here, or to shops like it, know to bring cool boxes with them, packed with freezer blocks.

Grace takes the butter she needs, and chooses some pork chops. She moves round the narrow aisles, chatting to Tom about what to buy. She finds some imported Polish jam, and adds three jars to the trolley. At Tom's insistence, and against her better judgement, she picks up a packet of the local biscuits, House of Manji orange creams.

'Are they alright? The name's putting me off.' A woman speaks to Grace as the biscuits land in the trolley. 'I can't decide whether to risk them.'

'They taste of soap powder,' Grace tells her, 'But they're strangely addictive. At least, to two year old boys and thirty year old husbands.'

The woman laughs and stretches out her hand. Grace sees a dark haired woman of about forty, dressed simply in a well cut khaki coloured shirtdress. It is the kind of thing Grace sees advertised in imported American magazines labelled 'safari' clothes, and which she is sure no safari hunter would be seen dead in. She smiles and takes the proffered hand.

'Grace McIntyre,' she says. 'This is Tom.' Tom beams at the new face, his smile a sickly, sticky green from the lollipop.

'Helen Frazer. Are you local? Working here?' The woman sounds interested.

'Not in Eldoret, out in Marigoi, off the beaten track. 'A one horse town without the horse', my husband says. He teaches at the school there. And you?'

'I work for The Standard, short articles. I'm up here to get some background on a story we're following. My editor has it in his head that this area's a hive of activity.'

'Does he?' Grace sounds dubious. George buys the Standard and the Nation every day, but she never gets much further than the headlines.

'The university was closed down at the beginning of May, all the students sent home. The government thinks it's a hotbed of sedition. There are rumours running round Nairobi that local politicians from up here know more about it than they should. I'm just chasing leads.'

'My *shamba* boy was a student. I've been wondering why he's back home; that'll explain it.' Grace laughs. 'Though I can't see him mixed up in anything. Too pompous.'

'It'll probably come to nothing, you know Kenyan politics. I'm in Kisumu till the weekend digging around. So, no time to hang around chewing the fat, I'm afraid. I have to get going.'

Helen moves on, foregoing the biscuits. When Grace and Tom get to the counter to pay, she is disappearing out the door. On the spur of the moment, Grace searches around in her bag for a piece of paper, borrows a pencil from Mr. Awar, and scribbles down her name and address. Abandoning Tom, sitting in the trolley with the groceries, she runs out into the street, glancing each way till she spots Helen, and hurries over and thrusts the address in her hand.

'Here,' she says. 'If you're up here again, get in touch.'

Helen looks taken aback, but takes the scrap of paper and pushes it in her pocket. She points over Grace's shoulder. 'I think someone wants you.'

Grace recognises the piercing wails soaring across the street, and rushes back to Tom, who is squirming in Mr. Awar's arms outside the supermarket. The shopkeeper hands Tom back without a word, but the purse of his lips and his narrowed eyes speak volumes to Grace about what he thinks of neglectful mothers. While she pays, she notices the weeping Tom has dribbled a trail of sticky, green slime from his lollipop down the back of Mr. Awar's pristine shirt. A frisson of sheer joy rushes up her spine.

It comes to her, now it's too late, that she should have asked Helen Frazer for her address or phone number. They don't have a phone themselves. None of the teachers does, though she expects there's one in the big house by the gates, where Mr. Chegwe, the headmaster, lives. But a reporter living in Nairobi is bound to have one. Helen has long gone when they leave Awar's, and Grace is so cross with herself for not thinking sooner, that she puts Tom in the back seat, gets behind the wheel and drives straight off. She forgets to tip Jacob anything at all.

'Let's go down to Kisumu at the weekend.' Grace makes her suggestion as she and George are getting ready for bed that night.

'Maybe. I might be on duty at school. We'll see.' George climbs into bed, rolls on his side, and pulls the sheet over him 'Can we go some other time? When I'm not so busy?'

Grace ignores his questions. Switching off the light, she pushes herself close to his back, wraps one arm over his shoulder, and kisses his spine gently. She feels him relax against her.

'It's not too far. I looked on the map and the road looks quite a good one. It'll be lovely to see Lake Victoria with our own eyes, won't it? We'll be able to write home and tell everyone about it. Think how jealous they'll be. Kisumu's a lot bigger than Eldoret anyway, more to see. It'll be fun to go somewhere different for a change.' She holds him tighter, her fingers inching down his body. George sighs.

And so it is decided. They will go on Saturday.

Chapter Four

George has thrown caution to the wind and put on a pair of the shorts he bought in Debenhams in Canterbury before they left, assuming he'd be able to wear relaxed dress for work here, but that idea has gone by the board. George soon realised anything but long trousers are viewed as lacking in respect for his colleagues. The Africans present themselves in tailored trousers and decent shirts every morning, and, to Grace's amazement, the women who work in the bank in Eldoret wear dresses her mother might have worn to a smart dinner party, all chiffon and satin.

'It's ridiculous,' Grace has said more than once. 'Shorts are so much cooler.'

'Harks back to colonial masters,' George explains to her patiently. 'They have long memories.'

The drive down to Kisumu has been entertaining. Once they are past the herds of skittering sheep and goats clogging the dusty murram road through Marigoi, and are onto tarmac, Grace is surprised how quickly the town is out of sight, and how different the landscape is. Where they are, over seven thousand feet up in the Nandi Hills, they are surrounded by rich acres of tea plantations stretching into the distance; the bushes flourishing in fresh, misty air. Grace and George often watch the pickers moving among the bushes, like locusts. Skirting the edge of the forest today, they wonder about the grey smoke coiling above the canopy in its heart. They imagine someone is cooking up his lunch, though Grace thinks the smell reminds her more of autumn bonfires in England.

At the lower altitude it is much hotter than at Marigoi, and the humidity envelops them, a physical blanket of moisture. They are expecting the heat, but not this dampness soaking into their clothes and hair. Tom has beads of perspiration glistening on his forehead and his dark hair looks as if he's oiled it.

Grace and George are soon surprised to find themselves amid long billowing rows of sugar cane, which they aren't expecting. Field after field fills the valley, stems ten or twelve foot tall.

'Looks like overgrown grass.' Grace comments.

'It is,' is the only answer she gets, and then Grace and George can tell they're passing the sugar refineries when the sweet cloying smell of caramel that hangs over the road wafts through the windows.

'Smell that Tom. It's like treacle.' As Grace says it George brakes abruptly, shooting her and Tom forward in their seats.

'Look at that!'

A boy dashes out from nowhere and picks up a sugar stem that's been lost over the side of a lorry in front of them. He's oblivious to any danger and goes off sucking out every last bit of sweet juice, a look of pure delight on his face.

'He might have been killed, damn fool.' Grace is quite shaken. 'Have they no sense?'

'Probably gold dust to him. Free food. He's hardly likely to be able to go in a shop and buy sweets, is he, Grace?'

Eventually, after an hour, they arrive in Kisumu and Grace's face lights with joy at seeing somewhere busy, full of people and traffic. It's the biggest place they've seen since their overnight stop in Nairobi when they arrived, before the school driver picked them up and they had the long, long drive through the Rift Valley to Marigoi, and Grace said goodbye to civilisation.

Looking round now, Grace can see proper concrete pavements, rows of tidy shops selling anything you could wish to buy, and well laid out roads branching in all directions.

'This is a bit of a change from Marigoi,' George is pointing at traffic lights, but he hasn't missed the happiness in Grace's eyes. 'We should get away more.'

Grace places her hand over George's bare knee and squeezes it gently. She is determined to enjoy her rare day out with her family.

'I'm hot.' Tom stands between the front seats and jostles George's arm.

'Sit down. You can't come in the front while Daddy's driving, we'll have an accident.'

Grace pushes him firmly back in his seat and stems the crying she knows is about to start by finding him a biscuit. George is driving at a snail's pace, crawling over a long sequence of tall speed bumps in front of the hospital to avoid damaging the suspension of their small Peugeot, and Grace persuades Tom to count them with her to divert his attention from a tantrum.

Tom is counting each bump as they lurch over it, though, as he can only count up to ten, Grace guesses he'll run out of numbers long before bumps. His little voice has just completed 'eight' when a battered Toyota pick-up truck roars past, horn blaring, and forces George to swerve into the gutter. The open back is full of men, squashed in together like sardines, and, as the truck hurtles ahead, belching out black exhaust fumes in its wake, the men gesticulate and jeer at George and Grace, '*muzungu.*'

'What are they saying?' Grace hasn't picked up any Swahili, but she can hear the venom in the men's heckles, and knows instinctively it's not pleasant.

'White man,' George tells her succinctly. 'It means white man.' He filters back into the stream of traffic and Grace hears 'one' as Tom begins to count all over again.

A mile up the road, Grace catches sight of the pick-up truck again, parked in a side turning outside a large house that is set well back from the road. The men have jumped down and each of them is busy, unloading holdalls and small crates, and hurrying inside. In that fleeting moment as they drive past the end of the turning, she feels sure recognises one of them. She swivels back in her seat to make sure, but it is too late.

'That was Isaac with those men. I'm sure of it. What on earth is he doing here?' By the time Grace has spoken, the house is far behind them and

George doesn't catch a glimpse of the men or the truck.

'Was it? Really? Well, he is allowed to come to Kisumu, you know, just the same as you. You employ him, you don't own him.'

'I know that. It just seems a bit odd. And they all had so many bags and boxes. I wonder what they're up to.'

'Grace, they might be maniacs on the road, but I don't suppose they're up to anything. If you reckon they were shifting boxes, they're probably helping someone move. It's nothing to do with us. Mind your own business. Look, we're here.' He turned into the hotel car park

Sammy Wambui, one of the biology teachers at school, has told them about The Sunset and its lovely swimming pool. It sits right beside Lake Victoria, so they enjoy the wonderful views while they swim. When they first arrive at the pool, there is only one other family there, an Asian couple with a little girl about Tom's age, and a tiny baby. Grace is conscious of the fact that, while the husband and his daughter splash and play in the water, his wife, hidden under layers of bright sari cloth, is sitting at the edge watching them, her face expressionless, and Grace feels suddenly exposed in her bikini.

Tom has taken to the water straight away, and is enjoying being thrown in the shallow end by his daddy, where he bobs like a cork in his bright red water wings.

'I recognise that happy face, young man.' Grace is pleased to hear a voice she recognises. Helen

Frazer has come through the doors from the dining room, and is squatting at the edge of the pool talking to Tom. Grace jumps up and introduces Helen to George, who calls the waiter over to order them all a beer. The two women move the sun loungers around, removing damp towels, so they can all sit together.

'I didn't know you were staying here. I thought you'd be back in Nairobi by now.' Grace knows this isn't entirely honest, and she has been hoping to run into Helen again while they are here.

'There have been developments,' Helen confides, artificially lowering her voice. 'The stakes have been raised where the politician's concerned. One of our 'sources' - Grace can hear the parentheses – has left me a message with dates and times of meetings here, in Kisumu. It's too good a lead to leave and go rushing back to Nairobi.'

'I think I saw my *shamba* boy, the student, earlier.' Grace also whispers, in her case to stop George overhearing. 'With a crowd of other men. Up near the main road, taking stuff into a house. They called us *muzungu.*'

Helen glances at Grace, but says nothing, though Grace is aware that she has piqued her interest somehow.

'Where does the politician you're interested in live?' she asks in innocence, arranging herself on the lounger to sunbathe.

Helen throws her towel on a chair beside Grace and pulls off jeans and a cotton shirt. Grace is heartened to see another bikini, and can't help

casting a sympathetic glance at the Asian mother.
She feels sorry for her, wrapped up in this heat.
She doesn't stop to wonder what the woman thinks
of her and Helen.

Chapter Five

On Monday morning, while Tom is occupied in helping Esther polish the wooden floor in the living room by skating up and down with pieces of lambs' wool tied over his bare, brown feet, Grace goes out into the garden to see if Isaac has made a start. It is past ten o' clock, but he hasn't knocked to say he's arrived. Grace has tried to talk to Esther about him, to find out more about what he's doing in Marigoi, but Esther's English is very poor this morning, much worse than normal, and she gets nowhere.

She can't find him anywhere, not in the maize or washing the car. She tries the door of the old servants' quarters, but it is securely locked with a heavy iron padlock and lockable bolts at the top and bottom. She's sure Isaac hasn't moved in, but he has made the building safe. Very safe for a few old tools, and it reminds Grace that he hasn't yet given her a key.

She strolls round trying to decide what flowers might grow in this heat, whether roses might cope. The jacaranda next door is wonderful now, and she finds a passion flower opening, tangled among the canna lilies that grow wild. The lemons are just ripening on the tree, and Grace is breathing in their glorious perfume, eyes closed, when Isaac comes up from the fields and pushes through the shrubs. He joins her by the lemon tree.

'Very good for gin and tonic,' he says. 'You'll have to pick them fast, or the kids will have them.'

Grace, opening her eyes, is taken aback. He is very forthright. None of the other Africans she has come across, admittedly not many, are like this.

'I thought you'd be here earlier,' she tells him. 'I wanted to tell you what to be getting on with before it gets too hot.'

'I'm sorry. I was delayed. It won't happen again. But I could not get away earlier today.' He smiles, but he isn't apologetic.

'I saw you in Kisumu on Saturday afternoon.' Grace watches his face as she speaks. 'Did you not get back?'

Still the same smile, as if he is trying to charm her.

'No, it wasn't me. I haven't been in Kisumu in a long time. Since I was a student.'

'I'm sure it was you, with a lot of other men. Your truck nearly drove us off the road.'

Isaac's smile remains on his lips, but it no longer reaches his eyes. He looks her straight in the face and repeats,

'I haven't been to Kisumu. You are mistaken.'

He turns abruptly and walks away, disappearing round the corner of the house. Grace stares after him. She thinks about what George said about her being nosy, and lets him go. After all, as long as he does what he's meant to in the garden, that's all she can ask. But it was him, she knows it was.

'Mummy!' Grace's knees are tackled from behind as Tom catapults out the door and launches himself at her. She falls on the floor with him, rolling down the slope of the newly shorn grass.

'Look.' Tom lies on his back and waves his legs in the air, showing Grace two polish covered feet, the thick brown cream reaching almost up to his knees. 'I helped.'

'It looks to me like you need a wash after all that hard work.' Grace hauls him to his feet, chases him across the grass and up the steps into the house.

When Tom is as clean as cold water can do, no electricity today, the pair of them goes to find something to drink. Isaac is in the kitchen with Esther, draining a glass of water, and having a heated argument by the sound of it. Grace can't understand a word, she thinks it probably isn't even Swahili, but one of the hundreds of other languages they speak in Kenya, but she can tell they're having a disagreement.

'Isaac,' she says pleasantly. 'What do you think I can do about the maize?' Isaac casts an odd glance at Esther, almost a warning, picks up the new *jembe* from the table and affixes his beaming smile.

'Let's go and see.' He hoists Tom onto his shoulders, where the boy curls his fingers into Isaac's thick hair for balance, and the three of them go back outside.

'It's the mousebirds,' Isaac decides when he looks at the damage to the corn. Grace looks blank. 'Those little brown birds with faces just like mice?' he continues. 'You've seen them?'

'They love to eat the maize,' Isaac is telling Tom. 'Your mother must put some twigs round the cobs to keep them safe.'

'I know the ones you mean,' Grace joins in. 'We do get all sorts of fantastic birds in the garden, but I don't know any of their names. I'm useless.'

Isaac unwinds Tom's fingers from his hair and slides him back to the ground. He pauses, considering, before making his suggestion.

'Some time when I am not working I could show you marvellous birds, more than you see here in the garden. Perhaps when you husband has a free day.'

Grace considers for no more than a second. The idea sounds very tempting.

'I'd enjoy that,' she tells him. 'Tom would love to see more birds, I'm sure. I don't know about George, he's very busy at work, exams going on. It might be better if Tom and I came to get out of his way while he's marking.'

She knows full well that, busy as he is, George would happily join the party, given the chance, and she won't admit to herself why she is so reluctant to include him. But Isaac is an enigma, a puzzle to be unravelled, and Grace wants to be the one to do the unravelling. She doesn't understand the fascination he holds, when he irritates her practically every time she has a conversation with him, but she has no intention of telling George about what she's planning. A day out bird watching will be lovely, especially if she manages to get beneath the skin of the man. It will be Grace's little secret. What harm can it do?

'We have to go to Nakuru to do the marking.' George is explaining to Grace why he will be away for three days. He's incredulous, but has learnt all the schools have to send their scripts to be marked together in one place. 'Presumably they don't trust the markers. We're going tomorrow, in the school bus.'

Grace can't believe her luck. With George away, she won't have to resort to subterfuge after all to cover her trip out with Isaac. She can go with a clear conscience. She'll tell George all about it afterwards, show him the pictures she's planning to take.

'You'll be okay, won't you?' George sits on the bed and pulls her onto his lap. 'Not too lonely.'

Grace links her fingers behind his neck and kisses the top of his head.

'I'll be fine,' she reassures him. 'Tom'll keep me busy. I can find plenty of things to do.'

Chapter Six

Grace is a cautious driver, and when she stops at the end of the school drive, leans forward over the wheel to check if the road is clear, as if she were tackling a particularly busy junction during rush hour at home. Opposite the drive is a cluster of mud huts and small shops, *dukas.* Grace knows one of the huts is Esther's, but has no idea which one. George often walks over, for *mandazi* or to buys beers and sodas, but she's never crossed the road.

She's never had to.

Isaac is waiting for her outside the Catholic church as they have agreed. He is going to take her to the forest, where he says you find the biggest variety of birds in the whole of the province. He settles himself in the passenger seat, solemnly shakes hands with Tom, and points out the route to Grace, almost identical to the one she and George took to Kisumu.

'I'm surprised you haven't been to more places while you've been living here,' he says. 'Kenya is a beautiful country, and this area the best.'

'So far, we've had one night in Nairobi and one day in Kisumu and that's it. We're going down to the coast for August, when the school has a holiday. We want to go to a game park.'

'Go to Masai Mara if it's August,' Isaac reliably informs her. 'See the migration from Tanzania. Or Tsavo, that's good for elephant.

When you go to Mombasa you'll go right through it.'

He says nothing more until he guides Grace off the tarmac and steers her towards densely wooded land along a dusty track. When they are out of sight of the road, he tells her to turn off the engine.

'My husband and I saw fires here when we went by last week.' Grace recognises the general area. 'We weren't sure what they were. Where are we?'

'This is the Kakamega Forest,' Isaac tells her. 'Many people live here. I will show you later.' He turns and helps Tom into the front and sits him on his lap. 'You must look hard,' he tells him. 'Find the birds.'

'There!' Almost immediately, Tom bounces up and down and points excitedly. Grace has a clear view of a grey parrot flying above the shrubs close to the car.

'African Grey,' Isaac tells them. 'One of the most famous birds of Kakamega. Many of them here, many. But there are plenty of others we must find. You'll see how beautiful they are. I know them all.'

They leave the car on the track and walk into the forest along pathways that Grace guesses must have been made by countless feet over hundreds of years. Tom dashes ahead, noisy and excited, but if Isaac says, 'sh,' and holds his finger to his lips, he stops, quiet as a mouse, to see what Isaac has found. Grace wishes she had the same knack. Isaac's eyes are sharper than Grace's and he notices a lot that she misses. The Great Blue

Turacos are unmissable, with their glossy blue and yellow plumage and bright red bills, but Grace would never have pinpointed the tiny sunbirds and bulbuls without Isaac to guide her.

Isaac knows a tree, an Elgon Teak, he informs them, where there are hundreds of weaver birds nesting, and the adults spend several minutes watching the birds construct their intricate nests, weaving grass into a perfect ball.

'They only leave a tiny hole for the parents to come and go, to protect their eggs from scavenger. They are very good at raising chicks.' Isaac is almost speaking to himself.

Tom is prodding the dirt with a stick and jabs it into a mound of red ants. They are much smaller than the safari ants, and don't bite, but the acid they squirt stings badly, and when the ants feel their nest being disturbed, they swarm up Tom's legs, crawling through his toes and under the hem of his shorts, till he screams in pain and panic.

Grace flies to him, beating at the ants with her hands, but there are so many of them. Isaac pushes her aside, lifts Tom well clear of the mound and strips off his clothes, throwing them to one side, where they seem to move with a life of their own for the ants still wriggling through them. Tom's legs and stomach are a mass of tiny red welts and he scratches at them, sobbing, but Isaac picks him up and holds his arms tight so the boy can't move. Tom's screams echo through the forest.

'You're hurting him,' Grace is distraught, oblivious to the rash burgeoning on her own arms. 'Let me have him.'

'It will be worse if he scratches. But I know where we can get some help. Local medicine to soothe the pain.' Isaac heads deeper into the trees, the track growing more and more difficult to follow.

'Where? Where are you taking us?' Grace stumbles along behind, desperate not to lose sight of her son, whose screams have settled into sad whimpers.

'You wondered about the fires you saw, Mrs McIntyre. I will show you. I'm taking you to meet some friends of mine who live here in the forest and who will know the right plants to help Tom. I am taking you to meet the charcoal burners.'

Chapter Seven

It is dark inside the hut. So dark, that the pale gecko skittering around the tops of the walls shows luminous against the gloom, though the flies his quick tongue flashes out at remain invisible. Grace knows they are mosquitoes only by their whining, and, when there is a momentary silence, she waits, anticipating the sharp sting of a bite. When one comes, she slaps it away, and the whining resumes. She thinks of what her mother's told her about the doodlebugs that were launched over their corner of Kent during the war, waiting to see if you'd be hit. The moment of silence is what you hate.

Tom is sleeping, stretched out on a makeshift bed that has been made from dried mud built up into a wide ledge. There is a wooden table in the middle of the single room, and a solitary chair. Grace squats uncomfortably by the bed on a low stool, her knees almost grazing her ears, and waits. Part of her wants to shake Tom, wake him up, grab him from the bed and run back to the car and drive him home. But part, too, now he is peaceful and tear free, appreciates these few moments of quiet.

Through the doorway, she can see the shadows cast by Isaac and the owner of the hut, Juma, as they sit outside, beyond her direct view. Their shadow arms rise and fall, but Grace can't tell if they are drinking or smoking or simply gesticulating. When they arrived here, and Isaac burst into the hut, Tom was by then hysterical, but Juma seemed to know immediately what was wrong. He took the child gently and examined him, peering closely at the bites. He keeps an old sack, full of small clay pots, hanging on a nail behind his door, and he sorted through them, rejecting one or two, before he made his choice. The old man bathed the ant bites and smeared them with the thick green paste the pot held, talking to Tom quietly all the time in some, to Grace, unrecognisable language. Tom stared at him, round-eyed, but let him touch his sore arms and legs without a murmur. Grace was surprised at his compliance.

'He makes all these things himself,' Isaac assured her. 'He is known all round this area as a good healer. He learnt from his father. People come with all sorts of problems. He can fix anyone.'

Grace stands up from the stool, stretching her stiffness away, and rubs at her own arms. She realises they are bitten in several places and can't decide which are from mosquitoes and which ants. She picks up the pot of salve from the table and sniffs at it gingerly, but is pleasantly surprised by the fresh, almost astringent, aroma. She dips in her finger and dabs at the biggest bites with the sticky mixture. There is the sound of urgent voices outside, and Grace looks up to find the two men studying her through the door.

'Juma says you need to put it on more thickly,' Isaac calls to her. 'Don't be sparing.'

Grace uses all the pot, scraping down to the bottom with her nail to tease out the very last dregs, and covers every blemish she can find. She feels her arms cooling straight away. She goes out into the daylight to join the men. Even though they are deep in the forest, the trees have been partially cleared near the hut, and enough sunshine still filters through to dazzle her after the darkness inside, and she shields her eyes with her hand.

'I've used all his ointment,' she apologises. 'Does he want some money?'

Isaac doesn't even bother to consult Juma.

'No. He's a good friend of mine. He won't take money from you, especially for helping a child. He'll go out foraging in the morning, ready to make some more. He doesn't need money for foraging. Some day, perhaps you will be able to do something for him instead.'

Grace thinks that very unlikely. Now she's not in the state she was an hour ago, she glances round the clearing and realises there are more huts nearby, each with a fire outside, and several more people milling around. It's quite a little village here in the forest.

'Do they live out here all the time?' She wants to know. 'Do they work?'

Isaac translates what she says, and the old man, Juma, chuckles. He says something to Isaac, waving his arms about, and laughs again, a rough, hoarse cackle.

'Yes to both your questions, Mrs. McIntyre. These people live here because they work here. They are charcoal burners. It's their fires that make the smoke you and Mr. McIntyre were so curious about seeing last week. Come, I'll show you. Juma will watch your son.'

Isaac guides Grace behind the hut, further back through the trees. The charcoal burners have built the kilns far enough away from the huts they live in for flying sparks not to cause trouble. The flimsy structures would go up in no time if one caught light. There are several kilns, some smouldering and some lifeless, but the air is heavy with the smell of damped down embers. Two young men stand over a kiln that's been newly opened, raking out the black gold it contains with long pieces of brushwood.

'They could do with one of your rakes,' Isaac says solemnly. Grace's immediate instinct is to bristle at the perceived sarcasm, but, when she looks, sees genuine mirth twitching at the corners of his mouth, and gleaming in his eyes. He has made a joke, and not at her expense, but as a friend, an equal. Grace herself considers it would be far easier for the men to have a good strong metal rake than rely on the branches they find lying around. But she's not prepared to say so; she doesn't want to force an argument with Isaac, not now. She doesn't want to spoil the moment.

'All these other ovens are out now. The people that own them have to let them cool down, a day, perhaps two, before they can get their charcoal out. When they want to burn again, it takes more days to get the fire in the pit hot enough. They cut the wood from here in the forest, the oak and the teak. It's very hard work. They have to live here to protect their ovens.'

'How do they make them? Why doesn't the whole thing burn down when the wood burns, if it's that hot?' Grace has moved from the open kiln to one where smoke still hangs in the air, rising gently over her head. Smuts of ash cling to her hair, and when she brushes at them, she can feel the last vestiges of the fading warmth on her skin.

'They pile up their wood, they know exactly how much they can put in, and then cover it up with earth. A thick coat of earth, many layers. Sometimes people use grass, big pieces cut from the ground like squares of matting.'

'Turf,' Grace says. 'We call that turf.'

Isaac nods, taking in the new word, and points at the open kiln again.

'They stoke up the fire, then have to watch it all the time to keep it at the proper temperature. They damp it down with water to make it smoke. The men always look grey; they are covered in ashes the whole day. It's filthy work.'

'What do they do with it? Sell it? Who uses so much of it?' Grace pictures only the fine sticks of charcoal she has seen artists use, and can't imagine how many sketches one of these kilns might produce.

'All of us Kenyans use it to do our cooking. Haven't you seen them firing up their little *jikos* outside their homes? Have you not noticed them in the village? Little ovens on an open fire?'

Grace hasn't. She hasn't ever wondered how Esther cooks her own meals when she has left her working day behind her.

'We sometimes get men coming to the door, trying to sell charcoal pictures, of the lake or the trees. They seem to know where all the Europeans live.'

'Some of it goes like that, too. Many of them, artists, are here in the forest. Or down at Kisumu by the lake. I see them a lot when I'm there.'

Grace recognises, even as the words leave his mouth, that Isaac realises his lie has been exposed. It hangs there, unacknowledged by a word from either of them, but heavy in the space between them. He can't unsay what he has said, but his regret is palpable. Grace feels some satisfaction; after all, she knew, didn't she? She knew he was there. But some part of her wishes it was five minutes ago and she could still pretend to believe his lie.

'Let's go back to the car. We must be leaving, before it gets dark. I'll carry Tom for you.' Isaac turns abruptly back to his friend's hut and, finding Tom awake, gets him to clamber on his back for a piggyback. Juma looks up from stirring the contents of a pot over his fire and mumbles something to him. When Isaac gives a sharp nod of the head, the old man spoons some of the warm salve into a container made from a discarded coffee tin, wraps it in a twist of old newspaper, and hands it to Grace. The men say their goodbyes and Isaac sets off back down the trail at a jog, Tom bouncing up and down as each footstep pounds on the earth. Grace follows them in silence. There is nothing to be said.

Isaac sits it the back with Tom and the silence lasts as they go on their way. When they emerge from the forest and are back on the main road,

Grace is surprised at how bright it is and has to reach for her sunglasses. With them on, she risks looking at Isaac in the rear view mirror without being obvious, but he is staring off into the distance, noticing neither her glance nor anything else. He is lost in his own world. When Tom jumps up and starts asking questions about something he has seen through the window, it is left to Grace to try and answer them. The journey home seems long and sombre compared to the happier start to their adventure.

As they near Marigoi, Isaac suddenly leans forward and says, 'Stop here. Let me out here. You know your way back now.'

Grace does as he asks, but when he leans to close the door, she twists in her seat and takes off the sunglasses.

'It doesn't matter, Isaac. I don't care about your secrets. I liked being out in the forest, seeing the birds. I liked meeting your friend, even though I was so worried about Tom.'

He looks at her for the first time since they left the forest, and sighs. Her hand is resting on the back of her seat as she is swivelled round to face him, and he covers it with his, just for a second. It is the first time there has been any contact between them, and the touch is almost nothing, as light as a butterfly's, but Grace is overwhelmed by the gesture. She snatches her hand away and turns to put it back on the steering wheel. When Isaac stands away from the car, she drives off too fast and the gears grind and the car stalls. Flustered, her face suffuses with colour, and it takes long seconds before she finally engages first gear and can pull away.

Until she rounds the bend in the road, she can see Isaac standing where she left him at the side of the road. She cannot tell if he is looking after her or simply waiting. She can't explain to herself why, but part of her hopes it is the former. She wishes she were not rushing off, it has put her at a disadvantage. The man was just being over friendly. What has she to be embarrassed about? She will make sure he has no chances in the future to be so presumptuous. She'll make sure she avoids any awkwardness. It wouldn't be right.

After Tom is safe in his own bed, and Grace is sorting his clothes for the laundry, she is assailed by the smell of smoke coming off his shorts and T-shirt, mixed with the fresher scent of the herbal ointment. She knows instinctively that Esther would be scandalised if she knew that Grace had been in the Kakamega forest with Isaac, it would cross the fine line drawn between white employer and black servant. So, as she can't face doing washing herself at this hour, she bundles the clothes in an old sack and carries them out of their compound, down the school path, and deposits them in one of the large bins near the kitchens. Grace has never been a secretive person before and is astonished at how easily she has taken to deception. She has no nagging doubts and no regrets. Only curiosity.

Chapter Eight

Finally, towards the middle of June, the rains come. They are very late this year, and the local gossip, among the teachers and up at the market, has been filled with an awful foreboding at the possibility of a full-blown drought. They worry endlessly about whether they will be able to save any of their crops, and how they will feed themselves if they can't. What will become of them? As it is, one day, which starts off just like the one before, the clouds burst and rain torrents down on the parched earth, great fat globules splattering into the murram and turning the tracks through the school compound into red rivers.

Grace has never seen such rain. It looks as if an unseen hand has poked a stick up into an invisible canopy, and all the water it was holding is cascading to the ground in one great gush. George, rushing in at lunchtime, feels the full force of it and is saturated in the fifty yards he has to cross.

'Listen to it!' He is already peeling off his damp shirt and trousers. 'Can you hear the noise it's making?'

'I know, it's unbelievable.' Grace fetches a towel and rubs his back for him. 'How long is it set in for, do you think?'

'Half an hour, if you can believe what they tell me in the staffroom. I'm never sure when they're joking.'

'It must be longer than that,' Grace snorts. 'Look at it. It looks as if it'll last all day.'

But, sure enough, by the time George has to go back to school, the flood has become a light drizzle, the sun is shining as brightly as ever, and the sunbirds are back among the cannas, their long curved beaks probing deep in the flower heads for nectar.

Over the next few weeks, the pattern is repeated at the same time every day and Grace gets used to having a fresh set of clothes ready for George at lunch times. Tom is fascinated by the deluge and traces the path the rain makes on the window panes with his podgy finger. As soon as the worst is past, he rushes out to play in the puddles and the squelchy soil. Grace has bought him a pair of green wellingtons from Bata, but he splashes and jumps in the eddying water with such relish that the muddy ooze surges over their tops and his feet are permanently red.

Isaac comes to the garden most days, but he works as far away from the house as he can, and spends much of his time cleaning the garden tools in the outbuilding, or cutting overhanging branches from the perimeter trees. If he needs to ask something, he catches George early in the morning and talks to him. Grace has seen him from the house, but hasn't been out to speak to him, and he hasn't approached her. When the clouds burst, he locks the shed early and walks off at his steady pace, oblivious of the rain soaking him, and making the shirt on his back cling like cellophane. On the very worst days, when hailstones the size of golf balls drop like missiles, shredding the maize leaves, he locks himself inside the shed to wait it out. Grace never sees him leave on those days, but supposes he must.

On the last day of the month, Wednesday, while Grace is choosing a shirt for George from the pile Esther has freshly ironed, she hears a knock on the inner door. She is surprised. Esther doesn't need to knock, and anyone else would use the outer door. When she puts her head round the bedroom door she sees Isaac, waiting for her at the end of the corridor.

'Isaac,' she says. 'You startled me. Have you been knocking on the other door? Is there a problem?'

'No, Mrs. McIntyre, no problem. I was in the kitchen drinking *chai* with Esther, so came through. I didn't think you would mind me being in the house. But perhaps you do. Perhaps you think I shouldn't be in here.'

'Oh, Isaac, don't be stupid. I was just surprised, that's all. What do you want?'

'I'm letting you know I will be away from work for a few days. I have to go to Nairobi. I hope it will not be inconvenient for you. I will be back after the first week of July.'

'No, it'll be fine. There's not much you can do while it's so wet. How are you going down? On the RVP from Eldoret?'

Grace and George used the mini bus service once, before they bought the car, and it wasn't too bad, just long and tedious.

'No, I have friends who need to be there also. We will all go together in their car.'

Grace can't help herself and blurts out, 'In their Toyota pick-up, you mean?'

For a moment she thinks Isaac is going to walk off, that she has pushed him to anger again, but he steps into the narrow corridor and closes the door to the back of the house behind him. He leans back against the wall and crosses his arms and he looks at her steadily. She returns the look, keeping her head high, struggling not to lower her eyes.

'Mrs. McIntyre, there are many things you don't understand.' His voice sounds weary, sad almost. 'There are things happening in Kenya you don't know about, you Europeans. You have a nice life here for a while, but then you go home and forget about us. But we have to live here all the time, and for many of us it is hard.'

'I know it can be hard. Look at Juma out in the forest with the others.'

Isaac laughs and pushes himself away from the wall, shaking his head in amusement.

'Mrs. McIntyre, I don't just mean hard physical work. There are far worse things a man has to put up with than that. There is so much corruption in this country, in this government. It has to start to change. People want it to change, and they are getting impatient.'

'So you're one of them, wanting change? Is that what you do in Kisumu, have political meetings? Like forming an opposition? Will you be at a conference in Nairobi?'

'Yes, Mrs. McIntyre, you could call it that. A sort of opposition conference.' Isaac brushes past her to open the door and steps back into the living room. 'I will see you in a few days, maybe a week.' He starts to leave, but hesitates. 'When I am back, I know somewhere else you might enjoy visiting. We will go when I return, a short *safari*. You and Tom and me.' And then he is gone.

For the first time, Grace catches sight of Esther, kneeling by the fireplace with polish half applied to the hearth, waiting in complete stillness. Grace wonders if she has been listening at the door. She certainly would have heard their last few words, but her English is so poor she wouldn't understand them surely. When the outer door closes on Isaac, Esther resumes her polishing, buffing the stonework to a silvery gleam.

Grace crosses the room to go and call Tom from the garden, and as she passes Esther, the woman, head still bent over the hearth, says something to her. She speaks quietly but very clearly. She could be talking to herself.

'He bring trouble, that man. Leave him, Mrs. McIntyre. Leave him.'

Grace is perplexed. What on earth's got into the woman? Who brought Isaac to them in the first place? She ignores her and goes out on the veranda in search of Tom. He is skipping round the garden in his shorts and lovely wellies, wafting a large banana frond from their tree above his head as a make-shift umbrella. Grace has no idea where his T-shirt might have gone to. She leaves him for several minutes, watching him play, letting him enjoy himself with such uninhibited joy. On the other side of the bushes she can also see the Chebele children, staring at Tom solemnly, their

13

dark eyes round and unblinking. One of them is chewing on a corn cob, but none of them says a word. When they see her looking at them, they startle like deer and run away.

Grace can't see why they find her so frightening. It upsets her. What do their parents say about her and George when they are home? What do they really think of them, these Europeans parachuted into their community? She realises she has been living on this school compound for seven months now, and has never been inside one of the other teachers' houses, nor invited one to hers. She is surrounded by families, yet she is more lonely than she can ever remember. At least she has her lovely boy.

'Tom, come in. Daddy will be here soon. Shall we walk over and meet him? You can bring your new umbrella. Pull one off for me too, help keep Mummy dry.'

Tom chooses a large frond and rips it from the banana plant. He has to tug so hard the tiny hands of unripe bananas quiver on their stems and one falls to the ground. He hands the leaf to Grace and looks at the fallen bananas for a minute, thinking. Then he picks them up and hangs them over the stem as far up as he can reach. Bending over again, he picks a handful of odd leaves and places them carefully on top of the bananas.

'There. That's better. I've sticked them back. I've mended them like the man mended me in the forest.'

Grace hesitates. Tom hasn't spoken about what happened to him before now and nor has she. But now she wonders how much he remembers, and how much he may have said.

'Did you tell anyone else what happened, Tom?'

'I told Daddy, but he didn't believe me. He said I was a silly. I'm not a silly, am I, Mummy?'

No you're not, thinks Grace to herself, but perhaps I am. By the time George got back from Nakuru Tom's rash was completely cleared, so she has let sleeping dogs lie. If Tom has said something, why has George never mentioned anything to her in all this time? They usually share Tom's cute remarks and nonsense, laughing together in the evenings over a cold drink. It's not like George to keep something to himself.

'Daddy's pretending because he knows it's our secret. We'll keep it our secret, just for us. Are you ready? I'll race you to Daddy's class. You start.'

The heels of the green wellingtons disappear through the gap in the hedge and it is only when Grace sets off after them she realises she is still wearing the rubber flip flops that make her slip and slither over the wet grass. She pauses and takes them off, and carries them in her hand the rest of the way. She is half aware of curious African eyes watching her from inside the row of classrooms as she careers across the football pitch after Tom, splashed to the ankles in murram blotches, like giant teardrops. What will the teachers think of her barefoot? If a pair of the watching eyes happens not be African, but European blue, what will George think of her?

Chapter Nine

They are all dressed in dry clothes, and are still sitting over their rice and beans, when Grace suddenly announces that they ought to throw a party, invite the people off the compound.

'What's brought this on?' George wants to know, forking a final slice of onion round his plate. 'You barely talk to any of them.'

'Exactly. I just think it's time we did get to know them a bit more, the people you work with. Everyone.'

'Who do you mean by 'everyone'?' George is wiping up the last of the spicy sauce with some bread and offering it to Tom, who opens his mouth like a baby bird and takes it.

'Everyone at the school. The teachers. Everyone.' Grace wishes George would pay more attention. 'Stop doing that. He's had plenty. Listen, concentrate. What do you think?'

'Mr. and Mrs. Chegwe? The secretary? The groundsman? Esther? You plan to ask all of them.'

'The Chegwes, yes, of course. Glory? Why not? She's very pleasant when I go in the office to collect the post, very good English. Obviously not Esther. I'll probably get her in to help. Not the groundsman either.'

'You'll need to buy in loads of sodas, most of them don't drink. And a crate of beers for those that do.'

'I'll do an English buffet. See if they like it. It'll be good.'

16

Grace pauses and George smiles at her, the same smile he gives Tom when they're playing together. She appreciates he's being indulgent, like humouring another child, but she can bear it if it helps to persuade him. She can't remember when she was last so enthusiastic about anything; certainly not since they first set up home in Marigoi. The poor man is bound to be pleased to see a bit of spark in her after so long. She knows if it makes her happy, he'll play along. He says to Tom,

'What do you think? Is your Mummy bonkers?'

'Yes' they all say in unison. George leans across the table and kisses her forehead.

'Go on, then. You sort it out. I'll leave the organising to you. I'll jot down all the names before I go back.'

There is only one week left of the term. Soon, the teachers will vanish back to their home villages to lay a new dung floor in the family hut, or tend to their *shambas,* and the compound will be all but empty, with only the clerk and caretaker on hand. The party needs to be soon, if they're going to have it at all, and Grace chooses the following Thursday. Once her mind is made up, she may as well get on with it, and informs George she'll go out this afternoon to invite people. George gives Grace a list of names and tells her where to find each house, all spread out across the compound and half hidden behind hedging. Grace and George's bungalow is close to the office but some are so far back, behind the dormitories, that Grace has never seen them.

Grace waits till the rain has completely stopped before she sets off. She has the list in her hand, baffling over which way to go first. The school compound is criss-crossed with tracks leading in all directions, pathways carved out by successive generations of feet tramping over them, but none of the houses is numbered. George has tried to identify them for her by writing helpful clues like 'small house next to labs.' or 'bungalow like ours behind water tank' beside each name. He has also made a note of the families where they have dogs, so when she gets to them she can keep a tight hold on Tom. For the rest, he dashes about while they go round, sometimes trailing behind and sometimes rushing ahead. All the time he chatters away, providing a running commentary on their circuit.

Grace knows Sammy Wambui's house, because his wife keeps chickens, and many of the other teachers go there to buy their eggs. When the hens have stopped laying, Mrs. Wambui sells them off for the pot and Grace has seen them being carried home upside down by their scrawny legs. Occasionally, one flaps a wing feebly, but usually they hang still and acquiescent, accepting their fate. Grace has sent Esther over for eggs, but never a bird. She can't bear the idea of killing one; the mere thought of wringing its neck revolts her. It has never occurred to her to ask Esther to do it.

When Tom knocks, a sharp tattoo, the side door opens and a young girl peers out. All Grace glimpses are brown fingers wrapped round the edge of the door and dark, almost black eyes. Their whites have a strange pale yellow tinge to them, like thick clotted cream. She stares at the visitors, but says nothing. Before Grace can speak, a voice calls out something from deeper in the house. The girl continues to look at her blank-eyed until the owner of the voice appears. Mrs. Wambui opens the door wider, acknowledges Grace with a small bob of her head, and furrows her brow.

'Go to the front door, Mrs. McIntyre. This door is for servants. The front door is for guests.' She lapses into English for Grace's sake, and firmly closes the door.

Grace understands she has made a faux pas right away; Kenyans are very prickly about proper protocol. She guides Tom round to the front door and they are allowed in.

'Would you like a drink, Mrs. McIntyre? Fanta? Sprite?' Mrs. Wambui is affable now etiquette has been observed.

Grace takes stock of the room. The house is the same as theirs, furnished with the same standard issue sofa and chairs and ornately carved table, but there the resemblance ends. Every surface in the Wambui living room is covered with pieces of violently coloured macramé or crochet work. A long runner in orange and lime flows the length of the table, and another across the width of the mantelpiece. Antimacassars and arm rests with dangling tassels adorn every chair, and blue and purple and acid yellow doilies litter numerous small side tables, a rainbow rippling through the room. Grace can't help feeling she has been transported back to a Victorian parlour, with added African vibrancy.

Instead of George and Grace's framed prints – Van Gogh, Monet – and single black and white photo of Tom as a tiny baby, the Wambui walls are covered with pictures cut from magazines and newspapers stuck up with Sellotape. A picture of the president hangs conspicuously in the middle, flanked by a national flag to the left and a large plaster crucifix to the right. Throughout the room the walls are pockmarked by small white patches where previous pictures have served their time and been roughly torn down

'Sit, sit.' Mrs. Wambui adjusts the bright cloth wound round her head, knotting it tightly with a flamboyant bow at the nape of her neck. 'What can I do for you, Mrs. McIntyre? Do you need eggs?'

'Grace, my name is Grace. No eggs, not today. I've come to invite you and Sammy to our house next Thursday. We're having a little party. About six o'clock.'

Mrs. Wambui stretches her eyes wide and Grace is reminded of a rabbit caught in the headlights. She practically jumps from her seat and seizes Grace's hand. She holds it tight, imprisoning it in a cage of rough brown fingers, and Grace can feel her wedding ring as it cuts into her flesh.

'That is kind of you, Grace, very kind. I am Prudence. I will ask my husband but I believe he will be so happy. My husband, he likes all the Europeans. Every one he meets, he says, 'they are good people'.'

With no little difficulty, Grace extricates her hand from Mrs. Wambui's grasp, and stands up.

'Are you going so soon, Grace? Let me give you a soda.'

'I must go; we've a lot of houses to visit. I've no idea how to find half of them.'

Tom has already disappeared out of the door. Grace finds him chasing the chickens that are left to roam free throughout the garden, pecking and scratching and laying eggs where they please, but which are now clucking in panic and scurrying into the shrubs to escape Tom's attempts to catch one. Grace snatches his hand and hauls him off, followed by Prudence Wambui's sing-song lilt.

'Are you sure you don't need eggs, Grace? Better than the market.'

Grace ticks the names off her list as she goes. The Chebeles will come, they can leave their children with the maid, who Grace knows is no older than twelve herself. Glory is very happy to be invited and asks if she can bring her husband, who has never been mentioned before. The Nyamas, the Ochiengs, Jackson Karui; they all say they will come. By four, when she should be thinking of going home, Grace has only one name left; the headmaster's.

The large blue-washed house, the only two storey house in Marigoi, is hidden behind overgrown hedges and a tall wooden gate watched by a guard, the *askari.* Mr. Chegwe is meant to be on site at all times; who knows when he might be required to administer a beating or admonish the cook for wasting money on oranges or meat.

21

However, as with many rules in Kenya, Grace and George understand full well this one is routinely ignored, a technicality easily circumvented. The headmaster disappears as soon as the teaching week ends on Friday, and is not seen again until he struts out on Monday morning to conduct assembly. Grace often watches as the Kenyan flag is ceremonially raised, the national anthem sung and the president respectfully acknowledged. The Chegwes' own children are at boarding school in Nakuru and are never seen in Marigoi at all, even in the holidays.

Grace senses from snippets she hears via George that Mr. Chegwe is not popular. Most of the teachers working here in Marigoi are from one of the local tribes, Nandi or Kalenjin or Luo, and don't like a Kikuyu being appointed as headmaster. The rumour is that Mr. Chegwe is a friend of the education minister in Nairobi, that influence has been used. Money might have changed hands. Grace and George don't believe half of what they hear, but, worryingly, that still leaves a lot they generally do.

Mrs. Chegwe remains a mystery. There is talk in the staffroom that she has some kind of job of her own, but nobody has any concrete evidence to the fact. Conjecture is far more rewarding. She is even more elusive than her husband and keeps her distance behind the high fences, only seen when the *askari* opens the gates and she sweeps out at the wheel of a blue Mazda. She is the only African woman Grace has seen driving, and the little

Mazda is the only car on the compound apart from the McIntyres' own.

The *askari,* even in this heat, is dressed in an old army greatcoat, marking him out as a veteran. Whether of the East Africa Corps or Mau Mau, Grace doesn't speculate. He greets Tom with a loud '*jambo*' and a wide smile, showing a lot of gum and a minimum of teeth, stained a gingery brown, the result of too much fluoride in the water.

'Madam not home,' he informs Grace. She can see the car parked in a lean-to beside the house, and looks at it pointedly.

'Are you sure?'

The *askari* clarifies the matter. 'Madam working, very busy.'

'I won't keep her long.' Grace pleads. 'Only a minute.'

'Madam busy.' The old soldier continues to grin, but he is implacable. He's been told what to say, and he says it. He will repeat it all afternoon if necessary.

Grace admits defeat. She picks up Tom, who is visibly drooping, and props him on her hip. Going home, she makes lists in her head of things she plans to cook and what she'll need to buy. Will she be able to get it all here?

She can write an invitation and leave it in the headmaster's pigeon hole if his wife is so busy. What can she be doing, anyway, that's so important she can't leave it for five minutes?

Chapter Ten

Grace has been in the kitchen all day. She's roasted meat, baked biscuits, sliced and filled bread for tiny sandwiches and tossed salads. George went for the crates of drinks, and a tall tower of them stands either side of the door, beers to one side, soft drinks to the other. Grace has persuaded Esther to work tonight, to hand round the drinks and do the washing up. Grace stays in the living room, encouraging her guests to try the new foods she's put on offer.

'Do you eat this every day? Is this typical English food?' Mrs. Chebele, Winsome, is talking while spooning mouthfuls of creamy trifle between her plump lips, her tongue searching out the tiny pieces of glace cherries clinging to her teeth. Grace is mesmerised when the pink tip slides out and flicks round Winsome's lips to catch every morsel. 'It is delicious. We Kenyans, we love sweet things.'

The evening is going well. Apart from Prudence and Sammy, who were on the doorstep at exactly six, the other guests, working on Kenyan time, wander up at their leisure, as if they were passing and just happened to notice the open door. Grace is momentarily disconcerted to see the uninvited groundsman walk in, but it turns out he is the husband Glory spoke of in in the office. He tells them he is Hezekiah, and that is the sum of his English, so Glory spends her evening as a translator, which is okay for 'have another drink', but useless for jokes.

24

There is some awkwardness at first. None of the women drinks, they are good Christians, and a few of the men avoid the alcohol, but once the drinkers have a beer, the atmosphere lightens. The women huddle together, a flock of colourful birds in their *kikois* and *kangas,* comparing the cost of tomatoes and unreliability of maids, and everyone relaxes and starts to enjoy themselves. Grace hates to be seen as the only woman drinking, so pours vodka into a Fanta bottle and sips it through a straw as she moves from one group to another. She learns a lot, just by listening in on conversations, and everyone has lots of questions about England.

It is not only Winsome Chebele who is enjoying the food. Apart from the trifle, the sliced ham, the cold beef, the eggs in mayonnaise, the sandwiches; all have been consumed with gusto. George tells Grace he expects they're not used to such a choice, and so much of it, that they're acting like starving men. He says they'll all complain of belly ache tomorrow, and skip classes and he'll be in trouble with the headmaster. The headmaster who hasn't come.

The younger male teachers, all of them unmarried, have found the stereo and are playing Grace's albums. Jackson Karui runs back home to fetch some records that he's been buying, waiting for when he's saved enough for a record player, and soon African music is booming out into the dark Marigoi night. The young men, keeping hold of their bottles of Tusker or White Cap, begin half dancing and half swaying to its rhythms, careless of whether beer splashes onto the floor. Grace is normally driven mad when she hears *benge* blaring out of shops and bars, so discordant and repetitive to her British ears, another thing she hates. But tonight, the music and the men's swaying are hypnotic. After topping up her own bottle, she goes over to the stereo, turns the volume up full and moves close to the speakers. Carried away by the insistent beat, she joins in the dancing with the men, stamping her feet and waving her arms above her head. The music from the drums and trumpets is pumping round her body like her blood, and she can't distinguish one pulse from the other.

'Grace, Grace!' George's voice is low but urgent, and his hand is on her arm, pulling her away from the circle of dancers.

Grace, cross at being distracted, expects him to ask her to fetch more pastries or snacks from the kitchen, and tries to shake him off and move back to the stereo.

'Esther's in the kitchen, she can help.'

'Grace, calm down. You're not behaving very well; you're making a spectacle of yourself. Do you see the other women making an exhibition of themselves?'

When she looks, the wives, women she now knows by their first names, have ceased their lively chattering and are sitting in silence. Glory flushes with embarrassment and casts her eyes down to her lap. Prudence and Winsome look scandalised, and the other women, Anne Negu and Primrose Ochieng and Sahanga Biri, are looking at their husbands, as if waiting for guidance. Someone turns the music down, and the young men stumble out onto the porch to finish their beers.

George drops Grace's arm, takes the Fanta bottle from her grasp and puts it on the table, among the debris of biscuit crumbs and spilt mayonnaise. He picks up bowls of crisps and nuts and passes them round, easing everyone away from awkwardness, so they can all begin to act as if nothing untoward has happened. Grace understands only too well that tomorrow she will be the talk of the compound. 'Did you see how the white madam behaved?'

As soon as she is not the centre of attention, Grace pulls her wrap around her shoulders and hurries out the side door, collecting a beer as she goes. There are no lights in the school grounds and she walks to the back of the house, as far from a window as she can get, and is soon invisible to anyone indoors. She stands in the blackness of the garden, staring up to the sky, and takes long gulps of the warm beer. Tears of frustration threaten to spill. When did George become so pompous? She was only dancing. She was happy, for once.

A small noise, no more than a scrape of wood against wood, disturbs her. When she brings her eyes back from the heavens and peers ahead, she can make out a faint light glimmering from inside the tool shed. She drops the beer bottle on the grass and goes closer. The padlock is swinging open in the latch, but when Grace tries turning the handle, the door is firmly closed, bolted from inside. She knocks. There is absolute quiet, an unnatural stillness. She knocks again, louder, and puts her mouth close up to the panels of the door, searching for a gap to call through.

'Who's in there?' But she knows who it will be.

She hears the bolts being slid back, smooth and well-used, and the door slowly swings open. There is a glimpse of blue-black skin, but Isaac stays hidden in the shadows. Grace hesitates, then steps as far as the threshold.

'I didn't know you were back yet. What are you doing here? Why aren't you at home? Your own home?'

'There are difficulties. I can't go home right now. I thought I would sleep here tonight and you would not find out. I saw all you and your friends enjoying yourselves as I came up the path, so I have been very quiet. I did not wish to disturb you, and it is better they do not know I am here. It is safer.'

'Safer for whom?'

'For both of us, I think, Mrs. McIntyre.'

The door swings back in a wide arc and the feeble flame of a kerosene lamp in the corner throws a narrow spotlight on Grace's face. Isaac studies her and, when he speaks, there is concern in his voice.

'What is wrong, Mrs. McIntyre? Why are you sad?' He turns down the lamp and steps closer to the doorway. His kindness is her undoing.

'Isaac, I'm so miserable. I don't know what I'm doing in a place like this. I don't know how I'm meant to behave and now George is so angry. I was having such a good time.'

Grace's weeping is inevitable and, when it starts, unstoppable. She does not bother to wipe the tears away, but lets the wet, salty drops track down her cheeks unchecked.

'Mrs. McIntyre, if you want you can come inside until you are feeling happier. We can close the door and nobody will find you till you want them to. We can talk, or we can be quiet.'

'I'd like that very much. You can tell me some more about the forest and the birds, but most of all, I'd like to sit and not say anything. And, please, don't keep calling me Mrs. McIntyre, I'm Grace.'

'Well then, Grace. You are most welcome.'

Grace stumbles over the rake as she negotiates the rickety step in the dark, nearly falling, and Isaac has to catch her to steady her. With his hand cradling her elbow, she finds her footing again, and lets him lead the way into the shed. When she is safely inside, Isaac closes the door against the world.

Chapter Eleven

Sometime in the deep hours of the night, Grace hears George in the garden calling for her. His voice breaks the cocoon she's made in the sanctuary of the hut, but she closes her ears to it. Isaac looks at her, but she shakes her head, and he, too, remains silent till the voice fades.

Grace hears Isaac leaving long before dawn, but she resolutely ignores him and feigns sleep. She listens to him moving round the small room, gathering up his *panga* and the lamp, before he inches round the door and is swallowed up by the navy blue pre-dawn. She pictures his long, deliberate strides carrying him towards the fields, making not a sound. Grace recalls what the older expats say; that the Africans are as stealthy as the animals they once hunted, they can make themselves invisible.

When she does stir, prompted by the desire to be indoors by the time Tom wakes, it is still not light, but birds are beginning to sing and over in the Wambui garden she can hear the first tentative crowing of the cockerel.

She makes her way back to the house across the dewy grass, evening chill still in the air. Bright blue glossy starlings are making an early morning visit to the garden and Grace watches them dabbling in tiny puddles, plumping out their iridescent feathers. She is relieved to find the door unlocked and creeps in, careful not to make a sound. When she reaches the living room, George is sitting out on the porch in one of the rattan chairs, facing out across the hedges, but she can't tell if he is asleep or awake. She takes off her shoes and tiptoes across the room, expecting at every minute to hear her name called, but she reaches the corridor unremarked. She hasn't begun to think what she's going to say to George to explain her absence, to excuse herself. On impulse, she goes into Tom's room and crawls into bed beside him. He smells of delicious small child and she buries her face in his hair and cuddles him tight, squeezing him against her chest. Tom wriggles in protest in the midst of his dreaming so she loosens her grasp and lays, holding his warm hand, until dawn fully breaks.

'Mummy, what are you doing? Why are you in my bed? Did you have a nightmare?'

Tom tugs at her arm then proceeds to clamber over her, sitting astride her stomach and patting her face gently.

'No, poppet. I just wanted to see my favourite boy as soon as he woke up. Did you hear all the noisy people last night? I bet you did.'

'I'm pretty sure he didn't.' George has come into the room and is watching them, standing with his hands deep in his pockets. Grace can see the tautened sinews of his forearms and she knows that, hidden by the pockets, his hands are clenched. Whether from fury or fear, she isn't sure.

'George…'

'Not now, Grace. Not in front of Tom.'

'Not in front of Tom, what, Daddy? Is it a secret?'

'I don't know. You'll have to ask Mummy later.' George crosses the corridor to the bathroom. 'I'm going to shave, get changed. I've got work today.'

Grace notices the sag of his shoulders and the way his head has shrunk into his neck; he wears his dejection like a heavy overcoat. In that instant, Grace is overwhelmed with tenderness towards him, a fierce unconditional love. His whole body has crumpled, in much the same way as the trousers and shirt he's sat up in all night, and she knows that is her fault, she is the cause of it.

'I'll get you some breakfast, shall I?' Grace asks as the bathroom door closes. 'I'll scramble some eggs, if you like.'

There is no answer, but Tom slides off the covers to the floor and pulls at her skirt.

'I want rambled eggs. Lots of rambled eggs.'

He tugs until she is on her feet and allowing herself to be dragged along to the kitchen. Passing by the bathroom, Grace is certain she can detect soft sobbing, the sound of misery seeping under the door.

She makes a special effort for a weekday morning. She lays the table and brews coffee in a large jug and, when the toast is exactly the right shade of golden brown, finds a proper rack to put it in. Tom collects the jam, every flavour they have in the cupboard, and lines the tins up in order of their colour; blueberry, strawberry, mango, pineapple.

George comes through at last. He's shaved and clean, but, in Grace's view, still seems shrunken

32

somehow. Diminished. He walks through the kitchen without stopping, merely ruffling Tom's hair in passing.

'George, I've done breakfast.' Grace cries after him in desperation.

'Not for me. No time. Too busy.' Weighed down by books and files, he goes without so much as a glass of water.

'Daddy's not eating. It's just us this morning, young man.' Grace hoists Tom onto a chair.

'Good! That means lots more for me.' And, true to his word, Tom demolishes every last slice of the toast, testing all the jams in sequence. 'The red one's my favourite. What's your favourite, Mummy?'

Grace doesn't know. She hasn't eaten anything. She scrapes the scrambled eggs and toast crumbs into the bin and begins to stack the plates, but, suddenly, it is important to her to wash them herself. She boils a kettle and adds it to the tap water to make it as hot as she can bear, and drops the crockery into the sink piece by piece, near scalding splashes thrown up like eruptions from a geyser. She scrubs everything twice over till it gleams and piles it, still steaming, on the wooden draining board. She has to balance everything very carefully to stop it clattering to the floor and shattering on the concrete.

Grace is watching the sun streaming through the window and refracting off the last of the of the bubbles that are swirling down the waste pipe, creating tiny prisms of colour, when she realises Isaac is arriving through the gap in the hedging, side by side with Esther as usual. She was not expecting to see him this morning. For some reason, she thought he would stay away today, probably stay away altogether from now on.

Esther lets herself in, carrying the beer bottle she's picked up on her way. She stacks it back in the crate, and turns to the kitchen. Esther expects to wash the dishes first, her practised routine, and when she sees them on the board, already clean without her, takes the broom and a pan instead and goes to sweep the bedrooms. She doesn't greet Grace with '*jambo*' today. Isaac waits at the step, examining the bananas that are fast yellowing.

'Go and help Esther sweep,' Grace tells Tom. 'Hold the pan for her.'

She waits for him to scamper off before stepping outside. She stands as close to Isaac as she dares and joins him in his scrutiny of the bananas, as if they were the most interesting thing in the world.

'You pick them before they are all yellow,' he tells her 'Otherwise the fruit flies eat them.'

'Do they keep well?' Grace doesn't care if they keep well or not, but must say something, anything.

'Not really, they go bad very fast. Give them to your neighbours, or give them to the kitchens. The boys here don't get fruit, it is too expensive.'

Grace knows a large hand of these tiny bananas costs a shilling at the local market, the same as six eggs or a Kimbo tin full of rice, so dreads to think how little is spent on the boys' food. It reminds her of her buffet being hoovered up by Winsome and

Hezekiah and the others, and thinking of them, she is forced to confront the rest of what she remembers of yesterday evening.

'You left very early, Isaac. I thought you said it wasn't safe to go home.'

'I think now it is safer not to be here. People are watching, watching all the time. They notice a lot of things, even if they do not talk of them. You cannot trust everybody. I will not go to my home. I will stay with people in Kisumu. They are my people there, Luo, I will be fine.'

'Luo? I thought you were Kalenjin.'

'Kalenjin!' The word spits out, scorn in every syllable. 'Don't compare me with them.'

Grace shrugs back her confusion and doesn't pursue it. Tribal pride, she assumes.

'What are you so worried about since you got back? Nobody's going to bother if they saw you here last night; I'm the one who's going to look the fool.'

'You have no worries. In a week they will be gossiping about something else. But I have to be careful. My meetings in Nairobi did not go as well as I hoped, as I expected. I want to stay in my own place for a while, down by the lake. We Luo help one another out. I'll be fine.'

Grace has thought all this time Isaac was a Kalenjin, since that first morning he came to the house and she saw his long, loose limbs. She doesn't understand the complexities of all these tribes in Kenya. Aren't they meant to be one country now? Hasn't the president just made it a one-party state? She's sure she remembers George reading out a piece in *The Standard* about it.

'Are you going to stop working for us? I'd miss you being here, in the garden, teaching Tom about the birds and the trees. And my husband might wonder why you've gone so suddenly.'

'I will have to return to Nairobi in a few days, there is more to do there for me. I will stay in Kisumu till then. When I come back next time, I will come and sow the beans, and you can tell me what you have decided about flowers. But you can't eat flowers, you know.'

'It's Tom's birthday on the seventeenth. Will you be back by then?'

'Eight days? That's plenty of time. I will make sure I'm here. We can go on that *safari* I told you about.'

'Isaac, about last night…'

'You do not need to say anything. I am glad I was able to help you.' He turns quickly and goes back the way he came, halting any further discussion. They have not looked at each other once.

Grace reaches up and twists the stem of a single banana to test it and it drops into her palm. She peels back the greeny-yellow skin to reveal the tempting cream fruit, and bites into it. It is still unripe, hard and tasteless, and she spits it out onto the grass. From nowhere, flies swarm over the chewed morsel, and others hover near her face, scenting out the uneaten part she still holds. Grace throws it in the dustbin by the door, and when the flies follow it, crazed for food, she slams the lid down on all of them. She stands and listens to their futile humming, trapped in the metal prison.

Chapter Twelve

It is only after Tom is in bed that they talk. At lunch time George sent a message with one of the boys to say there was an emergency and he was too busy to come home, but Grace doubts it was true. How can he be so busy that he can't even stop for a sandwich and a cup of tea? His deceit worries her, because, in all the years they have known each other, he has never acted like this before. They often have pointless arguments; petty squabbles about things that don't matter. Their marriage is littered with such incidents, always has been, but it is Grace who is the stubborn one who won't let things drop. George is a natural peacemaker, and she has come to rely on him to smooth things over, calm the waters. But this time things are very different.

'What do you think you were doing, for God's sake, Grace? As if it wasn't bad enough you acting like a fool at the party, and making me a laughing stock with the people I have to work with, you then disappear into the night. Have you any idea how worried I was? Anything might have happened. We're not at home now, with friends round the corner to run to.'

'I know. I'm sorry. I was just so upset; with you, with myself. I went out to get some air.'

'You weren't out getting air anywhere I could find you. I even looked in the car. Tell me you didn't go walking off the compound altogether. And when on earth did you crawl home?'

38

Grace breathes more easily; George really doesn't know how long she was gone. Perhaps he need never know about Isaac being there at all. He's furious enough, without that.

'Of course not. I didn't go far. I just hid in the tool shed and I must have fallen asleep. I can't remember. I came back as soon as I woke up.' Grace believes a white lie is acceptable under the circumstances. Why hurt the man any more than she has? 'I saw you asleep on the porch when I came back in and didn't want to disturb you.'

'Disturb me? It was a bit late for that.'

'George, I've said I'm sorry. I had more to drink than I meant to and got carried away. I've been so bored here, with you wrapped up in your work all the time, and I went a bit mad.'

'I'm here to work, that's the whole point. Don't forget, Grace, you were as keen to come to Kenya as I was. I didn't have to force you.'

In all the long months in Marigoi Grace has never considered this. Now she has to admit the truth of it. The day George came home with the advertisement Mr. Chegwe placed in *The Times Educational Supplement,* she urged him to apply. She thought it sounded exciting. It really isn't fair to blame him that, with hindsight, she regrets ever seeing the application form. She faces him across the table, where they are sitting as far apart from each other as they possibly could be, and reaches out her hand, willing him to take it.

'I know, I know you didn't. I suppose I didn't think we'd be so far from civilisation, so isolated.'

39

'What part of 'up-country' didn't you understand, Grace?' George ignores her hand and pushes his chair back from the table, rising to his feet. 'I don't understand you anymore. I don't know what you want.'

Grace is still at the table when she hears him slam the door of the bedroom. She gives a wry smile when she pictures how she must look; all alone there, sitting immobile with one bare arm stretched out in front of her, clutching at nothing. If someone were to come in and find her like that, they'd think she was mad.

She tucks the chairs neatly under the table, and scrapes a knuckle against a jagged gouge in part of the frieze carved round the edge that her fingers have never met before. Examining the table more closely, she finds more tiny shards of wood missing and scratches criss-crossing the surface despite Esther's thick layers of polish. She brushes her hand over the scarred wood. How many other couples have sat at this table over the years, laughing and eating and arguing?

Grace turns out the lights and trails down the corridor. She contemplates sleeping in with Tom for another night, to avoid George until he has begun to forgive her and they can be friends again. She hesitates outside the yellow door of the boy's room, unable to make a decision, and realises the big bed in the room opposite, her and George's room, is empty. George has gone to sleep in their spare room, the room they never use, so the decision is made for her. It is the first time they have ever shared a roof but not a bed.

Grace frets all night, but wakes in an entirely different frame of mind. She is not prepared to be the villain for as long as it takes George to thaw. She is weary of guilt. As soon as George comes into their room, as he must to collect his clothes, she confronts him.

'Are you talking to me today?' She may as well not be there, for the notice he takes. 'In that case, can you manage without the car for a day or two? Perhaps it will do us both good if I go away for a bit, give us both time to think and clear our heads.'

She has no intention of going anywhere, but wants to goad him into some sort of response. Even if he screams at her, calls her all the names under the sun, it would be better than this impasse. She is dismayed when he merely picks up the car keys from the dresser and tosses them to her. They sail across the room in a graceful curve and land beside her on the quilt. She is unnerved by George acting so out of character. She guesses he is daring her to go, and trusts she won't. Grace determines not to be the one to cede defeat first.

She springs up from the bed and drags a weekend bag from underneath it, and begins to pull open drawers and stack underwear and T-shirts neatly on the pillow. She acts as if she is calm and organised, in control of herself. She is boiling with rage inside, but she won't let George see that. She won't give him the satisfaction. She moves into Tom's room and chooses clothes for him, while he stares at her, bleary-eyed. In ten minutes, she has the bag packed, yet she still hasn't elicited any response from George. He is pulling on shorts and an old shirt, like any weekend.

It is clear that, for once, George is going to stand his ground. He may be able to break the patterns of a lifetime, but Grace can't. There is nothing else for it; she will simply have to carry out her threat, and go. She feels sorry for poor Tom, caught in the middle of it. Grace is only too aware that, now he's nearly three, he can pick up on any sign of a bad atmosphere between George and her. She's convinced he has developed special child antennae. To keep him happy, while he eats his cereal, she tells him she's taking him to Nairobi to find a big shop so he can choose something for his birthday.

'Is Daddy coming?' He looks at her over the bowl of his spoon as he raises it to his mouth.

'Daddy's got to stay here at work,' she answers. 'You'll be able to show him your present when you get home.'

'But it's Saturday. Daddy doesn't go to school on Saturday.' The spoon drops into the cornflakes.

'He's got to stay in case one of the boys gets ill, or the headmaster needs him for an important job.'

Grace is fully aware George is listening from the living room and prays that he doesn't suddenly decide to break his silence and contradict her. When he comes and kneels down by Tom's chair she holds her breath. 'If he says one word,' she thinks, 'One nice thing, I'll stay.'

'You and Mummy have a good time and you make her buy you something lovely.'

'A bike,' Tom announces. 'A red bike.'

'Go on, then. Daddy will teach you how to ride it when you get home.' George hugs Tom and kisses his milky mouth.

Angry and upset though she is, Grace is grateful George is not making things hard for Tom. She dreads him becoming a pawn in their ridiculous fight. What she thought would happen if she vanished into the night without a word, she can't say. She wasn't thinking at all. She is certainly stunned that the situation she finds herself in now has come about, shell-shocked by its onslaught. Grace convinces herself that, if only George would revert to form and offer her an olive branch, they could forget the past forty eight hours and carry on as before. She is wrong.

Instead, George loads her bag into the boot of the car and helps Tom settle in the back seat with his favourite Squidgy Bear, and reminds them both to stay sitting down on the busy roads. Tom giggles at his father's silliness. Grace fits herself behind the wheel, filling time by adjusting the mirror and sliding the seat to a better driving position. She winds down the window and waits for some final sign of appeasement. None comes. She starts the engine and pulls slowly away. The heat is already intense, and there is no longer any threat of rain. All along the school drive ahead of her, Grace sees the flame trees are forming a red avenue, each flower the colour of blood.

At the last minute, just as she turns out of their compound, she hears George call 'Drive safely', but it is too late to stop.

Chapter Thirteen

The fast fading light makes the city beyond the hotel window nigh-on invisible. The trees in the grounds stand ghost-like and the tall buildings in the distance blur into the night sky. Things take on a completely different perspective to Grace once she is settled into a room at The Jacaranda. 'Now what?' is the question that springs to mind. She booked in here because it is the only hotel she knows, from her visit with George, when they had to come to arrange his work permit. (And why that couldn't be done from Marigoi, she hasn't a clue.) Now, she is at a loss to know what to do on a Saturday night in an unfamiliar city. Moreover, one she has heard is full of potential dangers to white people who don't know their way about. One step beyond the regular tourist trail and all sorts of violent consequences might follow. That's what she's been told.

Tom brought a little box of favourite toys with him to keep him busy and Grace is down on the rug, helping him build a Lego castle. It dawns on her that all the shops will be closed tomorrow, Sunday, so she will have no chance of buying a bicycle for him then, or any other kind of toy. She didn't think of that before she rushed off.

She does remember Helen Fraser handing her a business card when they met that afternoon in Kisumu by the pool, and hopes she has it with her, and hasn't left it by the bed at home, or lost it altogether. A search of her purse finds it, creased and grubby with sun oil, but still readable, and

44

listing both an office and a home number. If nothing else, surely Helen will be able to give her some idea of where she can get a decent meal, or take Tom tomorrow.

When the last black brick is clicked into place on the battlements, Grace takes Tom with her down to the foyer to use the phone. She takes it for granted that the office number will go unanswered at this time at a weekend, so dials Helen's home number. It rings for a long time, the sound echoing in the earpiece, till Grace gives up. She pauses to consider, and rings the business number. Perhaps someone there might know where Helen is. If she's back in Kisumu, or anywhere else for that matter, Grace won't waste more time calling again.

'Standard. Copy desk. Who's calling?' The phone is picked up so fast, and the man answering so brusque, that Grace is put on a back foot.

'Grace McIntyre calling for Helen Fraser. It's a personal call. Sorry, but I couldn't get her at home.'

'Out on the town I expect. Hang on, I'll check.' The line quietens as the man apparently puts his hand over the mouthpiece, but Grace can make out barked questions and more faint replies. 'No, you're in luck. You just caught her, here she is.'

'Grace, what a surprise. I didn't expect to hear from you out of the blue. But make it quick, I'm done for the day, I was just off for a drink.'

'I'm here in Nairobi, me and Tom, only for a couple of days. I wanted to pick your brains about where to take him. I don't know Nairobi at all well.'

'God, where to start?' There is a pause before Helen continues. 'Where are you staying?'

'The Jacaranda, but I've got the car.'

'You don't want to drive. A few of us are going to go and get something to eat. Why don't you come along? I'll pick you up.'

'What about Tom?' Grace has no intention of leaving him with a sitter.

'He'll be fine. Haven't you noticed yet kids in Kenya get taken everywhere. I'll be in the car park in about half an hour.'

Her suggestion provides a glimpse of excitement for Grace. She doesn't remember when she last sat down and had a meal and a decent conversation with anyone but George. She and Tom race back upstairs and she takes him in the shower with her to save time, lathering the day's grime from them both. After dressing him, she slips an old dress over her head, the only one she brought, and a pair of flat canvas shoes. She drops a book for Tom in her bag, checks she has enough cash, and goes to wait for Helen in the foyer.

The receptionist stares at her, a woman without a man, from time to time and Grace begins to fidget. When she hears a car horn sound, she leaps up, dislodging Tom from her knee, and escapes the watchful eyes by dashing out to the car park. Helen is waving from an old VW Beetle that is so cluttered Grace has to throw piles of papers and laden boxes into the back seat before she can squeeze herself in, Tom on her lap, and they can go anywhere.

46

Within thirty minutes, she is sitting in a basket chair on the terrace of The Norfolk, feeling shabby and provincial among the smart city workers, and eating chicken curry from a scooped out pineapple half. She ordered a hamburger for Tom, thinking it simplest, but when it arrives, as big as the plate it's on, his eyes widen like saucers and he looks at her in wonderment. He doesn't know where to start.

There are two others at the table with them, colleagues of Helen. James is Australian, middle-aged, taciturn. He says nothing without careful consideration, weighing every word before he utters it, however mundane the matter is they're discussing. Ravi is younger, much younger in Grace's estimation; full of youthful enthusiasm. He has a habit of waving his arms about when he talks and slapping his fingers on the table to emphasise a point, much to the consternation of all of them sitting there, who expect to see a plate hurtle to the floor at any minute. Ravi is a Sikh, a Nairobi local, and his dark blue turban is a source of fascination for Tom.

The conversation veers wildly from the serious to the everyday, and Grace, persuading Tom to try the hamburger, is only half listening. Her attention is caught when she hears the word 'Luo.'

'I know someone who's a Luo. What are you saying about them? I didn't catch it.'

'We were just saying, if trouble comes, trouble for the president, they'll be at the root of it. They don't like being side-lined from the government.' Helen leans close to Grace, so her words don't carry. 'Remember, I told you about shenanigans when we met before. Kisumu's rife with it.' She laughs, and Ravi joins her, but James sits back in his chair, shaking his head.

'You won't be laughing if anything comes of it,' he pronounces. 'I wouldn't care to predict the consequences.'

'You sound very pessimistic. It's peaceful here, when you hear what goes on in most of Africa.' Grace drops her comment into a quiet lull in the conversation, and continues with her curry, relishing the creamy Korma.

It's as if she has lit the blue touch paper, and James, who has been so measured, erupts.

'You've been here five minutes; you haven't a clue what you're talking about. The Luo are clever. They want power. They expected power after Kenyatta died. The president is a Kalenjin, who's denying them power. Of course there's going to be bloody trouble!'

All around them, other diners are beginning to murmur and comment, but the more Helen and Ravi try to calm James down, the more carried away he gets, coming out with remarks that are both slanderous and racist, and, frankly, dangerous. Everyone's attention is on him.

Only Grace observes the African waiters. They move around the terrace balancing trays of drinks and food, and smile broadly, all white teeth and charm, when they put plates and glasses down in front of a customer. But, when they are finished serving, they congregate at the back of the bar, gesturing at James with tilts of the head. Some have faces like thunder and others look simply scared. They mutter at each other under their breath, and Grace can't believe what they're saying will be complimentary.

At last, Helen distracts James up with another beer, Ravi pays the bill, and soon they are going their separate ways. Ravi steers James off towards the city centre and Helen takes Grace and Tom back to The Jacaranda.

'If you can stay around till Monday, there are great shops in Biashara Street,' Helen tells Grace. 'Fantastic for fabrics and I'm sure there's a toy shop, a big one. All Asian, of course; they own all the shops round here. The president'll be wanting to get rid of them next.' She laughs her throaty laugh. 'As for tomorrow, if you like, I'll come and get you after breakfast and take you both out to Nairobi Game Park.'

'Game Park? In the city?' Grace finds that very hard to credit.

'Grace, it's famous. You really are green, aren't you? Didn't you find out anything about the place before you came out?'

No sooner are Grace and Tom out of the car than Helen slams the door and is gone, the VW coughing and spluttering. The suspicious receptionist has been replaced and the new man at the desk gives Grace her key with a cheerful 'Have a good night, Madam.'

'Tom-Tom. We're going to see some lions tomorrow. What do you think about that? And giraffe. And elephant.'

'Pigs?' Tom's little face lights up. 'Like in my farm book.'

'No, darling. Probably not pigs. But perhaps special horses, called zebras.'

'I like pigs best. Perhaps there are special pigs too.'

Grace hopes so for his sake. 'I can't promise,' she tells him. 'Let's wait and see.'

Chapter Fourteen

She is sitting barely fifty feet from a family of elephant, matriarchs and calves, yet Grace has only to lift her head to see the high-rise buildings of the city skyline, less than four miles away, shimmering in a heat haze. There is only a wire fence separating them and the towers blur into urban mirages, concrete oases at the edge of game park desert. It has been a revelation to Grace, a wonderful gem, and she can kerb her excitement no more than Tom, who is kneeling on the back seat of the car staring out and shouting every time he spots something move. Helen hired a Masai guide at the park gate when they paid their entry fee and he is teaching Tom the Swahili names of the animals. *Tembo, kifaru, duma.* Elephant, rhino, cheetah.

In front of them, grazing amongst the elephant, are vast herds of impala and gazelle, tails and noses twitching, every sense alert to danger. The smaller gazelle leap straight up into the air, as if on springs, whenever they're spooked and they spook easily. Giraffe graze on the acacia trees scattered over the plain, heedless of the vicious thorns that deter other, more delicate, mouths. *Twiga.* Grace has been listening to the guide too. She forgets a lot of the names already, they see so much. Tom keeps looking out for pigs, but, for now, is satisfied with the zebra, that he insists on calling stripy horses.

At noon the sun is fierce and unrelenting. Across the plain animals drift into the longer grass or congregate at the water holes in search of a cooler place to rest for an hour or two. A leopard languishes high up in the fork of a tree trunk, all but invisible. Even the vultures have ceased their circling and bleached bones and shredded skin are left unpicked on abandoned carcasses. Only the gazelle remain, constantly sniffing the air, waiting for disaster.

The guide signals to Helen to start the car and they move away slowly. They follow rudimentary pathways through the park, but they are rough and rutted and it is hard going in a saloon car at times. The guide taps Helen on the arm and points whenever he wants her to turn off through the scrub, and is clearly looking out for something in particular. His eyes scan the plains, seeing everything, until he puts his hand on the wheel and Helen knows to stop the car.

The male lion is huge. He is sprawled on a low rock, basking in the sun. His mane is a glorious thick halo that doubles the size of his head, and the feet that flop over the edge of the rock are the size of dinner plates. He casts one lazy eye in their direction before settling into a more comfortable position and slumbering on.

'Is it safe for us to get so close?' Grace is worried for Tom, who is banging on the window to attract the lion's attention. 'Would he attack a car?'

'Look at him. He's probably had a kill this morning and eaten fit to bust. It's as hot for him as it is for you; he doesn't want to be moving around. He's not going to be bothered with us.'

'*Utanyamaza.*'

'The guide says we must be quiet while we're here. We mustn't disturb the *simba.* Can you be very quiet Tom, like a little mouse?' Helen whispers in Tom's ear.

'Yes. When we saw the birds in the forest, I had to be very quiet. Isaac told me, or I'd frighten them all away. Isaac said I was good at quiet.' Tom lowers his voice to match his words. 'And I can keep a secret. Me and Mummy like secrets.'

His attention is drawn back to the lion when it stretches again and sits up. The male turns their way and shakes his massive head to dislodge the flies crawling round his eyes, his mane swirling. He shows his contempt for his audience by yawning widely, and his great gaping jaws bare sharp yellow teeth and a muscular pink tongue. Grace shudders in sympathy for the gazelle, appreciating their tremulousness. She'd tremble, too, in their fragile situation.

They are driving out of the park, nearly at the gate, when their path is crossed by a mother warthog closely trailed by two tiny piglets. Grace doesn't think she has ever seen such ugly babies.

'Look, Mummy. Piggies.' Tom's day is made.

'So, who's this Isaac? Friend of yours?' They are sitting by the pool at The Jacaranda sipping fresh lime juice. Tom is making friends with another little boy, whose father is helping them find lizards in the hotel garden. 'I don't think I've heard of Isaac before.' Helen swirls the straw in her juice and Grace can hear the ice rattle.

'He's my gardener, the student. I told you about him.'

'Did you enjoy the forest then? Did George?'

Grace catches the teasing tone of Helen's question, and, because she is already feeling guilty, gets cross.

'Don't be stupid. George wasn't there, as you've guessed. We just had a lovely afternoon. There's a lot of charcoal burning goes on in Kakamega and it was interesting to find out about it, as well as seeing the birds.'

'I bet you did. That who you meant last night, your Luo friend?' Helen drains her glass and waves at the waiter to bring another.

'Yes, but I didn't say he was a friend, just that I knew him.' Graces wishes she didn't feel as if she has to justify herself.

'If he's a student, he's probably a Marxist. They all are. That's why they don't like the president cosying up to the Americans so much.'

Grace laughs aloud at this. 'Marxists, for God's sake. You do come out with some rubbish, Helen.'

'You wouldn't believe how many of them graduate from Eastern bloc universities; Russia, East Germany. Doctors, academics, politicians; all the high fliers. Be careful, Grace. Don't get mixed up in things you don't understand. Sit back, stick to being an expat and you'll have a great life in Kenya. What the Africans want is nothing to do with you; you're only here for a couple of years. Let them get on with it.'

Helen reclines the chair and closes her eyes. Grace props her elbows on the table and tries to concentrate on enjoying herself.

The morning is cooler and more comfortable for city walking. Grace leaves the car at the hotel and sets off on foot, though she ends up having to carry Tom for most of the way. She passes The Norfolk and she smiles as an image of James firing off verbal salvos comes to her. She didn't notice last night that the hotel is opposite the university, which has had its doors locked to students and staff alike for two months now. She wonders if Isaac will ever get the chance to go back. She's never asked him what he's studying; she will when she sees him next.

Tom decides he can walk after all, and the two of them stroll hand-in-hand down the busy pavements. Tom is eager to find a toy shop, but Grace enjoys browsing and window shopping. She finds the street Helen told her about, Biashara Street, and turns down it. It is a little quieter than the roads surrounding it, running between two larger streets. The choice of fabrics here is vast; richly embellished sari cloth in jewel colours, printed cottons and everyday twills and ticking. Yards of satin ribbon and narrow lace tumble from spools, and, for a fleeting second, Grace longs for a daughter.

'Mummy, Mummy, there it is.' Tom sees the toy shop across the street before she does. 'Mummy, come on!'

The window is like a child's dream of Christmas. Dolls and cars and trains and teddy bears falling over each other, as if they've tumbled from an upturned sack. Inside, the shop is crammed to the rafters with boxes and shelves of every kind of toy and game imaginable, though a cursory glance at the price tickets makes Grace's eyes water. Hanging from sturdy chains around the top of the walls, like over-sized decorations, is a small selection of trikes and scooters and bicycles. When he sees Grace showing open interest in them, the shopkeeper manoeuvres the African assistant to one side and prefers to serve Grace himself.

'Can you get some down for me to look at? I can't see from here.' Grace points to the gently spinning bikes.

'I keep them out of the way. I don't sell so many, you see, only special presents. I need the room on the floor for the things I sell a lot.' The man indicates the array of items he has.

He unlocks the chains so the shop worker can lower the bikes carefully and separate them, lining them up for Tom to try. They have obviously been suspended out of the way for a long time, and a fine cover of dust coats the saddles and handlebars. The shop owner flicks the bikes clean with a soft cloth, whipping the dust into tiny tornados that swirl away and settle somewhere else. His worker goes and shuts the street door. Grace remembers Mr. Awar, and guesses half the reason the bikes sway so far above her head is that fear of thieves is an Asian obsession.

Sadly, there is no red bike in the shop, but after Tom tries every other one they have, whether his feet reach the pedals or not, Grace takes out her purse and counts out far more one hundred shilling notes than she was anticipating. The shop assistant is tasked with wrapping Tom's new pale blue bike in thick brown card and string. He hands it to her with a separate package containing the stabilisers.

She has no idea how she's going to carry it back to The Jacaranda with all her other packets and bags The owner, when she explains the problem, is so delighted at such a major sale, when it's not Diwali or Madaraka Day, that he loads bicycle, Grace and Tom into the gleaming truck that stands outside his shop and drives them himself.

There is nothing more to stay for. Grace has calmed down in these two days and is sure George will have too. She was forced into coming, but the break has been lovely. She feels quite refreshed. She and George must make the effort and come to Nairobi more often. Then Marigoi will be more bearable.

She drives towards home along the Nakuru Road, a thousand and one ideas swirling round in her mind. She has to sort out something to celebrate Tom's birthday, for one thing. Not another party, she quickly decides. She dreams up ways she can make things better between her and George. She wonders if there's anything she can do in Marigoi, some sort of work at the school, to help out.

Whenever a thought about Isaac pops into her head, she deliberately quashes it. Helen's been here a long time and is more than likely right in the opinions she holds. She's had more time to weigh up the situation, hasn't she? Grace should listen to her. Isaac is interesting, but she can't let herself get involved in his battles. Where would it lead? When she sees him again, she'll make it clear that there will be no more excursions. No *safari.*

Chapter Fifteen

The night air is heavy with the scent of datura and frangipani. Grace breathes deeply, drawing in great draughts of fragrance that infuse her whole body. Her hair and her skin are rich with its headiness. The daturas are protective of their perfume, storing it up till dusk begins to draw a curtain over the garden, when it bursts out to lure unsuspecting moths. It is too precious to squander on daylight. The waxy petals of the frangipani framing the porch glow like white butterflies among the leaves, fluttering up to heaven. It is peaceful in the garden tonight. No crying of babies and children, no boys sneaking out of homework and racing round the compound, no servants crashing and banging, and no neighbours talking long into the night.

Grace can hardly credit that only a week ago she was throwing open the doors of this porch and inviting those self-same neighbours into her home, full of confidence and hospitality. Look where that has got her. Rather than widening her social circle, she's constricted it. She's been living in self-imposed purdah since she got back from Nairobi, convinced that every scene from that night is being picked over by the entire compound, even those who weren't there. She imagines the rumour mill grinding through the offices and kitchens and even, what is worse, the dormitories; the details becoming ever more scandalous. The thought of turning a corner to find Glory or Prudence or Primrose gossiping is too much to cope with for now. Grace knows she can't be a coward forever;

it's not in her nature; she'll have to face them sometime, but not yet.

Grace has to face George, of course, but he doesn't make it easy. She hasn't been able to fathom out what he's thinking during these past three days. He is palpably delighted to have Tom home again, but nothing about his manner convinces Grace the delight extends to her. He is more guarded that he used to be, more circumspect. She doesn't like it.

The blue bike is a real hit and Tom wheels it out every day to practise. George follows him up and down the drive, over and over, one hand on the saddle till he finds his balance. George says their garden is no good for practice because the lawn is so bumpy, but Grace remembers the attention Isaac paid to it only weeks ago and the smoothness he achieved. She can't see how it can be any sort of problem for Tom with his sturdy stabilisers.

George is polite enough; no more interrogations, no more recriminations; but the old familiarity hasn't re-established itself. A distance has opened up between them, a subtle shift in their relationship, and Grace is treading cautiously, taking one step at a time. She's normally well-attuned to how the cogs in George's mind spin and slot into place and she isn't comfortable with this uncertainty. She is at a loss as to how to get the two of them back on an even keel, but knows she must. Seeing George with Tom, and their evident pleasure in one another, makes her heart melt.

'Come in before the mozzies arrive,' George advises her. 'We had to take a couple of the boys down to the hospital with malaria while you were away.'

'I'll be in soon. I've covered my arms up,' she reassures him. 'Are the boys alright now?'

'One's back here, but the other's pretty bad. Doctors think it might be cerebral.'

Grace is accustomed to boys being ferried to the hospital on a regular basis. None of them has anti-malarials. The school doesn't even run to mosquito nets, no matter what fees they charge to come here. She and George and Tom take their Paludrine tablets and Chloroquine syrup religiously every morning, ticking the days off on a chart.

'Could he die? Is it that bad?' She has never known anyone who has died. What must it be like to live in a society where it's commonplace, and the possibility of it lurks in the background all the time?

'I suppose so.' George shrugs. 'Cerebral often is. Still, only another day and they'll all be off home anyway. Their parents' problem then.'

It's unlike George to be so nonchalant about his pupils' welfare. When did this callousness towards them materialise? Or, perhaps, Grace has been so wrapped up in herself lately that it's always been there and she's never stood and taken the time to spot it before.

She sits a little longer, but soon joins George indoors. He has taken out the big map of Kenya and spread it out on the floor and is tracing a route to the coast. Now the holidays have all but arrived, he wants to go Mombasa and lay on a beach.

Grace pictures them all swimming in the Indian Ocean or shell seeking on the white sand. She dreams of coconut palms and pink coral, like she's seen on postcards.

'Depending on the state of the road,' George tells her, 'I reckon it'll take us seven hours from Nairobi. We'll have to stay overnight on the way down. Was The Jacaranda still okay last week?'

It's the first direct question he's asked about her trip since her return, and Grace takes it as a good sign. She tells him about the suspicious receptionist, hoping he'll laugh, but he just says he's not surprised, they must get all sorts.

'One of Helen's friends, another journalist, says there's going to be trouble. Thinks it's brewing under the surface. Do you hear anything at school?'

'They're very choosy about what to say and what not to say in front of me. But take my word for it, anything that does happen will wash over the top of us; we'll be bystanders to whatever they get up to. Having said that, I don't get the feeling anything's going on.'

'This journalist, James, blames it on one lot fighting with another; 'tribal conflict' he said. Talked about the Luo and the Kalenjin especially. I told him we were right up in Kalenjin territory and he said 'poor you.''

'They used to fight. The Luo didn't do so badly during British rule, not comparatively. The Kalenjin only really got together late on, they used to be lots of small groups. That's why the area is called Nandi, because they were all Nandi speaking. They have more clout as one big group. I don't think a president could have emerged from one of the smaller tribes, as they were.'

Grace is surprised George knows so much about Kenyan history. It's not something they ever talk about; she assumed he was as ignorant as she.

'Isaac is Luo, you know?' she says. 'He told me.'

'Did he?' George pores over the map, marking a possible route in red pencil.

Grace glances over his shoulder and points to an area surrounding his coloured line.

'When we go here, through Tsavo,' she informs him reliably, 'We should see plenty of elephant. You can see them from the road. And troops of baboon.'

'And did Isaac tell you that, too?' George doesn't raise his head.

'Yes, he did, if you must know. And he said if we wait till next month and go to the Mara, we'll see the wildebeest migration from the Serengeti. Thousands of animals cross.'

'Well, I'd hate to miss that, especially if Isaac recommends it. I'd hate to waste his expert advice.' George refolds the map along its neat creases and slots it back onto the bookshelf. He zips the red pencil into his pencil case and puts that in his briefcase. 'August it is, then. Second weekend do for you?'

Grace bites back the sarcastic remark that wells up, 'No, I'm busy that weekend. Didn't you know?' and goes to bed. When George comes in and flops on his back beside her, she rolls away.

Surely George isn't suspicious. She wonders if anyone's said something to him while she was in Nairobi. But what could anyone say? No-one knows anything. There's nothing to know.

George hasn't touched her since she's been home. He doesn't go as far as sleeping in the spare room anymore; God forbid that Esther should talk about them in the village. He lays beside Grace like a block of wood, which is somehow worse, as if he's immune to the tempting warmth of her body next to him and oblivious of her perfume infusing the sheets they share. She's given him time, waiting for him to make the first move, but if this physical rift yawns between them for much longer, they will never ford it. Grace fears that if she can't mend things here, in bed, she won't able to mend them anywhere. She rolls back towards him, touching him, encouraging him, desperate to restore their old intimacy. If only they make love, everything will be fine. It will make things better.

George's body responds to her touch, as she hoped he would, but he doesn't let down his emotional barriers so easily. He doesn't so much as whisper her name. The sex, for that's all it is, is perfunctory and soulless, quickly over. Afterwards, Grace feels grubby and worthless. Everything is not fine, and nothing is better.

Chapter Sixteen

Saturday the seventeenth has come. Tom is wearing a new black and white striped T-shirt Grace chanced upon in Biashara Street and couldn't resist. He looks like Burglar Bill, and George has printed SWAG on the bike's plastic pannier in indelible ink. Tom has been itching to expand his horizons, so, as a birthday treat, George is going to let him pedal to the village to buy bread and *mandazi* for breakfast. Grace expects it will take them some time. She's decorating the table with balloons and a banner saying 'HAPPY 3RD BIRTHDAY' that she has had hidden away for a long time. She peels and slices mangoes and whizzes them in the blender to make thick sweet pulp, ready to dilute into refreshing juice. It's Tom's favourite.

When she's got things ready, and is just waiting for the pastries to arrive, she takes her courage in both hands and goes over to the office. The door is wide open, as it generally is, and Glory is at her desk typing. Grace waits outside and takes a deep breath before she goes in. Glory has her hair scraped off her face and tied with a shocking-pink scarf that reveals her long neck. Grace is reminded of the giraffe in the game park. She's been worrying for nothing. Glory is peering over the keys, checking every word she types, and scarcely notices that she's no longer alone. Grace calls '*jambo*' and wanders behind the desk to sort through the letters in the pigeon holes.

'*Jambo,* Grace,' Glory smiles at her in a distracted sort of way. 'How are you?'

'I'm well thank you. I've come to see if there's anything for Tom. It's his birthday.'

'There is a parcel; I have it here. I was going to call with it later. It is very big.' Glory bends to one side and retrieves a brown paper box from under the desk. 'It is from England. I recognise the stamps.' Her smile is pleasant, her tone easy. She is soon concentrating on her work, and the clack of keys ricochets round the stuffy office.

Grace recalls her last conversation with Isaac; he said she'd be old news in no time and he was right. She takes the parcel and collects the rest of their letters, and glances through the envelopes on her way home. She can guess who most are from, only one or two have unfamiliar writing.

'Mummy, look. Look at me, no stables.'

Tom is pedalling towards her from the gate, his progress erratic. His face is a picture of concentration as he careers along the track, brow screwed up and teeth biting his lip. Jogging beside him, carrying the abandoned stabilisers, George is ready to steady him every time he wobbles. Tom hasn't learned how to brake, and crashes into Grace's shins, lurching sideways and falling off.

'I'm alright, it didn't hurt.' Tom is back on his bike in no time and struggling over the gravel behind the office. 'Beat you home,' he cries, wobbling as he looks back. 'Daddy, come on.'

George takes the parcel from Grace and chases after him. Grace rubs her shin. The mudguard has caught her below the knee and tiny pinpricks of blood swell through the skin, making a crimson seam against her bronzed leg. She wipes the droplets away but by the time she is home more are dripping onto her foot. Conscious of how easy it is to pick up an infection, she takes wipes and disinfectant from the bathroom and carefully cleans the scratch, pressing hard to stop the bleeding. She has to go into the bedroom to find a plaster. The disinfectant is beginning to sting so she sits in the chair, waiting for it to ease.

In her pocket, she still has the bundle of letters. There are five cards for Tom, grandparents and aunties, she's sure. Her friends at Canterbury Library have sent a postcard of the cathedral, and there are bills for George. The last envelope is an ordinary brown business one. Her name and address are written clearly in block capitals and there is a Kenyan stamp. She knows before she opens it, absolutely knows, who has sent it.

There has been no sign of Isaac since her Nairobi trip. He must have been there while she was; their paths might have crossed at any time. She pictures him walking down Koinange Street while she was round the corner deliberating over bicycles. He promised he'd be back for Tom's birthday, didn't he? But he won't. His message, four paltry lines, is simply to say he must stay in Nairobi 'for many months'. Grace folds the note back into the envelope. She hesitates, deliberating, and takes it with her to show George.

George is pouring iced water from the fridge over the mango pulp. He has laid all the pastries he and Tom bought on a big tray covered with bright cloth. As well as the white loaf and *mandazi*, there are small round buns with glazed tops that Grace has never seen before, and three large slices of sponge cake covered with shavings of coconut.

'I saw Isaac in the village, fetching water.' George says. 'Did you know he's staying at Esther's?'

'No!' Her shock is stark.

'He doesn't tell you everything, then.' George puts a small candle in Tom's piece of cake and lights it. 'He must have secrets too.'

Grace screws the brown envelope into a tight ball and thrusts it back in her pocket.
Tom blows out his candle after a lot of puffing, and Grace and George sing '*Happy Birthday*' to him. He has cake and buns and bread with his favourite jam. This week it is pineapple.

Grace leans over the kitchen sink, waiting. She has twitched the curtain to one side a hundred times, scanning the drive for the first sign of Esther's dumpy figure turning the corner. A hornbill has settled on the branches of the lemon tree, which droop with its weight, and one of the Chebele children has crept through the hedge and is stealing purple passion fruits. Grace wouldn't be able to tell you. Her mind is fixed on nothing but finding out if Isaac really is in the village. Why would he be, when he's written and said the complete opposite?

Grace glimpses a flash of blue and black *kikoi* bobbing up and down above the hedge and rushes out. Esther, surprised, is wary and

68

suspicious. When she hears what Grace wants, suspicion melds into an anxiety that etches itself on her face and fades the brown skin to grey.

'Mrs. McIntyre, it's not good for you to know him. He is not your friend.'

'No, it's work. He's been away for over a week and there's so much to be done.' Grace can see from Esther's eyes that she doesn't believe her for a second. 'Is he there?' She grabs the woman's arm, pleading with her. She's past caring what the gossip is when the locals sit outside their huts stirring their pots of *ugali*. She, Isaac and George will be a juicy titbit for them to chew over. 'Please.'

Grace tells George she's driving to Eldoret; says she'll go by herself, now he's home to watch Tom. If he doesn't mind. George gazes at her, blue eyes steady, and says he's happy to stay with his son. 'My son,' he says, not 'our son.'

She parks the car by the ramshackle *dukas*. A group of barefooted children is kicking a tin can around in the dirt. They stop and stare at her and the tin can rolls away, forgotten. The biggest boy swaggers up to the car and leans against it, both hands on the window. Grace hears him say '*muzungu*' and some other words that she doesn't understand and all the children giggle. It isn't a pleasant sound. The boy jumps back quick enough when she flings open the door, leaving two red imprints smeared on the glass. The group runs, scattering in all directions, shrieking and shouting. The village dogs join in, barking and jumping up, going wild. It is cacophony. People begin to poke their heads out of huts and shops to see what the fuss is about. Isaac is one of them. He regards Grace with the same steady look as George, locks the hut, and walks to the car.

'I will drive.'

It has never crossed Grace's mind that he might be able to drive. How little she knows about him. She slides across the smooth upholstery of the seats, and Isaac folds himself behind the steering wheel. Rather than turn on the ignition, he reaches for her hand and laces his fingers through hers. They sit. Words aren't important. When he does start the car, stamping too hard on the accelerator, he jerks away from the roadside without looking back, and is rewarded for his carelessness by the screech of brakes and a car horn blaring loudly. A blue Mazda swerves round them and roars through the school gate. It leaves behind it the smell of burning rubber.

Chapter Seventeen

Bamboo grows here, tall spires of green shiver in the breeze. Black and white colobus chase one another in and out the trembling fronds, babies clinging to their mothers' bellies. If Grace and Isaac's path strays too close, the monkeys freeze on their haunches, jittery, and a lone sentinel screams an alarm. Oak and teak fill the forest. They are at Mount Elgon. Grace thought Isaac would drive to Kakamega or Kisumu but he's brought her here, right up to the border. He tells her if they go any further west, they'll be in Uganda. It's where he's been planning to bring her, with Tom. Their *safari.*

'Come, I want to show you something.' He grips her hand and almost pulls her along, clambering over rocks and by the side of streams. The undergrowth becomes so wild and tangled Isaac has to force a path through, hacking at the leathery leaves with his bare hands or stamping down coarse grasses till they flatten into pulp. Where the branches are too strong for him, he holds them aside for Grace to scramble past. When he lets go they spring back, screening their passing. By the time they emerge at a rocky plateau, his arms and hands are covered in scratches, the welts swelling and oozing.

'Look at you,' Grace says, touching the scratches with her fingertips. 'You could do with some of Juma's magic. That'd soon fix you.'

'It's nothing,' Isaac insists, brushing off her hand, but he rolls down the sleeves of his shirt and buttons the cuffs, despite the heat. 'Come on.'

They begin to climb the rocks, which are smooth and well-trodden, until they reach the entrance to a cave. The opening is large but overhung by a rocky shelf which makes the interior completely black. Grace doesn't imagine the cave will be very deep; not much more than the caves carved out of the cliffs on the beaches near home.Remembering their trip to the forest, she expects they'll find be some strangenocturnal bird nesting there in the dark, and says so to Isaac. 'No, not birds.Plenty of birds out here, among the trees, but not inside the caves. I'll show you.'

They clamber the last few yards and into the cave, and stand just inside till their eyes grow accustomed to the lack of light. Grace, when she can see more clearly, is surprised at how large the chamber they are standing in is. The roof arches high above her head and the furthest end is impossible to judge.The shaft slopes away from them and they have to tread cautiously, keeping close to the wall of the cave. They descend for a quarter of a mile or more, Grace keeping one hand braced against the wall tokeep her steady. Isaac istracing the curve of thewallwith his palm and is obviously searching for something in particular. Gracecan see the white of his shirt sleeve as it brushes from left to right.

'Look here. What do you think these are?'

Isaac's voice echoes round the chamber

and from the disturbed silence erupttiny squeaks
and a muffled flapping that build into
a crescendo. Hundreds of bats that have been
hanging from the cave's roof unfurl their
leathery wings and swoop around their heads, their
high pitched 'eeks' barely audible.
The glare of daylight at the cave opening acts as
an invisible barrier they won't go
beyond, and they swirl and dive in the dark.Grace
tries to beat them off, dreading the
thought of them tangling in her hair, but Isaac tells
her to stand still.
'Ignore them; they are more frightened than you.
Soon, they will grow used to us. They are just
enjoying their little sleep.'

Grace, reluctant, does as he says and soon the
bats begin to roost again, hanging above their
heads like living stalactites.

'That's not what I brought you to see,' Isaac tells
Grace. 'Come here by the wall where I am. Can
you see these marks? What do think made them?'
Grace goes close to the wall, close enough to see
regular striped marks, and when she touches them
her hand discovers deep grooves worn into the
rock face, silvered with age.

'Is it some kind of erosion?' she asks. 'Does
water come through?'

'It is elephant,' Isaac says. 'They come here to
find salt from the cave walls.'
Grace is convinced he is back to making fun of her
and her European gullibility. 'How would they get
in here?' She shakes her head. 'They couldn't fit.
And elephant like the open savannah.'

'No, it's true. Whole herds come here, it is well known in the area. They come down here in the pitch dark and scrape away with their tusks till small pieces of the rock fall to the ground and then they eat them. It is the only salt around and they must have it. These are called the elephant caves. In other places elephant live completely underground.'

Grace realises he isn't teasing. She looks at the marks on the cave wall again, wondering how long it must have taken for such deep ridges to develop. Countless numbers of elephant must have come here over the years, generation after generation, wearing away at the surface. Habits so engrained that the herd is compelled to trudge for miles across the plains, through the forest and then make the awkward climb up the rocks. Family instincts.

Grace is stabbed by sudden guilt. She hasn't thought of Tom once, not since she left him with George this morning. Now she is panicked. They were driving for more than an hour before they reached Elgon and she has no idea how much time has passed since they arrived here.

'I've got to go back. It must be very late.'

Isaac can hear the anxiety in her voice. He turns to face her and takes hold of her hands, searching her face, then pulls her close against him and they stand with their arms wrapped about each other, his chin resting on the top of her head and they rock gently, as if trying to soothe away the tension. It is the first time they have been so close and Grace wishes they could stay like this forever, cocooned from reality. She knows it is impossible.

'What are we going to do, Isaac? We can't go on like this.'

'I didn't tell you I was back in the village because I thought we should not meet. I have too many problems. It was you who came to find me, Grace.'

'I was so worried. Esther tells me you are bad, I've no idea why. I don't really care. I just wanted to see you. I wanted to see you more than stay with George.'

'Grace, even without my present difficulties, you know it is very hard for us. Europeans and Africans do not often mix well here in Kenya. I don't know what it is like in your place.'

'Not always so very different.' Grace sighs and stands back from him. 'Do you think it's hopeless?'

'Grace, let me tell you. I think, between us, it would be hopeless at any time. Now, when I am involved in so much you do not know about, it is even more so.'

'Tell me then, so I will know. What have you got yourself mixed up in? Why is everything such a mystery with you?'

'Remember when we spoke before. My 'opposition meetings', you called them. I was in Nairobi to have more of those meetings. There are many of us and we are organised. We will fight for change if we have to. Last week we learned one of our group was a policeman, so we couldn't trust him. Those of us who do not live in the city came home and left him for our friends who live there to deal with.'

'Deal with? Deal with how?'

'However they think best. I did not ask. Then I will not have to lie.'

Grace, when she looks at Isaac, is shocked by how matter-of-fact he seems, how casually he implies violence. Surely she must have misunderstood.

'They won't hurt him, will they? They wouldn't beat him up or anything?'

'Grace, if they think he was spying on us, a beating would be a small thing. He would be lucky for only a beating.'

Grace drops her arms to her sides and moves back. She cannot believe Isaac is involved with men like this. She has to get things clear in her head.

'Have you beaten men yourself?'

'I have to do many things I do not choose to do. I told you, there has to be change here in Kenya, and sometimes only violence will work. It is always the way. You must understand that. Do you see how it is?'

'You sound like an old expat talking about Mau Mau, always excusing the atrocities.'

'Well the British taught us a lot.' Isaac laughs, but there is no humour there, only scorn. 'And we taught them much.'

Grace turns back to the cave entrance and finds her way to the opening, helped by the light filtering in.Isaac, unaware of how appalled she is, follows behind, telling her more stories of the elephant.

'We are like the elephant,' he says. 'We are all driven to do things by our nature.'

76

'I like to think we're able to be more rational,' Grace retorts. 'We're not wild animals.'

'We are, Grace, deep down. All of us.'

When they are retracing their steps to the car he continues to point out various animals and birds as they pass, but Grace takes in none of it. She can think of nothing but Isaac, a clear picture of him wielding a stick or his *panga*, or, what is worse, being at the receiving end of either.

Suddenly, she feels her arm grabbed as she is pulled to a halt.

'Look,' Isaac says quietly, pointing up to a large oak tree. Lying there, stretched along a thick high branch, Grace sees a huge cat, its spots half hidden by the dappled sun filtering through the leaves. It looks like any tame pet cat sleeping off its dinner.

'Leopard,' Isaac tells her. 'You don't see leopard easily. They are very hard to find. We are been very lucky to see him so close to the track. We have had a good day.'

Grace cannot fathom how a man can sound so relaxed, so happy, when, not half an hour ago, he spoke of violence. She wants so much to believe the best of him. When he sets off back to the car, she huddles to his side, a silent truce. With her arm around his waist and his across her shoulder, they walk along the path in close step, only separating when the undergrowth forces them to go in single file. When that happens, Isaac stretches his arm behind him as he forges ahead and Grace clings onto his fingertips with hers. She notices sticky, pale pink patches where his scratches have weptand leached bloody serum into the fabric of his shirt. She can't help picturing far worse.

Chapter Eighteen

It is nearly three o'clock by the time Isaac steers the car off the tarmac and pulls up on to a dirt road in the outskirts of Marigoi. Grace looks around, but they are in the middle of nowhere. A passing goatherd, a child, stares at the car but is soon distracted by one of his flock making a dash for freedom, and rushes to cut off its escape. She takes advantage of their isolation and leans over and kisses Isaac lightly, pressing her mouth to the hollow beneath his cheekbone. She has been longing to do this for weeks.

'Be careful, Grace. Consider what you are doing.' Isaac has on his scandalised voice, but Grace sees the beginning of a smile relaxing the muscles of his face, and leans to him again, edging across the width of the seats. She kisses him again, this time at the the very corner of his mouth, letting the tip of her tongue linger on his lips. Isaac's smile widens, but he doesn't kiss her back. He unlocks the car door, stretching out his long legs to stand in the dusty furrows that the car tyres have made.

'Grace, I'll come back to the garden tomorrow, to work. We will not talk about today there. We must keep out friendship very quiet. It is a private thing. Your husband must not begin to think bad things about you.'

'I don't care what George thinks.'

'You must. He is your husband. He is the father of your boy. You must think very hard.' Isaac says this, serious, and leaves her alone while he walks back down the road. Grace, looking round to watch him go, sees the young goatherdstaring at her, blank faced. The goats are running everywhere.

The house is empty when she lets herself in. There is no sign of George or Tom, and no note to say where they might be. Esther is long gone, but the cushions she plumped up while she was here are still smooth and pristine, and the woodwork she burnished to a gleaming finish bears no little boy's sticky fingerprints. Grace realises George must have left early, before Tom could create chaos. For a panicky moment she fears hehas taken the boy away altogether, but knows she's being irrational. He doesn't have the car, for one thing. She will have to wait.

Grace lays in the too short bath, her knees poking through scummy bubbles in the cooling water. One of the taps is dripping non-stop and the first rusty signs of corrosion are eating their way towards the overflow.The drips fall into the bath with tiny, regular 'plops', like Chinese water torture, that Grace has never noticed before. It must be a new development; a loose washer in all likelihood. George is good at practical things; she'll get him to fix it when he's home. When.

They burst into the house as she rinses the last of the soap from her body, drenching the sponge and pressing it against her neck. The water, now cold, cascades down her back. She hears their murmured voices and then little feet rush down the corridor and the bathroom door is flung open.

'Mummy, Mummy! I've got a puppy.' Tom is holding a small, wriggling body in his arms, squeezing it tight to keep a hold of it. Tom leans over the bath to show it to Grace, and the puppy, sensing itself dangled above the suds, whines and squirms all the more to escape.

'Be careful. You'll drop him in the water.' Grace pushes the puppy away. 'Where is he from? Whose is he?'

'Mine. It's mine and it's a her.' Before Grace can ask him any more, the puppy falls to the floor with a soft thud. It rights itself and scampers away, Tom chasing after it, calling, 'puppy, puppy!' as he goes. Grace can hear the two sets of feet, boy's soft shoes and animal's scratching claws as they cross the wooden floor in the living room.

Grace pulls the plug and sits on the rim of the bath to dry herself. Still wrapped in the towel, she goes to get an explanation from George. What has possessed him to get a dog without asking her? It's madness. It must belong to someone else. George is lying stretched flat on the floor with Tom and the puppy clambering all over him, both getting more and more excitable.

'What's with the puppy?' Grace asks. 'We can't keep a puppy.'

'It's a present for Tom, from the Wambuis. We can't give it back.'

George extricates himself from boy and puppy and rises to his feet. He picks black dog hairs from his trousers, one by one, carefully collecting them in the palm of his hand. He drops them in the waste bin and flops onto the sofa, squashing Esther's regimented cushions.

81

'Sammy came over to see if I could give him a lift to his mother's place, she's ill. I told him you had the car, but he said he'd have to go anyway, she needed food and blankets. So I said I'd go with him, help him carry things. Tom and I had nothing better to do, and I didn't know when you'd be back.'

Grace hears the rebuke. It doesn't bother her; it is the least of her worries today.

'How far?' Grace wants to know. 'How did you get there?'

'About ten miles, the road to Kericho. We took a *matatu*. Tom loved it.'

Grace has been in one of these death traps only once and swore 'never again.' The drivers are mad, in her opinion, completely reckless. She shudders at the thought of Tom in one.

'And how many did they cram in this time?' she asks. She remembers being squashed thigh to thigh with strangers, and more of them standing in the aisle right up against her face, until she felt she was suffocating. She remembers how the strong, musky smell of so many bodies being so tightly packed in the small space in the heat repulsed her.

'Eleven people, two goats and a crate of chickens inside, and three or four men hanging on outside. And Tom, of course.' George sounds amused.

'They could have at least put the chickens on top.' Grace is indignant for Tom.

'Well, they were Sammy's, for his mother.' George does find it funny.

The puppy, worn out by Tom's cuddles and shrieks, crawls out of his grasp and pads out of his reach. It flops in the middle of the rug and is soon curled fast asleep.

'And the dog?' Grace asks, set on finding a way to be rid of it.

'Mama Wambui's dog had a litter. When Tom said he'd just had a birthday, they gave it to him. They let him choose. It won't do any harm. It'll be nice for him.'

Tom is inching towards the little dog, keen to wake her up for more play. To give her some rest, George gets to his feet and picks Tom up in a fireman's lift.

'Let's you and me see what's in the shed that we can make a bed for your dog from. Perhaps Mummy can find an old sheet or something to put in it.'

'We can't keep it,' Grace says again, but she sees the way Tom is looking at the dog over George's shoulder, and they all hear the wavering in her tone.

Alone in the room with the puppy, she sits on the sofa, in the warm space George has left, and looks at it. Grace likes dogs. She just doesn't want the responsibility of one now, here, when so much is going on in her life. While she is looking at it, the puppy starts in its sleep and its legs twitch. Grace expects it's having a nightmare. She has to admit, it is very sweet. She can't help but bend down and pick it up, cradling it against the fluffy towel.

'The shed's locked.' Grace hasn't seen George come back in, she's so engrossed in the warm, soft weight on her lap. 'Where's the key?'

'I haven't got one. Isaac put a new padlock on for us.'

'So he might, but he must have given you a key.'

Grace has forgotten all about the key, it was so many weeks ago, another life. She takes it as a given that the shed is Isaac's space now, for him to organise and use as he wants. She hasn't been near it since the night of their party.

'He didn't. And I didn't ask.' Grace stands, handing the puppy to George, and moves out of the room. 'I'll go and sort something out from indoors for her.'

Grace finds an old curtain and an outgrown T-shirt of Tom's in the airing cupboard and collects a box, the one Tom's present from England arrived in, from his bedroom. She carries the box through to the kitchen and chooses the large bread saw from the knife rack. She hacks away at the thick cardboard till most of one side has been reduced to corrugated shreds, leaving a shallow ledge along the bottom. She lines the box with the curtain and rolls Tom's shirt into a pillow. The shirt is still redolent with the scent of him, and Grace presses it to her nose before she adds it to the box. She's pleased with her efforts and thinks it looks well enough, a cosy nest.

'Put her in here. She'll be okay for tonight. We can get the key off Isaac tomorrow if you want to find a crate.'

'I want to find a crate tonight, not tomorrow. It's ridiculous. What does he think he's playing at?' George is furious. 'It's our bloody shed, not his.'

84

'It's only a shed, George. He's not doing any harm.'

George stops shouting at her. He places the dog in the box and tucks it in a corner near the fireplace. Calm now, he looks at Grace.

'How do you know what he's doing? There or anywhere? Your trouble is, you try too hard to be matey with him. He's your *shamba* boy, Grace, not your friend. Remember that.'

A shiver runs down Grace's spine that comes from more than the chill of wearing nothing but a damp towel for so long. She recognises nascent suspicion running beneath George's words. He doesn't voice it, he may not be fully aware of it himself, but she can hear the worm of doubt deep in his brain begin to burrow to the surface.

Chapter Nineteen

Grace is exhausted, drained physically and emotionally by the events of yesterday, and sleeps late. She swims up from muddled dreams of Isaac and caves, elephant and leopards, only when it gets so noisy outside that she has to face reality. Esther is sweeping on the porch right next to the bedroom window and Grace is irritated by the scritch-scratch of stiff bristles dragging over the concrete. Esther is being unusually vigorous this morning and seems intent on banging the wooden head of the broom against the walls as often as she can; clonk, clonk. Grace curls deep into the tousled sheets, desperate to escape back into her fevered dreaming. What finally spurs her to sit up is hearing the faint, but distinct, tap-tap of a hammer from further away. If George is out the back, making the dog's bed, he's obviously been able to get into the shed and that can only mean that Isaac is here.

Once she realises he has arrived, is out there already, the fog of tiredness slides away and Grace can't wait to be up and in the garden herself. She longs to see him. She throws back the covers and jumps from the bed. She dresses quickly, impatient, and flies through the house. At the door, she checks herself and thinks about what Isaac said about exercising caution when they weren't alone somewhere private. It doesn't suit her nature to be circumspect so she is torn between reckless excitement at seeing Isaac and residual care for George's feelings. She opens the door and steps out. On the top step she pauses long enough to gain control of herself, and takes the time to look around as much of the garden as she can see from here. The length of the border at the side of the house is filled with ragged rows of newly opened marigolds with their strange, oddly unpleasant, smell. . On the other side of the lawn vivid daisies have sprung up and Grace thinks the swathes of orange and yellow and gold threading through the flowerbeds makes it look as if the sun has exploded and showered its fragments over the garden. Grace pauses to admire the flowers and realise how much it has changed in the past two months, but, while she does, her senses are all alert for a sign of Isaac; a sight, a sound. But she is disappointed.

Rounding the corner of the house, she can see the shed door propped wide open by the rake. George has pulled out the packing crate that their belongings were shipped out in from England, and has broken it into pieces. He's fixing wooden slats together, sawing lengths and checking angles at each step before committing hammer to wood. Tom, still in his pyjamas, is squatting next to him with a pile of shiny nails in a jar, passing them up to his father one by one as they are needed.They both have the same avid look on their faces, brows furrowed and tongues poking out one side of their mouthsin deep concentration. Grace is struck by how very alike they are. When she gets close up, Grace can make out the lading certificate from the import docket still stapled firmly to one of the slats

87

George is using. There is no sign of the puppy. There is no sign of Isaac.

'You got the key then.' She looks around again, hoping. 'Where's Isaac? I thought you might've got him to help.'

'He's gone.' George doesn't pause in the steady hammering. 'I thought that was the best way he could help.'

'What do you mean, gone? Gone for today or gone altogether, for good?' Grace tries to keep her tone neutral, though what George says hits her with a jolt. 'Why?'

'I just told him we didn't need him anymore. Now he's cleared the worst, we can keep things under control. I can do it while we're off school and we can get a young boy in later, if we think we have to.'

George is making it sound a rational decision, but Grace is all too aware that there is more to it than simple practicality. She knows him too well for that. George likes to have things under control, and know that his world is straightforward, and Grace understands her change in behaviour is a complication for him. He can't rely on the Grace he's known for nearly a decade, and he doesn't know how to cope.

'Has he gone already? I thought he'd say goodbye at least.'

'He went first thing. Collected his *panga* and left. I told him you were asleep.'

Grace, unable to believe what George is telling her, goes right inside the shed and looks around. The tools, cleaned and sharpened, are hanging on hooks in tidy rows, and at the back of the shed, propped on an upturned box, is the old hurricane lamp, its chimney cracked and body dented. There are piles of the rags Isaac uses to oil the tools stacked behind the door, and Grace could weep when she sees them. Everything in here evokes Isaac. How can he have gone?

She takes time to pull herself together and quell her rising panic before she goes back out into the sunshine.

'Where's your puppy, sweetheart?' she asks, crouching down next to Tom.' You haven't lost her already, have you?'

'Silly. Daddy shut her in my bedroom till her bed's done so she didn't run away.'

George hammers in the last nail and uses sandpaper to rub down the rough edges of the bed. He turns it onto its base and taps in on the ground to test its strength. Nothing splinters or wobbles; it's very solid.

'Decide what you're going to call her, Tom, and I'll paint her name on the back. What do you think?' His voice is bright, forced.

Tom gets up from his squatting position and leans over Grace, resting his full weight on her back, while he considers.

'Sungu,' he announces. 'I'll call her Sungu.'

'That's a funny name,' says George while he collects his tools together. 'Where did that come from?'

'It means ants,' Tom tells him. 'The man in the forest said it. The man Isaac took us to see. I told you.'

Grace doesn't say a word. She doesn't move. She can feel her heart thumping so hard in her chest she thinks her ribs might break, and she knows if she tries to stand up her legs won't hold her.

'That's right,' George says to Tom, 'You did. That's an insect name then, not a doggy name. Do you want to have another think?'

'No, Sungu's a nice name.' Tom peels himself away from Grace's back and begins jigging from one foot to the other. 'Sungu, Sungu, Sungu,' he sings.

'Why don't you go and get her? See if she likes her bed?' George suggests. 'I can paint her name another time.'

Still singing, Tom skips off to the house, and Grace waits till he is out of earshot before standing slowly, testing her knees, and stretching out her back where Tom's been lolling over it. He's getting a big boy these days and isn't her baby anymore. He notices things.

'Why haven't you said anything before now about the forest, if Tom told you?' Grace asks George, barely above a whisper.

'Why didn't you? I thought it wasn't important enough to worry about. I hope I'm right.'

Grace can't trust herself to say another thing, and turns on her heels in Tom's direction. By the time she reaches the house, he is already coming back with the dog, 'Sungu' she supposes she must now call it, and their paths cross near the steps with barely a pause. Grace is in search of Esther. She finds her still outside, though the sweeping is now complete. Esther has thrown the rug from the living room over the clothes line and is beating it to within an inch of its life. Something has upset her. Grace wonders if it's the arrival of the puppy, or something deeper.

'Esther, Esther.' Grace puts her hand on Esther's wrist to stop the beater thrashing while she is talking. 'Has Isaac gone back to the village? Is it your hut he's in?'

'No, Mrs. McIntyre. He goes long way from Marigoi.' Esther wrenches her arm from Grace's grip and goes back to beating the rug, giving great, hefty thwacks with the cane paddle. The puffs of dust that billow into the air catch at Grace's throat, choking her. As she splutters fitfully, trying to draw breath, Esther continues with her work, ignoring her completely.

Deep down, Grace really does accept that Isaac has left, but she has to check all the same; the temptation is too strong to resist. She hasn't washed yet, but after she has, and put on some shoes, Grace walks down the drive on her way to the village. When she passes the big blue house she waves at the *askari* and he raises one hand and salutes in reply. Grace is nearly at the road when she hears her name being called, 'Mrs. McIntyre, Mrs. McIntyre,' and she turns back, surprised to see Mrs. Chegwe striding out of her driveway, determined to attract Grace's attention.

'I'm sorry, I'm in a hurry.' Grace turns her back on the headmaster's wife and walks off.

'Mrs. McIntyre, I hope you are not going to the village this morning. It is not for you.' Mrs.

91

Chegwe doesn't raise her voice but every word rings out clear.

'It's none of your business where I go, Mrs. Chegwe. Your husband employs my husband, that's as far as it goes.' Rudeness is out not one of her normal character traits, but Grace couldn't care who she upsets at this moment.
Mrs. Chegwe catches up with Grace, and plants two large feet firmly on the drive in front of her, forcing her to stop again unless she physically barges past. For a moment the older woman says nothing, merely stands, quiet and composed, eyes kept on the nearby road and the huts on the other side of it. Grace thinks perhaps she is going to apologise, but she is wrong.

'Mrs. McIntyre, if you are foolish, your husband can soon be unemployed. I have seen you with this man, Kithu, and it is not suitable for you to know him so well.'

'Of course you see me with him. He's my gardener.' Grace is defensive, and her voice rises dangerously.

'He is not your gardener at four o'clock in the morning, or when he is driving your vehicle in the daylight when anyone can see you.' Mrs. Chegwe shows no emotion in what she says; she is fully in command of the situation.

Grace's stomach heaves at the thought that Mrs. Chegwe not only saw her and Isaac going off together yesterday, but she is clearly implying that the night of the party is no secret to her either. How can she know? Is there a chance someone has told her? Or did Mrs. Chegwe, when she was too busy to come to the party, watch from her window in the middle of the night as Isaac slipped away across the fields?

'Go home, Mrs. McIntyre. Go home and be a European wife and forget Kithu. Don't get involved in his business; in Kenyan business. He is a dangerous man.'

Mrs. Chegwe, when she has said what she intended to say, leaves Grace on the dusty path and goes back to her house. After she disappears through her gates the *askari,* with one last glance in Grace's direction, closes them after her. Grace wishes she'd been able to muster up some quick retort but she is shaken by the clear warning she's received, coming, as it does, from so unexpected a quarter. She so much wants to prove one way or another if Isaac has left or is still in the village, almost within reach, yet she would hate George to lose his job. On top of everything else she has put him through - is putting him through - that would be too much. She turns her back on the village and trails slowly home. That Mrs. Chegwe seems to know so much about Isaac, Grace finds baffling. What exactly she does know, and how on earth she knows it, Grace finds equally perplexing. She is mystified by the fact that the man she has grown to care for so much, is apparently seen so differently by the headmaster's wife and by Esther.

In the garden Tom is trying to persuade Sungu to stay in her box, while she clambers over the shallow edge every time he puts her on the cushion. Grace finds George in the kitchen, eating a late breakfast and reading a guide book. She slumps next to him at the table and pours a cup of tea from the pot into an empty cup. It tastes stewed and not hot enough, but she drinks it anyway.

'I think this might be a good place to start.' George pushes the tour guide towards her.

Grace glances down at the open page, seeing a picture of flamingo, and then up at George. She has no idea what he's talking about.

'Our holiday,' George reminds her. 'Game parks, the beach. I thought we'd set off next Sunday, stop off first at Lake Nakuru.'

George is going to carry on as before, Grace realises. He is determined to block out any problems. If he doesn't talk about them anymore, does he think they'll disappear?

'A week and a half,' he confirms. 'Can we get everything organised by then? Bookings and so on? Will you be ready?'

Grace stands and pours the dregs of her tea down the sink. She knows the yellow daisies are bobbing their heads outside the window, but she cannot see them for the prickle of tears rimming her lashes.

Chapter Twenty

Grace has got quite used to leading a double life. She wakes each morning, fixes a mask of normality on her face, and drifts through the days on auto-pilot. For more than a week she's gone through the motions of being the wife of George McIntyre, teacher, as he and Mrs. Chegwe expect, and kept her thoughts in check. George doesn't mention anything about what's been going on. Instead, he talks non-stop about their trip, a constant stream of wittering about plans that Grace couldn't care less about, which drives her quietly mad. Her lack of interest only serves to intensify George's garrulousness, but she notices he makes sure he stays well clear of saying anything that might open the way to voicing what she assumes must be on both their minds. God forbid they should stray into difficult territory, emotional territory, and talk about their marriage.

Grace simply acts as wife and mother. She buys food and cooks it, she cleans up after the puppy, she makes lists of things she needs to do if they are to go on this holiday George is so determined on; she thinks she may as well live in Stepford. After the coming weekend in Nakuru, George has booked them into a tented camp in Amboseli for a safari, followed by a lodge at the coast, and when each confirmation slip arrives he shows it to her and files it with the maps and ticks it off his list. She makes a show of listening, but could no more say where they're going than fly to the moon.

She's brought down Mothercare bags from the top shelf in the wardrobe and unpacked new, bigger, shorts and T shirts for Tom. She'll have to see about getting him sandals while they're in Nairobi. When she was last in Eldoret she remembered to pop into the pharmacy next to Mr. Awar's and stock up with sun screen and mosquito coils. A clearly reluctant Esther has been persuaded to come in and feed the dog while they're away, and Grace has picked the plump purple fruits from the passion vine to stop the local children scrumping them. No-one can accuse her of failing in her duty. Yet all the time she is putting tins into a shopping trolley or chopping onions for curry or cleaning up after Sungu or pouring coffee for George, she thinks of nothing and nobody but Isaac. Grace's head knows with absolute certainty that he's left Marigoi, but her heart still hopes there's been a mistake, a silly misunderstanding. Every morning, when she hears the handle of the back door turn, Grace can't help but glance past Esther's shoulder, just in case his tall figure is hovering there behind her on the step. It's as if an involuntary muscle has twitched. Yesterday, Thursday, she was stooping over the puppy, trying to prise sticky burrs from her coat, when she heard someone push through the shrubs from the field, then begin to pace steadily across the compound. She shot upright, expectant, a wide grin already breaking on her face, but it was only Hezekiah making his rounds. The daily disappointment is draining.

If she had Tom to occupy and entertain all day, it might at least ground her in reality, but, with the novelty of George home all day, Grace finds Tom is developing into a real daddy's boy. The two of them are trying to get Sungu used to a collar and lead, to make life easier for Esther while they're away, and they spend long stretches of time persuading the puppy to have the plaited sisal tied round her neck, then walking her round the compound. Grace feels sorry for her, she is so small and her fur so soft, it seems almost cruel.

'Isn't she a bit young for all that?' she says, watching the puppy twisting her head to gnaw on the collar. 'She doesn't like it.'

'She needs to get trained to a lead. You know how many animals get killed on the roads when they're running loose,' George explains. 'And it's very soft rope, it doesn't chafe.'

'She's playing. I expect she likes it really, Mummy. It will keep her safe.' Tom smiles. 'Daddy says we can get a little ticket with her name on to hang on her collar.'

'Tag, not ticket, Tom. Why don't we walk up to the town now and find if there's anything there we can use. We can all go.' George looks at Grace above Tom's head, but she brushes his suggestion aside.

'No, you go. I've got things to do before Sunday.'

'There can't be much left. Esther can give the house a good going over while we're not here to get in her way. Come with us.'

'No, not today. You go. Bring back some samosas for lunch.'

97

After they go, Grace goes back into the bedroom to make a start on her packing. She rattles the few clothes she has along the rail in the wardrobe in a desultory way, trying to summon up some enthusiasm, and a dress slides off its hanger and crumples among the shoes at the bottom of the cupboard. It's the dress she was wearing on Tom's birthday, and when she picks it up and shakes out the creases, she finds the note Isaac sent her still balled up in the pocket. Grace smoothes it out, easing the paper flat with the backs of her fingers. She reads it again; the work of a second, it is so short. She realises it is the only thing she has with his handwriting on; the only thing she has of him at all.

Grace's eyes dart round the room, searching for a hiding place, until they light on the photo frame standing on the table at her side of the bed. She folds the letter once and slips it between the picture and the backboard. She flops onto the bed on her side, looking at the photo of her parents on their wedding day, and curls into a foetal position, her knees to her chest, and rocks from side to side. Grace doesn't ever remember such an intensity of feeling for George; anguish engulfs her. Dry sobs rack through her and her chest feels constricted. She has an impression the room is hotter than usual and she feels as if she's suffocating there on the bed, barely able to breathe. She scrambles over to the window and opens it wide, leaning out as far as she can until the panic begins to subside. When she is calmer, Grace closes the window, standing motionless to stare out across the lawn.

Directly ahead of her is a straggly gap in the hedge. It's been broken down from being used as a short cut from the field; Isaac coming and going, and Hezekiah yesterday. All the compounds are seen as public footpaths at the school, and, though Grace hates the lack of privacy, she has had to get used to it.

It occurs to her that she has no idea of what's on the other side of the hedge. The beginning of the field can be seen from the house, but the land drops away after a few yards, and what it leads to is hidden. Common sense dictates it must go somewhere. Grace is taken with the idea that she has to find out, now, today. She puts on a pair of stout shoes, makes sure Sungu is safe indoors, and slips out the front door.

The lawn is dry and parched and crunches under Grace's feet as she walks. There are clear brown patches, like random pock marks, as if the grass has been infected with a virulent disease. Earlier in the year, the rains were late, and now everywhere is drier than it should be for the season.

Everything is out of kilter.

Grace pushes through the hedge. The part of the field she has seen is as she pictured it, scrubby and overgrown, but there are tracks weaving in several directions. She sets off along the most well-trodden, off to the left, but it ends abruptly at a wide pit, very deep, with the stench of rotting scraps rising from it. The school rubbish pit. Grace had no idea it was so close to her house. To be honest, she's never given a thought to where the rubbish goes after the big bins by the school are emptied. Standing at the lip of pit, peering into it, she gets a clear memory of her first day in the forest with Isaac, and wonders if Tom's discarded clothes are down there, buried under weeks of trash, the lovely herby scent destroyed by the obnoxious swill festering beneath her.

Another track leads in a straight line from the gap and Grace follows it, down the slope of the land. She is surprised to see that very soon the land becomes cultivated. A large maize field is well established to one side. On the other, the land is divided into lots of small plots, *shambas,* and there are women and children out working them now. Several of the women, even the older girls, have a baby tied to their backs with red or blue patterned *kangas,* lulled to sleep by the rhythm of their mother or sister hoeing or cutting. They pause and look up at Grace as she passes, but when she smiles and waves, they don't respond.

Eventually the field flattens out again, an untidy space of grass and dirt. There is a broken football post at one end, but otherwise it is bare. Grace shades her eyes with her hand and, squinting against the sun, sees the outline of buildings in the distance, built where the field begins to slope up again steeply. Another of the tiny communities, barely villages that Kenya is dotted with. Grace is curious, but debates whether she has the time to face a longer walk and some strenuous climbing. When she checks her watch she is concerned to see how close to noon it is, and decides she needs to get home. George and Tom are probably there already, and she can't face his questions. She simply can't be bothered to explain what she's been doing. When she turns round, she is astonished at how far she has come, and how invisible the school is from here.

Chapter Twenty-one

Grace pays no more attention to the sound of an engine in the cloudless sky above her than to register its presence at the back of her mind. Little crop sprayers fly over quite regularly, misting the tea estates with insecticide. Only when the sound becomes a roar does Grace register that this is a much bigger plane, completely out of place. When she does she stops, both hands shading her eyes, and looks up to the sky to follow its progress. The plane is flying from the east, low in the sky, and Grace watches, mesmerised, as it plummets down towards the field.

The first thing she thinks is that there must be something wrong, perhaps a mechanical failure, but she can't hear any stuttering from the engines, can't see any smoke. The plane, she thinks it's a fighter, closes upon her, louder and lower, and she realises it is flying directly at her. Before she throws herself to the ground, amongst the stones and stubble, Grace recognises Kenya Air Force markings on the fuselage. The plane passes so close she can feel its vibration in the air and the backdraft billows her skirt about her ears while she sprawls in the dirt. She can see the pilot's face clearly, and he is laughing at her. He knows what he is doing and a shiver of fear grips Grace's stomach. She has never been so scared.

When it seems almost too late, the jet climbs to a safer height and roars away. The pilot's had his fun. Nothing is left bar a long white vapour trail by the time Grace feels able to get up, brush the worst of the dust from her skirt and rush back to the house. The women in the fields must have heard the plane too, and this time, as she runs past them, their former silence is replaced by excited shouts and shrieks of alarm. Those working nearest the track call out to her, but she can't understand a word of what they're saying.

When she staggers into the kitchen, George and Tom are there. George is leaning against the sink and Tom is sitting on the draining board, legs swinging, while they dip samosas into ketchup and devour them like starving men.

'Didn't know where you were, thought we'd start.' George told her. 'There's no chilli sauce left, we're making do with this.' He taps the dish of ketchup.

'The most awful bloody thing just happened.' Grace holds the door jamb for support.

George takes notice of the quiver in her voice and is obviously shaken when he looks at her, because he hands his half-eaten samosa to Tom and helps her into a chair. He goes into the living room and comes back with a small tumbler of brandy, which he hands to her and watches while she sips it. Grace thinks she must look really awful for him to bring out the last of the Martell in the middle of the day.

'Look at the state of you. What on earth's happened? Have you had a fall?'

'I was down in the field when I was dive bombed. An airforce jet. The pilot laughed at me.' Grace swallows the last of the brandy. 'He laughed at me.'

103

'What were you doing in the field?' George takes the empty glass and sets it in the sink.
'For God's sake! It doesn't matter what I was doing in the field, I just was, and this idiot near landed on me.'
'We don't get big planes round here.' George crouches beside her chair, his eyes level with hers, all reasonableness and calm. 'No airstrip.'

'George, I'm not stupid. I'm telling you, a plane came over, a fighter I think, and flew so close I could feel it. It was threatening.'
'If there was a low flying plane, which seems unlikely, it was probably a young recruit showing off. No-one would deliberately fly at you; don't be so melodramatic. You're just a bit shaken up.'
'You weren't there, you have no idea. I tell you, George, he was menacing me.'
'Listen to yourself, Grace. Nothing's going to menace you and me around here. Possibly the odd snake, but we've never even seen one of them.' He lifts Tom from his perch by the taps, wiping ketchup smears from the boy's mouth with his thumb. He throws him over his shoulder in a fireman's lift and walks towards the door. As he goes through it, he turns his head to one side so his lips are level with Tom's cheek and whispers in his ear, like a conspirator.

'If Mummy had come with us to the market she wouldn't have got frightened, would she?'

Quiet as he is, Grace hears him. She thinks he meant her to. When she looks up sharply she sees only Tom's face, his lovely blue eyes staring at her, and a giggle bubbling up in his throat.

The rest of the samosas are on the table, cold and greasy, and the empty chilli sauce bottle has been knocked over. The residue of the ketchup George put in a saucer is congealing on the draining board, a red crusty puddle. Grace can't summon up the energy to clear it up, she simply can't be bothered. Instead of throwing it away, she leaves it all exactly where it is, closing the door to the smell of staling spices.

When she has washed her face and dabbed off her skirt with a damp flannel she feels better. Perhaps George is right, and she's making something of nothing. She's so wound up about Isaac that it must be affecting her common sense. The wardrobe door is still hanging open and Grace remembers she was trying to pack before she went walkabout. She thinks she may as well carry on, get it done. She sorts out shorts and shirts for her and George and finds her bikinis and carries them through to the spare room where she stacks them on the bed. The new things for Tom are already there, and Grace adds towels from the airing cupboard to the pile. Satisfied she hasn't forgotten anything, she leaves it for George to put in a case later on. He's so much better at packing than her; his organised mind, she supposes.

Through the window Grace can see George sitting on the top step of the shed. He's taken off his shirt and is leaning back against the warmth of the shed door. His eyes are closed but Grace can see his lips moving, as if he is speaking. Sure enough, Tom is with him, trotting backwards and forwards along a run of grass, holding Sungu on her lead. She isn't fighting with the rope anymore but is padding along quite happily beside Tom, and as her head bounces up and down, Grace can see the glint of something on her collar catching the sun. Grace is surprised at how very quickly the puppy has accepted her loss of freedom, and adapted to being controlled

Chapter Twenty-two

Afterwards, Grace will forever remember the exact time she hears the announcement. Twelve minutes past six in the morning. She will remember the chill against the backs of her legs as she sits on the concrete floor in the dark, and the hum of the fridge in the corner. The compound is slumbering, everywhere silent bar the disembodied voice from the radio.

Last night, before the start of the holiday, Grace expected Tom to be too excited to sleep, but he fell off as soon as she tucked him under the covers. George, too, slept soundly, stretched flat on his back across the mattress. He soon began to snore gently, little rumbles of breath like muted sighs, but it was enough to keep Grace awake. She prodded his side until he rolled over and there was a moment's respite, but the snoring soon started up again, louder than before. Grace stared up at the ceiling, willing herself to sleep, and failed. When George turned in his sleep and a long drawn out grunt escaped him, she abandoned any hope of sleep and stumbled from their bed before the faintest hint of daylight crests the horizon. She is in the kitchen. The oversized canvas holdall that George has packed so meticulously is waiting by the back door ready to be put in the car first thing so they can get away early. Tom's little blue duffle bag, so overflowing with toys and books that Grace waited till he was in bed before taking half the things out again, leans next to it. On top of the holdall George propped the radio. Why he decided he needs the radio, Grace has no idea. When is he going to listen to it on holiday? And he knows as well as her it's unreliable; she can guarantee the signal will fail after ten minutes.

It is to prove this point to her own satisfaction that Grace unwinds the cable and plugs the radio into the socket above the skirting board, and why she is sitting there on the floor, squashed between the oven and the fridge, listening. She is twiddling with the knob, searching out the BBC World Service and being rewarded by nothing but static crackling round the small room. 'I knew it,' she thinks to herself. 'Useless.'

Suddenly, the airwaves pick up a signal. The words aren't clear, there is a lot of distortion, but she hears enough. Someone on VOK from Nairobi is saying there's a curfew. The message is repeated at 6.14. There is a blast of music then a different voice, telling her the government has been taken over, the military is in control; the President has been overthrown for his 'violation of human rights.' Grace screams for George and he races down the corridor still naked.

'Listen! There's been a military takeover.' Grace pulls him by the hand to stand closer to the radio.

'Christ, I thought you were being murdered.' George switches on the light and leans on the pile of luggage. The broadcast is still on, and they listen together, staring at the radio as if that will make it all more understandable. The man sounds as if he is reading from a script. He is accusing the government of 'colonial' repression, of corruption.

He warns the people, *wananchi,* that anyone that opposes the new regime will face the same fate as befell the British before Kenya gained independence. He tells people to be calm.

'Calm,' Grace explodes. 'What does he mean 'calm'? He's staging a coup.'

'What a turn up.' George doesn't sound remotely concerned by what they've heard. 'I'm freezing. I'll get dressed and go out and see if anyone knows what's going on.'
Wrapping his arms around himself for warmth, he darts off. He's leaves her before a short pause comes in the announcement and so doesn't hear a second voice replacing the first, but Grace does, listening to every word.

'*We, the University of Nairobi students, register our wholehearted and unconditional support for the August 1*st *revolution organised by the Kenya Peoples' Redemption Council. We humbly request our new popular government to accord us the freedom we have always cried for.*'

The speaker isn't named, and the signal is wavering, but when the voice breaks through it carries a timbre and cadence that sound all too familiar to Grace. She has never believed for a moment that Isaac would get as deeply involved as this in an uprising and she realises how very much trouble he is in if she is right; how very much trouble they are all in.

George is soon back, now looking more worried. He pushes his fingers through his hair, combing it back from his forehead, and Grace stands up and stops him, holding his fingers tight.

'Does anyone know anything? What should we do?'

'There's nobody about much,' George tells her. 'Holidays. I went down as far as the headmaster's but couldn't get an answer; no sign of their *askari*. There's a lot of activity over in the village, though, so someone there's heard the news.'

They both start with shock when they hear the sudden knock at the front door. For a second neither moves till, wordless, they go together to answer it. Outside on the porch are two men, one of whom they recognise as an old *mzee* from the village. The other is younger, better dressed, with navy blue suit trousers skimming the tops of highly polished black shoes, though his shirt is crumpled and thesuit jacket is missing. He has the smooth, round cheeks of the well-fed, but fear is creasing the corners of his eyes and a grey pallor suffuses his black skin like the bloom on a mouldering grape.

'Mr. McIntyre, I am Patrick Chepkoech, the District Commissioner here, and this is Kaptum, the village chief. We are coming to warn you to stay in your house. There's…'

George cuts him off mid-sentence. 'We heard. Is it serious, even so far from Nairobi?'

'We are all Nandi here, Mr. McIntyre. The President is one of us so of course we are in danger. The soldiers and the fighting will soon reach this area; Marigoi won't escape.'

'We're meant to be going on holiday today,' George insists. 'Surely we'll be okay as far as Nakuru.'

The old man steps forward. 'Stay off road; soldiers.' He adds his warning to the Commissioner's. 'Nandi province dangerous.'

'They'll ignore us Europeans, surely.' George looks from one man to the other. 'We'll be alright?'

'You have no idea what they're planning. Stay indoors and pray for us all. This will be the end of the Kalenjin,' Patrick Chepkoech tells him. With that the men turn to go and keep their own houses safe. Grace takes note that each of them has slid a *panga* down the back of his shirt, the handles standing proud of the collars, ready to be drawn in a moment.

Grace shivers. She thinks that in normal circumstances the two Africans would have been scandalised by her standing at the door in her tiny nightdress, but today they don't notice; they have far more pressing things to worry about. Through the wall she can hear the everyday sounds from Tom's bedroom that tell her he's awake, abruptly amplified into high pitched wailing. George must have told him there won't be a holiday today; no *safari,* no beach. The cases stand, forlorn, by the door jamb. She'll unpack them later. Fingers of light are waking up the garden, tiny shards with no heat yet in them. Flocks of starlings, always the first arrivals, are squabbling over water and smaller birds are fluttering in to join them. It is a quarter to seven, a Sunday morning, and the first day of a new month. Grace knows, whatever happens, today marks a watershed in her life.

Chapter Twenty-three

The quasi-president, Senior Private Hezekiah Ochuga Rabela, lasts fewer than six hours. Grace and George leave the radio on all day, and, although VOK stops transmitting news, George manages to get BBC. In the middle of the morning it becomes clear the rebellion centres on disaffected members of the Air Force. By lunchtime they hear the coup has been defeated and the President is back in charge.

George gives Grace one of his 'I told you so' looks and acts as if it was all a fuss about nothing. He swings Tom round till he's dizzy and promises him they'll be going to see the animals soon. The bags stay by the door.

Grace is not so sure but, for a while, agrees they might have been panicking about their own safety too much. But, while she clings to the hope they're out of personal danger –especially that nothing's going to hurt Tom - she frets all the time about Isaac and is desperate to find out what's happened to him. The worry gnaws at her and, however she plays it in her head, the scenario she ends up with is always grim and dismal. She weighs up whether to confide in George or keep the dreadful things she's tormenting herself with to herself. But she has no choice; she will drive herself mad if she keeps her suspicions bottled up any longer.

'When you were out, before the Commissioner came, I think I heard Isaac on the radio, with the rebels.'

112

'Isaac? Don't be daft. What'll he have to do with it? He's probably lounging around in Kisumu.'

'It sounded like him. He's said things to me before about what he thinks of the President and the way Kenya's being run.'

'They all do that. You should hear the way Karui goes on in the staffroom sometimes. If Isaac has got himself mixed up in this, I wouldn't give you much for his chances. And if he was, I'd keep very quiet about knowing him if I were you. I've told you before, it's not our business.' George tilts her chin towards him, so she has to meet his eyes. 'Leave things alone, Grace. Let the Africans sort out their own affairs. Bloody load of hotheads, the lot of them.'

Whatever measure of relief they feel is short-lived. The President may be back in Government House, supposedly supported by his ministers and the Army, and telling the world he's in control, but the grapevine of rumour soon burns a path to Marigoi. Over the coming days, they pick up what information they can, but it changes depending who you talk to. First, there is no movement throughout the country and business in Nairobi is closed; next, travelling is 'no problem' and services in the capital are back to normal. On Monday, the newspapers report fewer than a hundred dead, most of them Air Force rebels; by Tuesday the figure has doubled. Between the hours of curfew George risks driving up to the town, and comes home with even more grim figures. 'Bumped into one of the managers off the tea estates at the Post Office. Says their understanding is that there's chaos in the capital; looting and people being attacked on the streets, women being raped. Lot more dead than the papers say as well, civilians.'

'Do you believe him? Will he be more clued up than the *Nation*?'

'Who knows, Grace? The white Kenyans do generally have their ears to the ground, but, then again, they always believe the worst of an African. And the President's in a risky situation so he's bound to try and maintain some sort of control over the press and the radio, keep up a show of strength.'

'And they'd be controlled?' Grace asks. 'Bend the truth for him?'
'They're realists, that's all.' George is only saying what they have both come to accept as normal in Kenya.

'I topped up the car and bought a couple of jerry cans and filled them, too, in case the petrol supplies get disrupted. Better to be on the safe side.' George picks up Tom, who's lolling against the sofa, and swings him round the room till he shrieks from dizziness.

'Stop it, George; you'll get him over-excited.' Grace pleads in vain, because George's answer is to spin faster and faster, Tom barely missing the wall. As they whirl round he gets the boy even more excited, and Grace more and more angry, by saying,
'Do you hear, Tom? Your Daddy has got lots of petrol to take you on holiday after all.'

'Don't say that, George. Don't make promises you won't be able to keep.' Grace snatches Tom mid-swing and sits in the armchair, cuddling him to her to try and restore calm.

'We can do Nakuru like we planned. We don't have to go on any further if things haven't calmed down. We'll be okay. They won't bother with Europeans.'

George has convinced himself that, as long as they're careful about the curfew, they will be perfectly safe. Who will hurt *muzungu*? Why would the army risk stirring up an international brouhaha? It's only the rebels that the government will bother with, he assures Grace, and they've probably been dealt with already. She points out that history doesn't bear this out, in more places than Kenya, but nothing she says can dissuade him.

She is tempted to tell him how Isaac feels, how frustrated and desperate, in the hope of that he might – *might* – listen, but she is wary of revealing too much of what Isaac's talked about. For one thing, Grace wants to keep the closeness she has to Isaac private, something just for herself to treasure; and for another, and she isn't sure what George might do with any information. For the first time, she wonders if she can trust George, and the doubt worries her.

The rest of the day follows a mundane routine. Esther hasn't been to the house since the coup attempt, but she arrives in the middle of the morning, says *jambo,* and, without another word gets on with cleaning and polishing. She sweeps around the heap of luggage and shakes the rug to flatten it where it has been scrunched into folds by the battering it took from George's pivoting feet.

Chapter Twenty-four

After dinner George takes Sungu for her evening walk. Grace is in the kitchen, expending furious energy on mundane chores in an attempt to take her mind away from obsessing over the last forty eight hours. It's a futile attempt; she may as well sit still and do nothing, because a tape is playing over and over in her head, a continuous loop of horrific images which grow in significance at each turn. Re- washing glasses that Esther has already washed perfectly well, or arranging the tins in the larder from large to small, and with every label facing front, aren't helping. Physical exertion is no distraction at all. Her brain is racing, jumping all over the place; George, Tom, the troubles, this stupid bloody holiday, Isaac; more than anything some news of Isaac. The longer she sweeps and tidies and cleans and sorts, the wilder her imagination grows, until she feels sick with anxiety.

 She notices an orangey mark on the table, no bigger than a shilling; the remains of spilt chilli sauce from last Friday, the day she saw the plane. She wipes it with a damp cloth, but the stain is ingrained and stubbornly refuses to move. She wets a scouring pad and rubs it across the streak, harder and harder, until her arm aches from the sheer pressure she's putting into grinding the scourer back and forth. The wire wool is tearing the skin on her fingers and she can feel the muscles in her neck and back tightening, but she is

117

determined – obsessed - with getting the stain to disappear, every last sign of it.

The back door has hardly had time to close behind George, when finger nails scratch across the window pane, jolting Grace from her absorption. She looks up, brushing strands of hair from her face, and there he is. Isaac. He is watching her through the glass, one hand pressed against it, and, for a moment she is rooted to the spot, pot scourer still in hand. They stare at each other through the window, Grace not quite believing he is there, for long seconds. She feels a great weight being lifted and a bubble of joy soars through her.

She shakes herself into action and rushes to the door. Isaac slips through it but, before Grace can say anything, before she can touch him, he slumps against the wall next to the small hill of luggage, and his legs crumple beneath him. When he is on the floor he draws his knees up and collapses his head onto them. Relief courses through Grace and, like a mother finding a lost child, it erupts in an explosion of fury.

'Where the hell have you been?' Grace shouts at him. 'And what have you come here now for? You're damned lucky George is out; what are you thinking of?' She hits out at him blindly and the forgotten scouring pad skids out of her hand and falls in a soapy puddle by Tom's rucksack. One hand connects with a hard crack across his shoulders and only then does he lift his head and speak, though he doesn't put up his arms to defend himself.

'I saw him go. I've been waiting out in the maize. I didn't know where else to go, Grace. I need you to help me, I am in much trouble. Things have gone very badly.'

His hands are clutched round his knees so tightly the veins and knuckles stand out as if they would burst through his skin. Grace, the sudden anger dissipated, squats in front of him and rests her hand on his.

'What have you done, Isaac? How have you got yourself in such a mess? Tell me you weren't in Nairobi. You know, for a while I thought I heard you, there at VOK, when the rebels took over. I got myself so worked up I convinced myself, though George said I was hearing things. I bet you think I'm crazy, don't you? Mad English woman in a panic.' Grace hears herself prattle but can't stop the words tumbling from her mouth. 'I am mad, aren't I?' A nervous giggle escapes her throat. 'Isaac?' she prompts. 'You weren't, were you? You weren't that stupid?'

She wants him to re-assure her, tell her she must have been hearing things and, of course he's not that stupid. She wants him to say anything to dispel the churning in her stomach and make the thumping in her heart vanish, but he can't. He has no answers, no explanation, he simply lifts his head and meets her eye, and she knows. The bubble of joy subsides, pricked by that unflinching look, and she feels as if her insides have liquefied.

The face looking back at her is not the Isaac she thinks she knows. Grace is shocked at how gaunt it has become, with grey etched into new creases around his dark eyes; his once beautiful eyes. Now they wear a haunted expression that comes of more than exhaustion, and their fierce intelligence seems dimmed. His clothes, too, tell their own story. His shirt is grubby and rumpled, his trousers stained and torn over one knee, and an aura of rank sweat hangs round him. On his feet he is wearing, not his good shoes, but a pair of the black rubber sandals Grace has seen for sale in the market, made from recycled car tyres. She can make out *Goodyear* across his left ankle. She has never seen him look so shabby.

She reaches forward and strokes his cheek, edging closer and closer to him till she is kneeling between his legs, enfolding him in her arms. His hunched shoulders drop and his arms tighten around her, crushing her, and, as if she were trying to soothe Tom, she whispers gently in his ear, one hand cradling his head and the other stroking his back.

'It's okay, you're alright now. I'll help you, of course I will. But what's been happening, Isaac? You must tell me, I need to know.'

'We thought we had a chance. We had everything planned so well for so many hours. But plans are no good if people do not follow them, if they do not do their jobs. We could not even trust our friends.' His arms relax their fierce grip and Grace slips out of the circle of his embrace and shifts her weight sideways so they are sitting shoulder by shoulder, holding hands.

'The soldiers were all over the place, screaming, beating, shooting. I thought it would be more orderly; that the military men would be disciplined.' Isaac's voice is as weary as the rest of him, his usual buoyant confidence utterly missing. 'I saw dreadful things, Grace. Dreadful.'

'But have you done dreadful things, Isaac, that's the point? Tell me you haven't.' Grace is holding on to hope, she so much wants to exonerate him from any blame. 'Where have you been since Sunday? In Kisumu?'

'The soldiers came so fast they must have known what was going to happen. Someone betrayed us. Someone was meant to arrest the President, but he went looting instead. Nobody stuck to our plan, nobody. We all ran when we saw what was happening. Some escaped to Tanzania, they had planes ready. Others went into hiding in the suburbs. I've been trying to get across the border into Uganda, but there are too many people looking for us; the army on the one hand, and the President's tribal followers on the other. We are hunted on both sides. I am fed up with running, so I have come to you.'

Grace believes that, as far as it goes, what he says is true, but she guesses he's carefully edited the whole story. Her common sense hasn't completely deserted her and, no matter how much love makes her want to trust him, she trusts her instincts more. But she will have to wait to find out more. Now she has to get him out of the house.

'You can't stay here now, George will be back soon and he'll have no sympathy. He'll throw you out as soon as look at you.' Grace stands and pulls him to his feet. She reaches on top of the kitchen cupboard and hands him a key. 'Go and hide in the shed, George won't go in there tonight. Don't light the lamp. I'll try and get out later, when he's asleep.'

She realises that he is probably hungry and wraps some bread and leftover chicken in a paper napkin. It looks so meagre, but there is nothing else in the fridge. She gets two bottles of beer from the larder and, at the last minute, takes some tins of corned beef and beans from the shelf, leaving jagged gaps in her newly ordered rows.

'Will you be able to get into them?' she asks. 'I can't let you take the tin opener.'

'I'll manage; someone kept the tools are very sharp, remember.' He manages a half-smile. 'I'll come out as soon as I can, listen out for me. We'll decide what to do then.'

Before he goes Grace leans to brush her lips against his cheek and give him one more gentle hug, but he grabs her head and holds it steady between his hands and kisses her full on, his mouth hard and his tongue thrusting between her lips, searching, greedy. Grace is shocked by his ferocity. They are locked together, two desperate people, till, at last, he is the one to break away. Isaac opens the door slowly, peering out to judge if it is safe, but by now it is so dark that even the shadows have disappeared. George must be making his way back home, and no doubt Hezekiah is prowling the compound somewhere making his rounds. Who knows who is watching? Grace has found before, to her cost, that there are eyes everywhere and no secret is truly safe.

When she closes the door behind him, Grace traces the shape of her mouth with her fingers. Her lips are tingling and, when she presses them harder, they are sore from the crush of Isaac's. She runs her tongue across her gums and tastes the faint tang of blood where her teeth have been pressed into the tender skin inside her mouth. Grace wishes it were only her mouth that has been bruised.

Chapter Twenty-five

The luminous green spots on the hands of the bedside clock are hypnotising. Grace watches them as they count away time, time she could have with Isaac, while she waits for George to drift off to sleep. Her frustration at how slowly the minutes pass is unbearable, till finally, as the spots close together at midnight, she hears the stertorous breathing that tells her it's safe for her to move.

She doesn't dare waken George by opening drawers or the wardrobe to look for clothes, and, anyway, nothing of his would fit Isaac, but she brushes her hand over the table on George's side of the bed to find the money he's taken out of his pocket and left there. She folds some of the notes, not all, into her palm and hopes he hasn't counted it. Grace creeps into the spare room across the hall and strips the blankets from the bed, wrapping one tightly round her own body and rolling the other into a neat bundle. She collects a new cake of soap from the bathroom and pokes it and the money into the folds of the blanket.

In the daytime Grace never notices the imperceptible creaks and groans of the door as it opens but now, as she eases the wood from the frame, Grace hears every one explode into the silence like a gunshot. She pulls the door to behind her, leaving it ajar, and steps onto the damp grass. Cold night air shivers through her and she wishes she'd had the sense to find some shoes, but she tugs her blanket tighter round her and hurries through the garden. In her rush, she doesn't notice an old ball the dog's been playing with, and trips, almost falling. As it is, she drops the bundle she's carrying and has to stoop down to pick everything up, swearing under her breath.

Quiet though she tries to be, Isaac hears her and has the door to the shed open by the time she reaches it, his hand outstretched for hers, and she is engulfed by the inky space. She is engulfed too by Isaac, his arms wrapping her to him. A strong, musky warmth enfolds her and, rather than turn away from it, she buries her face deeper into his chest, breathing in the reality of him.

Grace's entire sense of smell is heightened because she can't rely on her vision in the unlit space. The inkiness is broken only when occasional pinpricks of light glance off the tools swaying on their hooks, flaring for brief seconds like fireflies dancing round the walls. As it is, a stew of odours assails her. Some – turpentine, oil, sawdust – are old and ingrained, other are new additions; stale beer from the bottles Isaac has drunk and the waft of fat from the corned beef

'You managed the tins then,' she observes, voice muffled against his chest.

'Only one, with the chisel. I will save the rest.'

'I've brought you a blanket, and some money. Three or four hundred shillings, I haven't counted it. I though you could use the bus, they're still running.'

'It might be dangerous. But I know someone who will help if I can pay him. I might try the border again. I can hide at Elgon if I have to, there are many places.'

Grace remembers the elephant caves with a fond pang. 'Where will you go, though, if you can't get out of Kenya? You can't stay there forever.'
'I'll be okay. You're better not knowing.'

'Am I better not knowing about Nairobi, too?' She asks.

'Forget Nairobi.' Isaac says into her hair. 'I thought I was going to die, that's all you need to know.'

'But we heard so many people were killed, civilians.' Grace persists, 'Why did that happen? Was that soldiers doing the killing, or rebels?'

'Don't believe everything you read. In any case, people were told to stay off the streets. If they got hurt it is their own fault.'

'How can you say that?' Grace tears herself away. 'Listen to yourself.'

He pulls her back to him, stifling her comments. 'Grace, Grace. Don't spoil things.'
He peels back the blanket and begins to kiss her arm, tracing a line with his mouth from her fingers to the hollow of her neck. The nerve endings in her skin jump and twitch, sensitive to every touch of his lips. His hand moves down her back and rests on the sharp jut of her hipbone. She feels his long fingers through the thin cotton, his thumb tracing circles on the swell of her stomach, and her response is immediate, instinctive. She forgets caution, forgets doubt, forgets George and Tom. She is blinded by her own body's surge of desire. The blankets fall to the floor and lay ignored. Grace and Isaac, braced against the wall, snatch at

each other's clothes, their movements quick and urgent, driven by lust and fear and desperation.

Afterwards, she wants to cling to him, collapse onto the blankets and take time to relish the feel of his naked skin on hers, every inch alive and charged. But the luxury of time is what they don't have; Isaac needs to move on, get as far away from Marigoias possible, and she knows she has to let him go. He pulls away, suddenly brusque, and bends down to pick up the blanket and money, and Grace stays, back against the wall, feeling the chafe and rub of the rough brick for the first time.

'There's some soap too. The Chebeles are away; you can use their outside tap.' She wants to say so much, but all that she can come up with are banalities.

'Yes, it's not good not to be clean. I hate it.' Isaac voice is stilted, as if he finds talking to her as difficult as she does him. Sex, instead of fusing them in a closer bond, has made them awkward with each other. They both realise a line has been crossed.

'I will send you a message when I am settled.' He hands her the second blanket.

'Don't write. Don't take risks. Just come back when things are back to normal, when it's all over.' Grace peels herself away from the wall, waiting for some word, some crumb of hope.

'Grace, it will never be over.' Isaac wraps the blanket round him, like a Masai in his *shuka,* and puts the money deep in his pocket. He takes out the key and hands it back to her. 'I will come back Grace, as soon as I can.'

'Can you make use of any of the tools? The chisel, the hoe? Take anything you like,' she says. '*Take me*' is what she means.

'Better not.' Isaac strokes her hair and kisses her, his lips grazing her eyes and neck and, when they reach her mouth, the kisses are tender, ferocity and passion abated. 'I will think of you with your boy while I am away. Be careful, Grace.'

She wants to hold onto him, if only for an extra minute, but she doesn't. She lets him go without fuss, without tears. She listens to him walk away, straining her ears for the last fading sound of his footsteps. After he has gone and all is silent, Grace remembers, too late, all the things she meant to tell him. She hasn't told him about the plane dive-bombing her. She hasn't told him George is set on this hare-brained plan to go on holiday tomorrow as if nothing has happened. She hasn't told him she loves him.

When she crawls back into bed George is very quiet and Grace dreads him being awake, but he doesn't open his eyes and the only movement he makes is the slow rising and falling of his chest. Grace is so cold from being outdoors, she wishes she could rub her frozen feet on his warm leg and bury her nipped face in his neck, as she used to on cold Canterbury nights, but those days are behind them now.

Chapter Twenty-six

Grace doesn't want to let slip the slightest hint about Isaac's return to the area, even less her reckless behaviour, so she watches what she says. She hugs the memory of last night to her like a precious secret. Isaac may have got embroiled in a political situation she doesn't truly understand, but he's not violent. He's just got out of his depth. The man who she was with last night could never be violent; never in a million years. In a month or so, he'll come back to find her and they can decide what they're going to do. Last night marked a transition in their relationship, an implicit commitment.

She is happy, ridiculously so, and so awake and buzzing she can't stay in bed. She rolls out of it at dawn, full of life and optimism. She feigns sudden enthusiasm for the trip and has the car packed and Tom up and dressed before George has finished shaving. If George is surprised at her sudden change of mood, he doesn't say anything. Grace bites her tongue when he decides the luggage needs re-arranging and lets him take control. When the bags are stowed in the boot to his liking and an over-excited Tom is persuaded to sit still on the back seat, they're off. There isn't a single person out on the compound but as the car goes past the big house Grace sees Esther talking to the Chegwes' *askari*.

The tarmac road is equally quiet. There are a few Africans walking along the track at the side and the butcher is herding the cows to their regular

Wednesday fate at the market, but Grace is aware there is very little traffic. They tail a rusting Chevrolet whose driver gives George no room to overtake, and off in the distance a bus chugs a slow path to Eldoret. Grace hopes Isaac managed to catch a bus; perhaps that one. She is reassured that there are no signs of violence, as predicted by the Commissioner. If people staying at home is the extent of any evidence there's been a disturbance in the country, Grace is happy.

The potholes are deeper and more numerous than when she drove down to Nairobi with Tom in June and George has to weave around them, but that is the extent of their problems for thirty miles or more. They meet the roadblock when they are halfway to Nakuru. First they see a line of oil drums strung at an angle down the carriageway, narrowing the road to one lane and forcing them to drive on the right. Nobody's bothered to erect a solid barrier, but half a dozen men dressed in dark uniforms straddle the road. They wear the distinctive green caps of the GSU, the military police. .

'What have they got Special Forces out for?' George mumbles.

One of them stands in the path of the car and raises his gun, while the others cradle theirs loosely in their arms. George stays on his straight path, pulling to a halt almost at the man's boot tips, but leaving the engine running.

'Pull over!' the soldier barks, waving to the side. 'Over.' He emphasises his point with the gun.

George applies his foot to the pedals and manoeuvres the car a fraction more to the side.

He winds down his window and calls through it, 'There's a ditch. If I go any further I'll be in it.' He turns back to Grace and smiles at her. 'Damn fool, he'll be happy when I roll the car.'

The barrel of the gun, which Grace thinks might be a Kalashnikov, is rammed through the open window, stopping an inch from George's head. Neither of them has seen the soldier move from the front of the car, he is so quick. Tom, used to the smiling, waving policemen in Eldoret, begins to scream.

'I told you to pull over,' the soldier shouts. 'Are you going to do it, or do you want me to shoot you?' He looks as if he would enjoy it.

Grace notices the three stripes on his shoulder and realises that, as a sergeant, he won't be defied in front of his subordinates, especially by a European, despite George's misplaced confidence. Her happy mood vanishes in an instant, replaced by cold fury.

'*Shoot if you're going to and be damned with it.*' The instant the thought bursts into Grace's head she snatches it back, half-formed. *'I don't mean it, I don't mean it.'* How stupid. It's sheer panic that's affecting her. Panic at the situation they find themselves in, and panic at George's reaction to it.

'For God's sake, George, do what he tells you.' Grace barely speaks above a whisper; she doesn't need volume to convey how scared she is.

'I am over.' George moans, and Grace is reminded of a petulant child. But he does yank the steering wheel sharply down and the car drops off the tarmac, two wheels slipping down into the dry ditch.

'Get out of your vehicle. Give me your papers.'

The gun barrel retreats and the soldier steps back for George to climb out. The car is so lopsided over the edge of the road that he finds it hard to push the door and, when he forces it back, it scratches a furrow in the dirt and stops half open. George has to squeeze through the narrow space to get out. He reaches into his back pocket and produces their passports and residency permits. George is standing in the ditch and is forced to look up when he hands the papers over to the sergeant, who has stayed on the tarmac. Grace watches a look of satisfaction spread over the soldier's features and it sickens her. She stares through the windscreen at the other men in the unit, who stand immobile, faces expressionless, while the white family is humiliated.

They all look up at the sound of another vehicle approaching from the other direction. An RVP brakes too sharply and skids into one of the oil drums. It comes to a halt in front of their Peugeot, level with Grace's watching eyes. One of the waiting soldiers springs into life and starts yelling at the driver, just as he'd seen his sergeant do at George. All the passengers are forced off the minibus, and Grace sees the way the attitude of the soldiers changes, how their eyes light up, when two of them turn out to be Asian.

The soldiers make the men, only young boys, unload their luggage from the bus and open up every bag, there in the middle of the road. While the soldier that stopped the bus keeps a gun levelled at the men, his friends poke through the contents of the bags, scattering clothes across the road. One whoops with delight when he finds a watch hidden inside a sock, and puts it into his pocket.

Instead of keeping quiet and being sensible, the owner of the watch objects to its loss and demands its return. His shrill onslaught alerts the sergeant to what's going on. He is taking his time checking the papers George has given him, but, hearing the commotion, he narrows his eyes and takes stock of the situation. He waves the papers under George's nose then lets them slip through his fingers to the ground and George has to scrabble around in the dust for them. The sergeant says, 'You've been lucky,' and marches over to the RVP, sensing better sport than a white family obviously too stupid to stay at home.

He thrusts the butt of his rifle into the Asian boy's chest with such force Grace wouldn't be surprised if ribs were cracked. The boy collapses on the road and no-one moves to help him. The sergeant holds his hand out towards the younger soldier.

'Give me the watch,' he orders.

The soldier knows better than to argue with a superior and passes it to the senior officer without hesitation. When it is handed over, the sergeant holds it high in the air, turning it from side to side to admire it. Satisfied, he slides the watch onto his own wrist where its steel bracelet gleams against his dark skin. He moves over to the open cases in the road and uses the barrel of his gun to overturn them completely so nothing is left inside.

'\What else have you hidden?' He addresses the injured man's companion. 'Quick, quick. These other good passengers want to be on their way.'

When she looks, Grace can see the Africans from the minibus are distancing themselves from the Asian youths, edging bit by bit closer to the GSU. They may be frightened, but they have a common target. This is a golden opportunity for them to take a small bite of retaliation against all the Asians in Kenya who, Grace has learnt, every African in the country believes grab anything of value and bleed them dry. Grace knows enough to know there are times when tribal differences can be set aside. She knows that today, on this piece of isolated tarmac, there will be trouble.

The weight of the car has made it settle so much that it takes some time to force the driver's door closed again. George sits, head bent over the steering wheel, taking deep breaths before he can continue. Grace doesn't look at him as he bumps up onto the road and they drive away. She sits in silence, watching the scene being played out on the road, twisting her head further and further round to keep it in her sight till the roadblock is far behind them. Only then does she realise Tom is still screaming.

When she turns her attention to him to try and comfort him she notices the dark tell- tale stain spreading across the front of his new checked

134

shorts. Tom hasn't wet his pants since before they left England. It reminds her how comfortable her life had been once, safe and happy, and it brings into focus just what a place they've brought Tom to.

Grace explodes with sudden rage. She uses her fist to hit George on his arm and shoulder, over and over, till he has to stop the car before they crash. Even then she carries on pummelling until her anger is spent and her shock dissipated. Hot, angry sobs rack her body and she curls into a ball on the car seat. George waits, silent, while her fury is vented, a livid red patch showing on his bicep below his T-shirt sleeve. Only when she and Tom are quiet does he turns the key in the ignition and carry on to Nakuru.

Chapter Twenty-seven

'Some Air Force they musta had here! Where did they find those lunatics? I tell you, these guys over here are crazy,' Grace is trying to keep her temper while Larry Levinson waves a hand, heavy with gold rings, expansively at the captive audience at the bar, Grace included.

Larry is at the lodge with his wife Barbara. They tell everyone they're from 'Springfield, Illinois, home of Abe Lincoln', as if they bear personal responsibility for the fact. He's holding court before they go in for dinner, propped on a bar stool in the middle of the small group of visitors. There is a party of five volcanologists from Bremen University, who've taken a break out from conducting a geological survey based at Mount Longonot; a pair of young Texan honeymooners, all bright white teeth and cameras, and Grace and George.

Larry has been monopolising the conversation for the last twenty minutes, no-one could get a word in if they wanted to. His loud American voice is filled with certainty, brooking no argument. The man is insufferable. Grace feels her hackles rise and it takes enormous effort for her not to shout at him outright. She manages it by remembering that not so long ago, before she met Isaac, she might well have had some sympathy with his point of view, if not his bombast. If he shuts up, she'll ignore him. But he won't.

'What they're upsetting the country for I have no idea, it's way out of order. They have independence, they got the vote. It's a democracy here, goddam it, what more do they want? What are they complaining about?' Larry takes a long slug of beer and thumps his glass down on the bar with a satisfying thud.

The barman wipes the spills with a damp cloth as soon as they land. He says nothing, but Grace catches the small pulse in his neck twitch and wonders how much it must cost him to suffer fools like Larry for the sake of keeping a job. Larry hasn't even noticed the barman cleaning up after him because he is looking round the semi-circle of white faces, expectant, waiting for a chorus of agreement.

'It depends what you mean by democracy.' Grace comments in a low voice, twiddling with the stem of her glass. 'Perhaps Kenyans don't think what they've got at the moment is democracy. Perhaps they want more of a say in how things are run, a bit more fairness.'

'No need to go murdering tourists out on the streets. I've heard that's what they've been doing.' Larry nods, as if he has incontrovertible insider knowledge.

Grace, defensive, is quick to answer. 'I don't believe that.' She can't believe it, after last night. Isaac would have told her. 'You're not telling me you take everything you hear at face value? It'll be rumour, propaganda the government's spewing out. Plenty of people think these politicians are corrupt; they don't trust them.'

'Hell, none of us trusts our politicians,' Larry chortles. 'That's the point of democracy.'

What Larry intended as a barbed witticism falls flat. One of the young scientists bridles at the perceived heresy and takes issue with him loudly. Barbara, not to be side-lined, leaps to her husband's defence though, till now, she hasn't said a word, merely nodding in approval at every inane utterance that comes out his mouth. Seeing their colleague assailed from two sides by the older couple, the other men and women from the university group make a show of siding with him, and a minor squabble breaks out. The young couple moves to the other end of the bar and stays well out of it, nervous smiles plastered on their faces, and the Levinsons soon find themselves besieged by the Germans.

The atmosphere is getting more and more heated and the voices more strident. Grace is quietly pleased that she's pricked the bubble of Larry's smug complacency and forced some sort of debate, however rowdy and emotive. She's quite enjoying watching Larry and Barbara wilt under the onslaught till, to her horror, George drains his beer and weighs into the argument.

'I think Larry has a point. Kenya's done really well for an African country, post- independence. Haven't had the wars most places have. Haven't had the economic collapse. Some people just want to make trouble. I work with Africans; I know them.' He sets his empty glass on the bar.

Grace is speechless. What Africans does he really know? Cold fury at his arrogance, his self-delusion, sweeps through her and she grips the glass stem so hard it snaps. The bowl of the glass

138

falls to the floor and what's left of her Shiraz soaks her toes. Grace shakes wine from her foot and gets off her stool, handing the jagged stem to the barman, who is now looking at Larry with unconcealed contempt. Contempt that is lost on the brawling *mzungu.*

'You're all such experts on the situation in Kenya you don't need my opinion,' Grace snaps. 'I'm going to leave you to your dinner. I think I'll go and check on my little boy, make sure he's okay. He's hasn't had a good day.'

'He'll be fast asleep by now, he'll be fine. You worry too much.' George rubs her arm gently. 'Stay and have some dinner with us.'

Grace snatches her arm away, hating his touch, hating the way he prefers to ingratiate himself with this bunch of strangers rather than support her.

'No, I'm find I'm not really hungry. I don't want to eat with you. To tell you the truth, George, I think I might choke if I tried.'
The noisy argument subsides. George, reddening, pushes the stool away and rises to his feet. 'Do you want me to come?' he asks her. 'Keep you company?'

'No, George. You stay and chat, why don't you? Set the world to rights. I'm sure you can solve the problems of the entire African continent if you set your minds to it.'

As she makes her departure, splashes of wine squelch from her sandals and spray a trail across the wooden floor like tiny, red teardrops.
There is a moment of embarrassed silence when she goes till she hears Barbara-from- Illinois say to

George, 'Your wife sounds kinda tired.' Her saccharine tones only serve to irritate Grace all the more.

'She'll be fine,' George assures her. 'She does get het up about things. We ran into a roadblock on the way down, GSU waving guns about. Lunatics, like Larry said. I told her not to worry but she was very frightened and it's upset her nerves.' George lowers his voice. 'She does get very emotional.'

There is a murmur of understanding around the bar and Grace can almost feel the waves of concern directed at her back and the sympathy the rabble of people she's left behind exudes towards George. Infuriated, she plans to make her feelings obvious by slamming the bar door behind her with a satisfying crash, but the flimsy louvred partition merely swings to with a gentle swoosh, robbing her of even the petty satisfaction of a grand gesture.

Chapter Twenty-eight

The game in the park is very different from Nairobi. There are plenty of antelope; they see warthogs and giraffe, but no lions, no elephant. What they do see, in vast numbers, are birds. Maribou storks so ugly that Tom wrinkles his nose and squeals; drongos flying in a mass above the lake like a silver cloud; grey heron on their nests and egrets pecking between the kudu. On an islet in the lake a colony of pelican stands guard and, when she uses the binoculars, Grace can pick out fluffy grey chicks hidden, protected, in the middle of them. Vultures sit on the bare branches of tall trees, hunched in anticipation of their next scavenging expedition.

Loveliest of all, they see flamingo; huge numbers of them, from palest pink to a bright coral. As if at a yoga class, they're lined up in the shallows balancing on one leg, with the other folded up close up to their bodies; they are protecting each leg in turn from the caustic waters of the lake. The flamingo are on a fishing trip and, when something swims within reach, they lower their necks and skim their upside down beaks beneath the lake in one graceful movement. If they're lucky, long necks straighten in the air for them to swallow the shrimp they've caught.

Grace is confused. She feels guilty at how much she is enjoying herself. She doesn't forget Isaac and what's going on in the country or how angry George made her yesterday, but she manages to lock it in a separate part of her mind. Now, here by the lake, it is so beautiful and there is so much to see that she finds it easy to smile and talk to George and laugh along with Tom's infectious pleasure. She isn't sure it's natural to be so perverse.

'What do you suppose it's like up in the town?' She asks George. 'It's so cut off here in the reserve.'

'They make their money out of tourists; the last thing the country wants is to put them off. They're bound to make sure visitors are safe in places like this. You can bet the coast is carrying on as usual; too much money tied up there to risk.'

'But surely people will be put off coming if they read about things at home?' Grace pictures the scores of Italians and Germans who flood to the coast sitting over their breakfasts with *Il Gazzettino*or *Das Bild*, shaking their heads and cancelling plane tickets.

'Depends how much coverage it's had and how good the government here's been at playing everything down.'

Grace is unsettled by the thought that, just up the road, beyond the secure gates of the game park, ordinary Africans are having their lives disrupted while people like she and George take photographs of wildlife in perfect safety. It doesn't seem right.

'We could stop off tomorrow, if you like, on our way to Nairobi, see what's going on. There's a tannery, evidently; sells all sorts of things.' Where George has discovered this, Grace doesn't know. Larry Levinson, perhaps, he seems to know everything. She is more concerned at what else George has said.

'You're surely not still thinking of going down to Nairobi this week? I thought you said we'd come as far as Nakuru and no more.' Grace lets George feel the force of her astonishment.

'We'll be fine by now. Things will be back to normal, you'll see. We know how to deal with it now, if we see more roadblocks.'

'For God's sake, George,' Grace begins, but George puts a warning hand on her arm before she can tell him exactly what she thinks of his latest mad proposal.

'Sh.' George warns, putting his index finger on Tom's lips to quieten him. 'Take a look what's happening over there.' They turn their heads dutifully where he's pointing.

A young gazelle, far too young to be away from his mother's side, has wandered away from the herd and wobbled on unsteady legs down to the edge of the pool. He hasn't learnt to wait, to check for predators, and his inexperience lets him think it's safe to lower his head into the water and sip. He doesn't see what George is pointing out to his wife and son, a crocodile. It is almost indiscernible in the brackish water, just two hooded eyes breaking the surface and a V-shaped ripple of bubbles flowing after it. Grace and George watch, mesmerised, as the crocodile swims closer and closer to the unsuspecting kid, closing the distance gradually but determinedly. There is no sound from humans or animals.

143

It is already too late for the gazelle by the time he senses danger. His tail and ears twitch nervously and he suddenly rears his head up out of the water but he is not fast enough. The crocodile launches itself from the water, cracking the surface with loud splashes, and opening its jaws ready. In a second the razor sharp teeth have closed round the gazelle's exposed neck and he is lost. He kicks his hind legs in an effort to escape, but they find no purchase on the muddy margins of the pool. The kicks quickly become feeble jerks and he collapses to the ground at the water's edge, crocodile jaws clamped firmly around his throat. In one swift movement the crocodile disappears under the water with his prize.

'He bited it to death, didn't he?' Tom looks from parent to parent. 'Poor deer.'

'He doesn't kill things by biting them,' George explains. 'He has to take in right under the water and spin it round and round till it's drowned. Then he has to wait till it's all horrible and mushy before he can eat it.'

Tom squirms with macabre delight and, before he'll let them move off to look for more animals, drags George down to investigate the churned up patch of mud where the little drama took place. Only when he's satisfied that there are no souvenirs he can salvage – no lost teeth, no golden gazelle hair – does he agree to climb back in the car and be driven away from the pond.

George hasn't been in a game park before, and Grace tries to remember all the Swahili names she learnt for the animals in Nairobi, and tells him any she can. He doesn't seem at all impressed.

'As far as I'm concerned it's a warthog. When am I ever going to need to know it's a *nigri?*'

Grace can't be bothered any more. 'If I see a *nyoka* I'll keep it to myself then, shall I?' she mutters.

'What?' George looks at her.

'Snake,' she says. She spends several minutes trying to capture something else the guide taught them. Finally, it pops into her head. *Yenyesuma.* Poisonous. She doesn't tell George.

Thinking of the day in Nairobi reminds her of Helen. If George insists on going to the capital, it will at least be a chance to see her again and get some real idea of what's been happening. Reporters, especially if they live in Nairobi, must know everything, even if they don't publish it.

They spend the rest of the day out in the park. At one point they are passed by a zebra-camouflaged minibus with four Japanese inside, who must have just arrived from Nairobi. Though Grace is reluctant, in her present mood, to think George might be right about anything, she wonders if she has been over-cautious and they'll be safe after all. She'll see how George behaves at dinner tonight, and if he can redeem himself she'll agree to go. At least the Levinsons will have left by then, and she won't have to face either Larry's arrogance or Barbara's patronising pity.

The drive back to the lodge late in the afternoon takes them past the water hole where they spotted the crocodile. The animals have deserted it by now and the birds are beginning to roost in the overhanging branches, leaving a picture of calm and tranquillity. Any turbulence is hidden from view, masked by the glassy surface, but Grace has a vivid image of an underwater larder full of slowly rotting flesh, where death is strung out as long as possible.

Chapter Twenty-nine

The smell hits them as soon as they step through the doorway into the small shop at the tannery. Unbleached skins are crammed into every available space; stacked on dusty shelves, left in disordered piles on the floor and overflowing from bins. The skins range from pale cream to dark brown, their wool coarse and tough, and retain the unmistakeable shape of the bodies that once filled them. In the claustrophobic space the smell is overwhelming.

Grace, before she lived here, imagined Africa in technicolour; a vivid portrait of wildlife, vast skies and stunning landscapes. Those images, formed by television and colour supplement photography, were never scent-free. Now, it's the very smell of the place that epitomises what she thinks of as Kenya. The scent of flowers and gum trees in her garden, the choking reek off bloody offal at the market butchery, the aromatic fragrance that rises to greet her if she brushes against leaves on the tea estates, the rank, faintly tobacco-ish, odour from a herd of giraffe ; they all meld together to encapsulate the essence of the country. And, from today, the scabrous, eye-watering smell of lye-soaked hides at the tannery will join the mix, forever etched in olfactory memory.

At one side of the shop, squashed under a small dusty window that doesn't let in enough light, is a glass topped counter containing a meagre display of ready-made leatherware. It looks like a relic from a nineteenth century haberdasher's. There are purses and belts, mittens and hats, handbags and slippers. An elderly African hovers over it, the skin of his neck and hands as wizened as the creased hides themselves. He is using what little charm he can muster to try to persuade them to buy something. Grace expects he hasn't seen many visitors this week.

When he sees they are not impressed with what's on offer, the man pushes aside a ragged curtain and goes into the back room, coming back with an armful of sheepskin coats. Grace thinks she'd look like a Michelin man in one of them, but George tries one on, forcing his arms into the stiff sleeves.

'What do you think?' he asks her, turning this way and that.

It looks to Grace like a poor relation of the Afghan coats that were all the rage when they left home, and she tells George so.

'You look ridiculous. It's awful. I can just imagine you wearing that back home.'

'I'm not back home, though, am I?' he reminds her.

While they've been talking, the African has zipped Tom into a waistcoat, the undyed suede edged with curling dark brown wool, as dark as a Jacob sheep. Grace has to admit he looks very cute, and, against her better judgement, she lets George buy it, as long as he agrees to leave the coat behind. They pick out some small pieces they can send home as presents and some of the sheepskin floor cloths Esther uses, and everything is wrapped into a brown parcel. Grace prays the lye has done its job, and there isn't a colony of invisible parasites seething among the raw fleeces, ready to scuttle out at a later date and infest them all.

The tannery, for good reason considering the stench, is away from the hub of the town, over the railway tracks and down a dirt road. The local residents have stayed indoors; there are even fewer to be seen than in Marigoi. Grace and George pass two or three boys trying to sell tomatoes or plums at the roadside, but there's no sign of anybody about likely to buy them. As George brakes to avoid a cavernous rut, the boys scent a sale and rush up with bags of fruit, thrusting the bags through the car window and shouting '*shillingikumi',* ten shillings. When it becomes apparent that, even at five shillings, the car's not stopping, the boys go back to wait for the next chance.

A solitary old woman trudges along, bent-backed under an unwieldy stack of firewood and that is the only other person they see. Grace isn't too concerned at the air of desolation in this part of Nakuru. She is more disconcerted by the lack of activity in the normally busy town centre. The road through Nakuru is the artery of the Rift, with cars and trucks and belching buses going up and down all day. The town is large and prosperous, filled with shops and hotels and factories; the creamery is here, and the Rift Valley Club. She's heard many of the original white settler families established themselves on the farms around here, where they still manage to maintain their privacy and their privilege. Independence hasn't affected them too much.

Asian families, always sharp to good commercial enterprise, have businesses everywhere; shops, garages, dental practices; anything you need you can find in Nakuru. Whenever Grace has driven through before, the ranks of residents have been swelled by an influx of tourists. It's a good town to break a journey and stop off for a cold drink, or use as a base for touring the lakes and craters. She and George have done it themselves. Today she could count the people she sees.

Some African workers are unloading sacks of rice from a pick-up into a small supermarket and being shouted at by its owner, a man who reminds Grace of Mr. Awar. He has the same gleaming white shirt and maroon turban wound tightly round his head, and he is shouting at the workers in the same way for spilling a few grains of the rice as they heft the sacks. A handful of women are shopping and two young white men with heavy backpacks are consulting a map. A battered jeep and their Peugeot are the only vehicles moving on the road but some cars are parked up along the road. One of them is a little blue car that looks familiar, but, to Grace's relief, there is no Mrs. Chegwe, just a bored looking Kikuyu driver. The emptiness unnerves Grace.

She is distracted, just for a moment, when George parks on a corner in Kenyatta Avenue outside a shop advertising itself as the *Christian Bookshop*. The thought of innately religious literature amuses her. She taps George on the arm and points at the lettering.

'Do you reckon all the books arrange themselves on the shelves according to denomination; Catholic here, Methodist there,' she wonders aloud. 'No mixed marriages?'
'Is that meant to be funny? The shop's what it says it is,' George snaps. 'You have a weird sense of humour.' A sense of humour, Grace seems to remember, he once appreciated.

'George, it was just a joke. No need to bite my head off.'
'That is funny! Me, biting your head off! ' He marches off, Tom held firmly at his side. 'Talk about kettles and pots, Grace.'

Grace is pulled up sharp by his rebuff. Because he says so little and seems to ignore what she says so much of the time, she assumes most of her remarks sail straight over George's head and are lost in the ether. Yet, all the time, he must have been storing up every slight up, picking at it like a sore. Grace worries what he might dredge up in the future to use against her. She wishes she could crawl inside his head and find out exactly what he is thinking. She is scared to ask him outright for fear of the cataclysm she'll unleash before she's ready to face it. One day soon she will force the issue into the open and admit how she feels, about Isaac and about her own future, but that day can wait. She's made up her mind that this holiday will be the best she can make it in the circumstances, especially for the sake of Tom. Honesty will have to be put on hold.

151

Grace is so absorbed in her own thoughts she is oblivious to anything else. She doesn't notice George has stopped until she walks straight into the back of him.

'George! Watch out, for God's sake.'

Tom is leaning close to George's side and now scurries behind her. He hides his face in her skirt, clinging to her while hot tears begin to make a wet patch on her leg. She knows something must be very wrong for him to be so upset. George stands still but nods his head forward.

'Our friends again. They get everywhere. If I were paranoid I'd think they were following us.'

Ahead of them on the road armed police are patrolling, guns ready. Some of them huddle in the road and others walk up and down the pavements in pairs in front of the shops. From time to time one of them pushes a shop door open and Grace hears a muted exchange, though whether it's with a shopkeeper or a customer she can't tell.

'At least they're not GSU,' she notes. 'Just the regular police.'

'We don't often see this many. If they reckon they stamped the coup out so fast, why are they being so heavy handed?'

'Some of the coup leaders escaped. The President'll want them tracked down so there's bound to be a police presence for a while yet.' Grace tells him. 'It's only been a few days. I did tell you we ought to stay in Marigoi, well out of it.'

'How do you know they escaped?' George looks puzzled. 'The radio said they'd been taken.'

Grace nearly tells him, then and there on Kenyatta Avenue, but thinks better of it. She plonks Tom on her left hip and follows George down the road. Jacaranda trees grow on either side of the avenue, so heavy with blossom they mushroom like beautiful mauve canopies, but it is a beauty lost on Grace. Two of the policemen are standing in the middle of the pavement and, instead of moving back to let Grace and George go by, they stand their ground so the pair of them have to go in single file to squeeze past.

There is barely room for Grace as it is, with Tom on her hip. She swings him to her other side and edges by so close she can feel the policeman's breath on her cheek. and see his eyes glitter as they appraise her. His face glistens with sweat and Grace, despite her anxiety, smiles in sympathy at him having to wear heavy uniform under this blazing heat. She sees his eyes glitter as they appraise her, staring at her low neckline and bare arms. He looks at her as if she is a piece of rubbish blown in his path.

She cannot understand what prompts such scorn? What has she done to upset him so much? Why do so many Africans fester such hatred towards the whites after all this time? Surely Isaac doesn't look at anyone like that? The policemen turn their heads to follow Grace and George as they walk further down the street, and Grace can feel their eyes burning into her back. The air of menace spoils what is left of her day.

'Don't let's bother with a beer,' she pleads. 'Let's go.'

'Don't let them get to you, it's what they want. I thought I'd try the creamery for cheese. They make a cheddary one but it's meant to taste pretty ropey. 'Dunlop' people call it.' George strides off. 'Well, that's hardly a good recommendation, is it? What must it taste like? Anyway, what's the point? It'll only melt or be rancid before we eat it.'

'Have it your way.' George huffs. 'As usual. But I'm not going back by those two clowns. Let's cross over.'

As they step off the pavement they suddenly hear sirens screaming and a roar of noise and a black limousine with shaded windows speeds past, flanked on either side by GSU trucks. The policemen lower their rifles, stand straighter and salute till the phalanx of vehicles disappears on its way to Nairobi. The dust it has churned up spews everywhere, and Grace can't avoid being caught up in its fallout.

Chapter Thirty

Somewhere in the garden, on the other side of the heavily barred window, unseen frogs are croaking so loudly Grace assumes they must be bullfrogs, but Helen assures her they're not. The sound that booms from the pond is made by yellow specks no bigger than a thumbnail that swell their throats with air and send it out in this incessant song, air sacs collapsing like shrivelled balloons.

'It's the males, trying to attract mates,' Helen says. 'They have to advertise or they'd never find each other.'
They are sitting in Helen's house in Parklands, safe inside four bricks walls and with the added security of a Kikuyu guard at the locked and chained gate armed with both a *panga* and a cudgel. What they would have done without Helen, Grace doesn't know. It doesn't bear thinking about.
The drive from Nakuru is threatening enough, with police at every turn and a huge GSU presence at Gilgil with another roadblock. Sagging from exhaustion, and with nerves frayed, Grace and George and Tom finally arrive at the Jacaranda to discover the manager won't let them in. All George's meticulous planning has been for nothing. No matter how much he waves his precious booking reservation and shouts, the manager is adamant; apologetic, but adamant. There is no room for them. International flights have been cancelled since Sunday and tour buses failed to arrive to carry guests off on safari, so

those who should have left days ago are holed up in the hotel, some terrified, some belligerent, but all refusing to move out of the rooms.

'You must find a place very soon,' the manager tells them. 'Curfew at six, you must not be out after that. They will shoot you if they see you.'

George argues but it does him no good. He argues for so long the sun is already disappearing by the time he gives up and Grace can't think of anything else to do but ring Helen. The manager, clearly reluctant, but anxious to be rid of them, lets her in as far as the lobby to use the phone, and Helen takes pity on them and offers to take them in for the night. Grace writes down the address and the manager shows her on the map how to find it, only a few streets away.

'Not far, five minutes,' he promises, though Grace knows from experience of the people she lives among that five minutes could be fifty. 'Go at once and you will be fine.' He locks the door behind her.

They drive through almost deserted streets. The last hawkers and stragglers are scurrying back home in the fading light, heads down to avoid the unwanted attention of any armed police they run into. Once, in the distance, Grace hears what she takes to be a gunshot, followed by screams, but otherwise she has never known Nairobi so quiet. At least there is none of the typical African exaggeration in the hotel manager's claim, and George quickly finds his way to the address Grace has copied down. There is some delay while the guard unlocks the padlocks and draws back the bolts, but they are soon indoors, a drink in hand, and Grace can relax for the first time in hours.

Helen's bungalow is smaller than Grace and George's, but better decorated and furnished. The kitchen is fitted out from the pages of a style magazine, all gleaming worktops and laminate cupboards and full of labour-saving appliances that would often be defunct in Marigoi, with its unreliable electricity supply. The fridge is a huge, gleaming avocado-coloured monster and an automatic washing machine whirrs beneath a worktop. Grace can't decide if Esther would be envious or plain terrified of it.

'Missionaries from Kansas before me,' Helen says. 'They import everything from home; no third world for them. I bought it all off them for peanuts when they moved on to convert China.'

'Oh, well, that's Americans for you. I met a couple from Illinois the other day, very sure of themselves.' Grace tells her. 'They were just so self-righteous.'

'Just because he had a different point of view from yours it doesn't make him self-righteous.' George butts in. 'He was alright.'

'Alright!' Grace raises her eyebrows and shrugs at Helen. 'This was a man who told me categorically that foreign tourists were being killed on the streets here. Who made out the President was right to be so draconian.'

Helen hesitates before she speaks. 'There have been incidents. You don't get to read half of it in the papers. You have heard of censorship, I imagine.' The sardonic tone in her voice is matched by the slight arch of her eyebrow. 'What about 'seek for the truth' and all that? Isn't that the journalists' code?'

'More like the missionaries',' laughs Helen. 'Grace, of if you work in a place like this the 'journalists' code' as you put it is to stick to the rules, even if they're not spelled out. If we print something they don't like they'll tear up our work permits and have us on the next plane home before we can turn around. What good would that do? At least while we're still here we can have a stab at digging out what's really happening.'

'But killing tourists? The manager at the Jacaranda went on about the army being trigger happy but I didn't take him seriously. What purpose does it serve?'

'Grace, you haven't got a clue. What makes you think anything that's been going on this week is the result of purpose? It's mostly just reaction and opportunism. Go into the city centre tomorrow morning and wait till you see the state of the streets and the shops. There's been so much looting going on it's like a full scale war zone.' 'But tourists?' Grace persists. 'Caught in crossfire? Accidental casualties?'

'They were certainly in the wrong place at the wrong time; at least the two that I definitely know about. A Japanese man and his son, shot right outside the Hilton for taking photographs of the looters. The police say they warned him, but who knows if they did or not, or if he understood them if they did. There are rumours of more.' Helen's resume of life in Nairobi over the past five days builds one horror upon another, till Grace is overwhelmed by hearing it.

She remembers Isaac saying he saw dreadful things, but she's never analysed how dreadful that might be. It isn't so much that she has been wilfully blind, as that these events are so far beyond her realm of understanding that she hasn't been able to absorb their enormity. There is something about the matter-of-fact way Helen counts the incidents off on her fingers that suddenly wake Grace up and she wonders, for the first time, if she should place such implicit trust in Isaac. If she is right to trust him at all.

Helen is ready to change the subject. 'Come on. Let's get you sorted with another drink while I find us something to eat. Does Tom like omelettes?'

'Tom eats anything,' George laughs. 'Fish or fowl, fruit or vegetable.'

'What's fowl?' Tom asks.

'Chicken,' George tells him. 'You love chicken, don't you?'

'And eggs,' Tom adds. 'Eggs are chickens. Like Mrs. Wambui's.'

'Well, my eggs aren't from Mrs. Wambui. Mine are from the supermarket.' Helen moves over to the fridge and takes out a box of them. 'Are you going to help me beat them up? Then, after we've had our dinner, you can watch a video on my television.'

'What's a video? He asks again.

159

'These days Tom's favourite word is 'what', closely followed by 'why'.' Grace points out. 'Three is an inquisitive age.'

'What's quisitive?' Tom looks up from stirring the eggs with a fork.

'Nosey.' George takes the bowl of eggs and whips them into a froth. 'And if you're too nosey you find out things you wish you hadn't. Better to keep your questions to yourself and live in happy ignorance.'

Grace and Helen exchange glances. They understand George is not talking to Tom.

Chapter Thirty-one

There is only one spare bed so Tom snuggles in with Grace and George. He starts off tucked up between them, but during the course of the night he wriggles under the covers to escape the cloying warmth and the two adult bodies are pushed further and further apart by his spreading limbs taking over more and more bed. George clings to his side, immovable, but Grace is nudged into such a narrow margin that, despite her tiredness, sleep is impossible. When a small foot kicks into her ribs for the umpteenth time, she sighs with resignation and gets up. She picks her clothes off the floor and wanders through to the kitchen, as quietly as she can to not disturb anyone, only to find Helen already there, dressed and drinking coffee.

'You're up and about early, you've only just caught me.' Helen pushes the coffee pot towards her and points to the shelf of mugs. 'I'm popping into the office. You can tag along if you like, see what town's like.'

'What?' Grace pours coffee and leans against the counter top.
'After what we were talking about last night, I thought you might be interested.'

'I would, if I won't be in the way,' Grace says. 'See how many body parts I see littering the streets.' She laughs but Helen doesn't join in.

They leave the house before George and Tom have stirred. There is heavy dew on the ground and coolness in the air, but the light is a clear pale yellow and promises of unremitting heat later on.

161

As they drive through the Nairobi roads, the early starters are beginning to move. Elderly Kikuyu women out to sell eggs with baskets full of them hanging down their backs suspended from a strap over their foreheads, girls with long slender legs striding out with tins of lard or margarine balanced on their heads, old men sweeping twig brushes along the gutters. There are no other white people on the roads yet. There are police, but they are still, watchful, lounging against walls and waiting for the temperature and the action to heat up.

Helen drives down Tom Mboya Street and Moi Avenue, weaving through the streets for Grace to see the damage. When they pass along Koinange Street, Grace gets her to slow down while she looks for the toy shop and its wonderful window display, but it is almost unrecognisable. The windows have been smashed and their eclectic selection of toys ransacked. Grace can see fragments of jigsaw and crumpled playing cards dropped among the shards of glass on the pavement. Deep inside the emptied shop she can see a single bike left swinging eerily on its chain from the ceiling like a forgotten Christmas bauble.

The fabric shops all along Biashara Street have been treated with the same wanton destruction. Inside one or two of them, Grace and Helen see people rummaging through the last remaining bolts of cloth, though whether they are late-comer looters or shop keepers desperate to salvage what's left of their stock, they can't tell. Suddenly, from nowhere, the sound of running feet pounds up the road followed by louder, heavier steps. A boy, no older than the ones George teaches, is staggering towards them under the weight of a television, his eyes wild and frightened, and being chased by two policemen. They shout at him to stand still, to put down the television, but, despite his fear, he won't give up his prize so easily.

The policemen don't warn him again. They both raise their rifles and shoot. Whose bullet hits him Grace doesn't know. He wobbles for a few more steps, trying to hold on to the television, and collapses in front of them, his head bumping off the car bonnet as he falls. For a moment, a mere heartbeat, Grace freezes in disbelief then quickly yanks the handle of the car door, ready to leap out to help him, but Helen grabs her arm and pulls her back.

'Lock the door. Sit still. Don't get involved.'

'He's still moving, for God's sake. We must do something. We can't just leave him there.'

'There isn't anything you can do. Just sit.'

The policemen don't lower their rifles as they approach the dying boy. They stand over him, barrels aimed at his head, and wait till he is completely still. One prods the body with the toecap of a gleaming military boot and, satisfied he is not going to leap into life again, they lower the guns and swing them over their shoulders. They look at Grace and Helen through the windscreen for only a second before they walk back in the direction they came from, laughing, leaving the boy's body where it fell. One dead arm is stretched out, its fingers touching the broken television.

Grace begins to weep. 'Helen, what do we do? Don't we have to tell someone?'

'There's not much we can do now. I wish I had a camera with me. I might have got a picture in the paper.'

'He's only a boy. They can't just shoot him like that.' Grace wipes her arm across her face, mopping up the tears.

'I've been telling you; it happens.'
They drive through the ravaged town to *The Standard* offices and Grace, legs wobbling like jelly, follows Helen up to her desk on the second floor. James is there, sleeves rolled up, marking off a sheet of typescript, deleting odd words and whole paragraphs with savage scratches of his pen. He looks up when they go in, surprised to see Grace there.

'Where have you come from? Not down from Eldoret this week, I guess.'

'You guess wrong,' Helen tells him. 'She and her husband drove down yesterday from Nakuru, where they'd been since Wednesday. Mad, or what?'

'Definitely mad,' James agrees. 'Lots of activity in Nakuru, I bet. See much?'
'Roadblocks. Lots of police.GSU escorting some sort of convoy in this direction. Gilgil was just as bad.' Grace perches on the corner of James's desk, unable to talk, so Helen answers for her. 'They thought Nakuru would be calmer.'

'That's where they hid the President at the start of it,' James says. 'He has a farm in that area. The commissioner up there, Wachira, pretty much closed the place down. Same in Gilgil; General Musumba closed the road completely to stop rebels moving west, and it's rumoured to be him that's mopping up the other plotters now, here in Nairobi. We got unconfirmed information about a major arrest there yesterday. You must have found yourself in the middle of it.'

Grace doesn't recognise any of the names James is bandying about, but she sees Helen nodding in acknowledgement of what he's saying and understands the import of it. Despite her uncontrollable shaking, she asks,

'This Musumba, how long will he keep it up, this hunting people down?'

'As long as it takes. The government has long arms and an even longer memory. They'll be all over the city until they find who they're after and then they'll wrap their tentacles round their hearts and squeeze till there's nothing left. When everyone's either dead or in prison, then he might stop.'

Grace's shaking becomes worse, till James can't ignore the trembling legs and shaky voice. He looks at Helen.

'We've just seen a looter shot in Koinange Street,' she tells him. ' Grace is understandably upset. She's not used to seeing dead bodies before breakfast. Can we get a photographer down there sharpish? The body was still there when we left.' She gives Grace's shoulder a reassuring hug.

'Lot more dead bodies out there,' James says. 'Ravi's found someone at the hospital who can get us into the morgue. Do an unofficial body count.'

165

'I could go,' Helen volunteers. 'I'll drop Grace home first. Who do I ask for?'

Grace shakes her head. 'I think I'm alright. I'll come. I don't want to go back to the house yet.'

Helen finds a press ID card in one of the other desk drawers and gives it to Grace.

'Better take this, in case.'

Grace reads it and sees she is meant to be *Janet Barber,* another Australian. She clips the plastic onto her waistband.

'What's that for?' James's tone conveys both curiosity and worry. He stops editing the galleys, pencil poised, and swivels round in his chair. 'Don't get her into trouble. Or us.'

'She's going to be my assistant.' Helen gives the swivel chair a push so it swings him back to his desk. 'You get on with that. And don't forget about sending a photographer down Koinange Street.'

'Where will you be later, for when I need to send out the search party?' he calls after her, already back to slashing copy.

'After we've counted the corpses the government says don't exist, that's me done. The rest of the weekend's all mine.'

Chapter Thirty-two

If Grace thought the smell at Nakuru tannery was bad, this is far worse. She and Helen have been whisked through the corridors of the city mortuary down Ngong Road by a young doctor wearing the distinctive maroon turban of a Sikh, who turns out to be a cousin of Ravi, Helen's colleague. At the door there is some huddled conversation between him and Helen and the green-smocked African attendant, and 200 shillings disappears from Helen's purse into the attendant's pocket. *So that's how it's done.* Grace has been wondering how James was so sure they'd be let in, given that the death toll has been repressed so effectively up till now.

The metal door swings wide on a scene of carnage. Grace imagines this is how it must have looked at some medieval battle; Acre, perhaps. The blood-flecked floor is smeared with a slick of human remains and the only pail in the room overflows with brackish, filthy water. There are mortuary tables, like Grace has seen in police dramas or medical documentaries, but each one has at least two bodies on it, mostly not even covered by a sheet. The attendant has no embarrassment at letting Grace and Helen see all this. He leans by the door, oblivious to their western sensibilities, and only moves to extend a foot and stamp down hard when he sees a cockroach scuttling over the foetid linoleum.

When Helen asks, 'Are there more?' he rouses himself to nod towards a small window and when they force themselves to go further into the room, alternately slipping on or sticking to what's beneath their feet, they can look through it and see more bodies piled up in the yard outside with concentration camp abandon. There is no dignity in death here. Flies hover everywhere, a deafening buzz, and the smell fills the women's lungs, their eyes, their hair. Grace gags and tries to cover her face with the sleeve of her thin cardigan. Why she bothers, she doesn't know. Nothing can form a barrier to this.

'And they told us seventy,' Helen notes with disgust. 'You can times that by as many as you like.'

A rusting trolley is pushed close up to the wall in the corner and a pale, coffee coloured arm protrudes from under the dirty, ragged sheet over it. Grace sees Helen flick the top edge of the cloth away, and reveal the face of a young, and still beautiful, Asian girl. In the middle of her forehead is a round, dark mark. It is not a bullet hole, but the distinctive tilaka of a Hindu. Indeed, in contrast to most of the bodies there, this young woman seems unmarked by violence.

Helen calls through the door to Ravi's cousin, who is keeping watch outside, and he peers round the door.

'What's happened here?' Helen asks. 'She's not been shot.'

'Indian tourist, raped by looters. She committed suicide afterwards.' The doctor's voice is resigned, too worn down even to be indignant. 'There was a German woman too, the same.'

Grace's stomach finally rebels and she heaves a thin orange pool of acid onto the stinking floor. She rushes from the room and lurches down the corridor, desperate for air, desperate for respite. As her feet rush away from the charnel house, her mind rushes away from accepting the reality what is happening. As her fingers fumble to unlatch the door, she remembers the contemptuous look the policeman in Nakuru gave her, she remembers the poor shot boy and his television and she remembers the girl on the slab not a hundred feet away, dead from savagery and shame. Mostly, she remembers how Isaac refused to meet her gaze when he spoke about last weekend in Nairobi, and she is haunted by his silence. She is flooded with shame when she thinks how readily she slunk out to him on Tuesday night, without question. What has she done?

She feels a touch on her elbow, and Helen is with her, signalling it's time to leave. The city is far busier now, the roads have a steady stream of traffic, and people seem to be carrying on as best they can. The heat augured when they left home has burst through and blisters through the windscreen. The sun dances off the white buildings lining the main avenues, so blinding it makes them near invisible. As Helen turns the car right into the Parklands estate, they pass the university, still in lock-down.

'Does your gardening student still work for you?' Helen asks in innocence, concentrating more on negotiating her way past a broken down *matatu* in the middle of the street than in what she's saying. 'They've been well in the middle of things, the students.'

'He doesn't work for us anymore, no. George sacked him.' Grace isn't ready to say more, not yet.

'And?' The *matatu* safely avoided, Helen stops at the Parklands shops.

'And, what? I think George thought I was too friendly with him.'

'And were you?' Grace tries to ignore her, but Helen won't be deflected. 'Grace, what's going on? It's more than the morgue, more than the shooting. I could have cut the atmosphere between you and George with a knife last night. Have you done something really, really stupid?'

Grace holds out for only a minute, but decides, after all, to trust Helen to be a friend and not a journalist.

'Isaac, my friend - at least I think he's my friend - was here last weekend. I think he's very involved with coup leaders. He came back to Marigoi a few days ago in a terrible state. He's in hiding now, in Uganda for all I know.'

It's a relief, after all, to have told someone. It's like putting down a burden she's been shouldering alone for too long. Helen, when she answers, isn't scandalised or condemnatory. She is calm and clear and Grace is grateful for that.

'The students' union, SONU, and many of the lecturers are very, very closely involved in what happened, Grace. The politics department especially, as you could guess. If the man you're talking about is one of that faction, he is in big trouble and that means danger. And I don't mean for him, I don't know him. I mean for you; for you and George and Tom. George is right, though he doesn't know why. Find another gardener when you get back. Cut your own lawn. Ignore him.'

'I can't,' Grace faces Helen, pleading for understanding. 'It's gone beyond that.'

'If you mean what I think you mean, you're a fool. I don't want to know any details but I will tell you to stop it. This man will cause nothing but trouble. You have a husband and a son and a chance to spend a couple of years in the sun building up a good bank balance for when you go home. Don't waste it on pipe dreams. Don't waste it on an African who will never be what you think you want. Go down to the coast with your family, swim in the sea and eat mangoes on the beach. Concentrate on that, only that.'

When they go through the door into the cool parquet interior of Helen's bungalow, they say nothing specific, they come to no agreement between them, but there is a tacit understanding that there will be no mention of the mortuary or the killing of the looter. George doesn't need to know.

Chapter Thirty-three

They have rented a villa right on the beach at Diani. They are lulled to sleep by the sound of the Indian Ocean lapping in the moonlight, pulled by its tides, and wake when they hear the bicycle bell ringing from the man who comes to sell fruit every morning. He trudges the shoreline from one end to the other every day, his feet massive from the effects of elephantiasis, and Grace and George take pity on him and buy something every day; enormous, sweet pineapples, pawpaws the size of small footballs, full of hard black seeds, and unguent, perfumed Lamu mangoes.

Though they have a little kitchen in the villa, they don't cook. At lunchtime or in the evenings they walk along the beach to one of the tourist hotels and eat there. Sometimes someone lights a barbecue on the beach and they grill barracuda or king fish, fresh from the sea. Once or twice they drive into Mombasa itself and find a proper restaurant, but it's too hot and too much trouble to have to put proper clothes on. At the beach they live in *kikois* and *kangas,* even George, and Tom runs barefoot up and down the white sand, collecting shells, carefree and joyous.

His favourite thing is going out over the reef on a glass-bottomed boat. He loved it so much when they first went that they've now been out three times. He loves to watch the brightly coloured fish swimming among the coral through the porthole in the boat's floor, and screams with laughter when George jumps overboard and joins them.

'It's a daddy-fish, it's a daddy-fish,' he cries in delight.

The tourists are handed bags of food to scatter over the side of the boat to attract fish to the surface. When they anchor, one of the boys takes Tom into the water, small white body held safe in dark brown arms, and when Grace dribbles her pile of crumbs into the turquoise ocean, Tom tries to touch the fish that flock round. He is both cross and enchanted when he misses every time.

He swims like a fish himself, leaping off the boat or the diving board at the pool, fearless and agile. Grace, a nervy swimmer herself, can only watch in wonder. Where did she get this beautiful boy from? How could she have been so mad as to risk him? She has George to thank for Tom, at least, and tries hard, so hard, to find some reconnection to him. They have little more than a year to get through before his contract finishes; perhaps back in England things will come right again. Helen is right. Family should mean everything.

Grace sets her mind to live by Helen's advice, and, when she's lucky, she finds whole days go by when she hasn't thought about Isaac once, and it isn't till night-time that his face swims unbidden to her mind and her skin seems to have a memory of its own, rekindled by imagining his touch. On the nights when these treacherous thoughts sweep through her, she damps them down, determined to win, but they are like demons goading her with memories and stealing her peace. She has to wait the torments out until the long, dark hours end. The days are easier.

The villa next theirs is rented by a large family with a rank of tall, blond children, all much older than Tom; practically teenagers really. They arrive one afternoon, squashed into a large white Mercedes bearing foreign plates, and talking a language Grace thinks she recognises, but when she asks, conversationally, where in Germany they're from, they look appalled and put her right very soon.

'We're Dutch,' the mother tells her, sharp and cross. 'Not German.' She is obviously horrified by the thought of being mistaken for one of her continental neighbours.

Despite this awkward start, the two families get along well. George and Piet pore over maps and discuss the relative merits of their cars on Kenyan roads, and Tom is spoiled and babied by the children. The boys take him exploring and the girls mother him. Their own mother, Hanne, forgives Grace her cultural lapse and the two families get into the habit of eating together and going on short excursions when they can bear to make the effort. They visit Fort Jesus in Mombasa and the old Portuguese settlement at Gede. Here they're entertained by local dancers and George and Piet make ribald comments about the women, who pad their bottoms with multi-layered petticoats to make them as fat as possible, which their tribe finds alluring.

On their last day Hanne comes over early in the morning, while Tom is still dribbling the juice of an orange down his chest down and George and Grace finish their coffee.

174

'There's a snake farm in a village up the road,' she tells them. 'We're going later, the boys want to. Why don't you come? Your little one would like it.'

George thinks it sounds interesting so they set off in convoy, Piet and Hanne and the girls in one car and the boys go with Grace and George. There's a steep climb up from the beach and the car wheels churn the arid, stony bank, but soon they're bumping along the coast road. Away from the ocean breeze it is humid and swelteringly hot and, in every village they pass, many of the local people loll by the side of the road, inert.

'Look at them. They don't do any work.' Jan, the older boy, spits the words out. 'My father says they're all lazy, these Africans.'

Grace thinks she'd probably loll under a tree if she was supposed to work in this cauldron all the time, but she says nothing. She does, however, exchange a glance with George who shrugs his shoulders and says mildly, 'Not all of them.'

The snake farm is a typically low-key Kenyan venture. Various large cages and vivaria hold a selection of local and imported snakes, from tiny corn snakes to long green or black mambas. In one part of the farm is a collection of reptiles that can be touched. Grace thinks of the petting zoo near Canterbury, but here, instead of lambs and guinea pigs and baby goats, there are juvenile crocodiles and non-venomous snakes.

One of them is a huge python, its body as thick as a man's arm, and the park keepers are thrusting it at the tourists, hoping to make them jump.

Grace, who learned enough in the reference section of the library when she worked there to know a well-fed python isn't going to hurt you, picks Tom up and poses for George's camera with the python coiled round their necks. The Dutch children think her very brave.

There is a large walled enclosure in the middle, open-topped, with a thin grey-barked tree growing in it, around the branches of which large brown boomslang snakes wind their sinuous bodies. Nailed to the tree is a sign saying, *If you drop litter in this pit, you will be sent to pick it up.* The children want to know why Grace laughs out loud at this.

'Boomslangs are deadly,' Grace tells them. 'They hide up there in the trees and drop down and sink their fangs into you without warning. The shock of their poison can kill you in no time.'

'Where did you know that from, about the boomslang?' Hanne wants to know as they go back to the cars later.

'Someone told me. An African.' Grace takes Tom by the hand and steers him away from the crocodile pool. 'When you've been struck there's no antidote.'

Chapter Thirty-four

The boys are drifting back for the new term by the time George and Grace climb up through the Rift valley again and arrive home in Marigoi. The lucky ones, those whose parents can find the wherewithal for a ticket, climb off the bus at the bus station by the market and only have to walk down the road to school. For the majority the walk is much further, and they often have to make their own way for miles from isolated villages in the scrubby hinterland. But they do it without question for the privilege of an education.

As usual, Grace is disconcerted at the size of some of the students. Secondary schooling doesn't come free in Kenya and many of the boys finish Primary school when they're ten or eleven and have to wait for years to progress to places like Marigoi High School. They spend the time working and saving every penny they can, or hoping their fathers will invest in the future and sell a cow. There are 'boys' in their twenties in some classes, still obliged to wear the compulsory short uniform trousers until they're sixth formers. Grace thinks it's degrading, but the boys don't seem to complain. They are just grateful to be at school.

Tom appreciates being home as well. He has an ecstatic reunion with Sungu, who has grown fat while they've been away. Although she has clearly been well fed, Esther has apparently drawn the line at taking her for walks. The dog jumps all over them and barks like a mad thing when they walk through the door and, once she's free of the confines of the house, races round the garden, circuit after circuit, as if she'll never stop. Tom chases after her, whooping and shouting. Boy and puppy are delirious to be together again. The grass has grown so much that, when the hurtling figures finally collapse from exhaustion, the two small bodies are barely visible above the stems, with only Tom's giggling letting Grace and George know where they are.

'We could lose them in that grass,' George notes. 'I'll have to get it cut before term starts.'

Grace takes the time to cast her eyes over the entire garden, and notices how unkempt it's beginning to get, beans running to seed and flowers falling over one another. She considers hiring another *shamba* boy and nearly suggests it to George. Heaven knows, there are always people mooching around the town looking for ways to make extra money, but she bites her tongue and doesn't mention it. There is something deep inside her that resists the thought of someone new tending the maize and scything the weeds, hoeing the beans and collecting up the fallen eucalyptus leaves. The idea of anyone but Isaac having a key to what she has come to think of as *his* shed, of a stranger's hands using the tools *he* spent so much time caring for, is more than she can bear. If George can find time to mow, she'll sort out the flower beds and the vegetables herself. It will keep her occupied. It will keep her in touch with Isaac, even if she can't see him.

The odd thing is that, though smells of fresh polish and disinfectant hang about the house and Sungu is obviously not starving, there is no sign of Esther once they are home. Grace expects her to arrive for work on Monday morning but eight o'clock comes, then nine, and there is no head wrapped in a scrap of colourful cloth bobbing above the hedge, no turn of the door handle. The next day is the same. After three days she sends George to ask around the village and he finds out from the bar owner that she has locked up her hut and 'gone home'. Where that is, Grace doesn't have the faintest idea; she always assumed it was Marigoi. She can only guess that, like so many of the Africans, Esther lives here for expediency, because there is work, and that she has a place somewhere in the vast country that she calls home. Perhaps she has family there. In eight months Grace has never found out if there is a husband or children.

George decides her absence is a Kenyan quirk and is very relaxed about it.

'She'll be back, you wait. We pay her too much for her to up sticks and go. She'll have got it into her head to go off and see someone; you know what they're like.'

Grace doesn't know. She's always found she could set her clock by Esther. She hopes George isn't turning into a quasi-colonialist, on top of everything else. For now, she hopes he's right about Esther, but she is disappointed that she's gone off just when there's so much post-holiday laundry to do. Grace has been spoilt these last months, used to relying on someone else to sort out the everyday grind of housework, and she doesn't relish having to take it all on herself, even as a temporary measure. She can't imagine ironing in this heat; it would be the final straw.

Life returns to normal; at least, as normal as it can. George, at Mr. Chegwe's insistence, teaches more classes and, as if he isn't busy enough with that, agrees to coach the junior football team. None of this extra work brings more money, which is why the local teachers are loth to take it on, but George relishes the challenge and thrives on it.

Grace, when she's not working in the garden, drifts back to her old routine. She cooks, she walks up to the market nearly every day, she entertains Tom. When Thursday comes round, she drives into Eldoret, fully prepared to listen to Mr. Awar ingratiating himself with the Europeans in his oily fashion and determined not to rise to the bait. She'll do her shopping, look round the town and come home.

She finds, instead, that Mr. Awar is in a more than usually serious frame of mind. The shop, normally so well stocked, looks neglected, with the shelves half empty and the freezer switched off. Grace thinks it's only to be expected that the recent unrest has caused a degree of disruption in deliveries but it's unlucky it's seemingly come at the same time as another power cut. Only when she hears a crackly roar from behind the counter does she register that Mr. Awar has a radio on, listening to the cricket, and that all the shop's strip lights are humming as they flicker orange above her.

'Is it a good match?' she asks, calling from one end of the shop to the other.

Mr. Awar leaves the cricket behind him and joins her by the defunct freezer cabinet.

'Very good. It is the Pakistan and England Test match from your Headingley. Do you know Headingley?'

'No, not really. It's a long way from where I lived in England.' Grace taps the freezer door. 'No butter, Mr. Awar? When will it be in?'

'No butter, no. No more, I am emptying everything. I am closing my shop.'

'Closing? Are you moving somewhere else? Somewhere bigger?'

'Moving? Yes, we are moving. We are being forced to move, to leave Kenya altogether. I am closing the shop and selling my house, selling everything while I can. Life is becoming impossible for us Asians now in Kenya, the President is making life very hard. He'll be happy when we have all left.'

'That's ridiculous,' Grace says. 'Why would he do that? I'd think he had more problems right now with Africans, not Asians.'

Mr. Awar, out of habit, takes a sweet from his pocket and gives it to Tom, barely noticing what he's doing. He crosses his arms shakes his head.

'Madam,' he sighs. 'Asians are blamed for everything in Africa. This foolish attempt to oust the President has just given him an excuse to do all sorts of things he's always wanted to. If we don't

181

leave the country soon, we'll have nothing left to leave with. It will be like Amin and our friends in Uganda ten years ago.'

Grace feels a small stirring of pity, even though she's never much liked the man.

'Where will you go?' she asks quietly. 'Have you got firm plans?'

'My brother is in Leicester, we will go there. My son wants us to go to Canada, he says he will have more future there, but we know nobody. It's better to go where there is family.'

'I'm sorry. I had no idea.' Grace is embarrassed for Mr. Awar, to see him so reduced.

She abandons any idea of finding anything in the shop she wants to buy and begins to wheel the trolley back to its place by the door. She feels a tug at the back of her shirt and, when she turns round, sees Mr. Awar trying to hold her back.

'Do you want to change money?' he pleads. 'Black market. Very good rates for sterling. I won't be able to get shillings out of the country.'

'I don't think so, Mr. Awar,' Grace is as polite as she can be. 'I'd be too worried about getting caught.' She slots the trolley next to its neighbour and tries to leave but Mr. Awar now holds onto her arm, his long fingers gripping her elbow.

'Mr. Awar!' She pulls her arm away and hurries Tom through the door, any residual sympathy forgotten.

'Ask your husband. Tell him, twenty five shillings to the pound.' The desperation in the shopkeeper's voice follows her into the street. 'I could perhaps manage twenty seven.'

182

Chapter Thirty-five

'It's happening to everyone,' George tells Grace. They are sitting out on the porch waiting for the sun to set. 'There won't be any more white teachers in these government schools after us and none of the tea managers are having their contracts renewed. The Asians are just part of the trend. Africanisation, that's the name of the game.'

'Mr. Awar said it's all come on the back of the unrest.' Grace sits back in her chair, basking in the last glimmer of sun. 'How he works that out, I don't know.'

'Just that the President is going to be even more careful to make jobs for Africans now he knows he can come under threat. His confidence must be shaken, despite it all being a storm in a teacup.'

'It's only a storm in a teacup for people like you, George. I imagine a lot of Africans don't think of it in quite so pragmatic a way. And the old Indian community obviously doesn't.'

'It's me I'm concerned about,' George retorts huffily. 'And you and Tom. We won't feel any repercussions, will we?'

He looks at her, challenging her to contradict him, but Grace merely looks back at him, silent. Her concerns remain unspoken, the repercussions that might come undiscussed.

One casualty of the Asian exodus is the stationers that stood opposite the supermarket in Eldoret. It's become an African owned bookshop, like the one in Nakuru selling mainly Christian literature, but, slotted between the shelves of bibles and hagiography, there are some imported titles for children, story books and school primers. On a whim Grace buys an eclectic mix and now her latest project is starting to teach Tom to read. She spends the evenings when he's asleep writing the alphabet in large letters on single sheets of paper and making word games and pinning simple flashcards round the house. *Bed, door, window, tap.* She gets carried away, and soon the house is festooned with banners of words, fluttering like bunting when they catch the hint of a breeze. George has to duck to avoid some of them and stands it for only a few days before he derides Grace for being so single-minded. 'Give it a rest, Grace, he's only three. Let him wait till he's at school.' He rips '*bag*' off his briefcase and drops it in the bin.

'He's enjoying it,' Grace insists, retrieving the card and pinning it back up. 'He likes learning new things. It'll give him a head start for when we go home.'

'That's ages away,' George points out. 'At least fifteen months, more if I extend.'

He drops this bombshell into the conversation so casually, as if they've been actively considering it, that it almost doesn't register with Grace. When it does, she is appalled.

'Extend? Here? You've never mentioned this before. I though we agreed, one tour and we'd go home for Tom to start school.'

'It's worth thinking about, that's all, weighing up the pros and cons. Life's so easy here for us, and so cheap compared to home, it's only sensible to give it some thought. Even if I left Marigoi there are plenty of schools I could get work; somewhere bigger if you like.'

'I don't like, George. I don't like at all. And how do you think you'll get another contract when you've just been telling me the jobs are all going to be earmarked for Africans from now on?'

'There are still plenty of private schools; Nakuru, Nairobi, Mombasa even. I'd easily get a job in one of them.'

'And what would you do when that job finished? Find another one and end up sending Tom home to boarding school?'

'Plenty do,' George retorts. 'Don't make out it would be the end of the world.' He rises to his feet and leans on the porch balustrade, watching the sun plummet below the horizon of the field ahead. 'You might be able to get a job yourself if we transferred to one of the cities. Take you out of yourself.'

Grace, who doesn't feel she needs taking out of herself, is dumbstruck. How long has George been mulling this idea over? Has there always been a little place at the back of his mind with it as a possibility, or is it a sudden impulse that's popped into his head from nowhere? She searches for the right words to explain to him that it isn't a sensible idea, not even worth thinking about, and, for her, sending Tom away would be the end of the world. The fact that she can't find those words, points out to her the width of the gap between them. They are both very different people from the young couple who arrived here. She has been so busy focussing on the changes in her since she met Isaac and blaming herself that she hasn't realised that George has changed too, is re-evaluating his own ambitions, and is forging a new path himself.

Grace turns on her heel and leaves him. She can't trust herself to say anything without shouting and, more importantly, crying. Crying is the last thing she wants to do in front of George. She hasn't forgotten him telling Barbara Levinson she was 'emotional' and she certainly isn't going to give him the satisfaction of being proved right. She will have to find other ways to dissuade him from staying in this country a minute longer than they have to.

When she passes Tom's bedroom she can't resist the urge to open the door and tiptoe in to stand by his bed. He has fallen asleep with one thumb in his mouth and she leans over him and gently pulls it away. There is a little plopping sound as it drops onto the pillow and Tom's face wrinkles and he makes a little moue with his lips, but it is only for a moment. Grace straightens the sheet, thinking that soon it will be cool enough at night for a thin blanket as well, and brushes the damp fringe back off his forehead. She kisses the small patch of skin her fingers have uncovered and listens to his even breathing. She watches his eyelids flicker, wondering what dreams he dreams, and wishing she could keep him happy and innocent like this forever, to protect him from the pain of growing up. While Grace watches and wonders and worries, Tom sleeps on, unaware that she is there.

Chapter Thirty-six

Esther re-appears as suddenly as she vanished. Grace knows the woman is illiterate, so has the wit to appreciate she couldn't have sent a note to let them know she was coming back, but thinks she might have called at the house to let them know she was living in Marigoi again before coming in at the usual time on the last Monday of the month as if nothing had happened.

'Where have you been?' Grace asks, while Esther busies herself with the laundry, which has been sadly neglected, and which now stands in sorted heaps on the bathroom floor. 'You should have let us know if you wanted leave.'

'Family,' Esther says, bending over the bath to scrub the clothes. 'I needed at home.' Her muscular arms plunge under the water and swish back and forth, frothing the powdery Omo into a lather. 'I go.'

'I know, but you should have asked first. It's not good enough.' Grace hears herself, sounding like a latterday *memsahib,* and hates herself. 'Is there a problem?' she probes in a more conciliatory tone. 'Can we help you?'

Esther carries on steeping George's shirts up and down, her face wreathed in steam, but says nothing, blocking Grace's presence altogether.

'Well, I'm glad you're back. But I mean it; anything we can do to help you, we will. If someone's ill or if you need an advance on your wages, just tell us.'

187

Esther doesn't go so far as to turn her head and actually look at Grace but she says, as if talking to the shorts of Tom's that she's draped over the rim of the bath and is now scrubbing at roughly with a small, stiff brush, forcing out the ingrained grass stains,

'Not ill. No.'

The scrubbing becomes more vigorous and Grace has visions of the fabric being worn into holes. It's clear she's not going to find out anything more today but she's convinced, as she leaves Esther on her knees amongst the puddles on the concrete floor, that there is something still unresolved between the two of them.

She almost falls over Tom who has been sitting on the passageway floor outside the bathroom, evidently listening to her and Esther. She sits down beside him, hugging him close.

'Mummy, why is Esther cross?' He pulls out of her grasp.

'I don't think she's cross,' Grace tells him. 'Just a bit worried about something, I think.' She leans over to tickle his tummy but he shuffles back and avoids her.

'I think it's a cross face,' he insists. 'Or a sad face. Have you made Esther sad? You make Daddy sad.' He slides further away from her and crosses his arms.

Grace, already feeling ignored by her housegirl and now rebuked by her three year old son, snaps. She gets to her feet so fast her elbow cracks into the wall, and she hauls Tom up after her, pushing him towards the kitchen.

188

'Don't be so silly, Daddy's not sad about anything. Don't poke your nose into grown-ups' conversations. You don't know anything about it.' Tom wails in protest at her rough handling and tries to pull away from her tight grip. Hearing the noise he's making, Grace loosens her hold but Tom takes advantage of her relaxing fingers and pulls out of her clutch altogether and sits down again. He kicks at the wall with his heels, over and over, until a sizeable chip of pale green paint peels away from the wall and drifts to the floor, followed by powdery flakes of plaster. 'You naughty boy,' Grace shouts at him and, before she knows what she's doing, slaps his leg hard.

'Mummy!' Tom screams, too shocked at first to cry until he sees the red welt swelling on his thigh. Then he stretches full length and sobs uncontrollably. When she hears him, Sungu sniffs her way from the living room and nuzzles round him, whimpering until he flings his arms round her neck and pulls her onto the floor with him. 'Sungu loves me,' he wails, voice trembling with accusation. 'She wouldn't hurt me.'

Grace storms into the garden, shaking with remorse and anger and frustration. She crosses the lawn into the maize field and, only when she is out of sight of the house, collapses onto the dry earth and cries as if she will never stop.

At lunchtime, when George comes in, Grace is on tenterhooks, waiting for Tom to say something about his awful mother, but, though he makes even more fuss of his father than usual, he stays mute on the subject of the smack. All the while she is cutting thin slices of bread and rolling them round sausages to make the closest they get to hot dogs, he looks at her through lowered lids as if she were the enemy. He pours far too much ketchup over his sausages, as if daring her to object, and, when she doesn't, he smears it round the plate with his fingers, making wider and wider circles, till his fried onions collapse over the lip of the plate onto the table.

'Tom, what are you doing?' George snatches the plate away and uses his paper napkin to wipe Tom's fingers. 'You're not a baby. If you can't eat properly, don't eat at all. What's it to be?'

Tom looks from one parent to the other. He thought his Daddy would be an ally and has to weigh up his options. He looks at the sausage wrapped in its jacket of bread before mumbling a half-hearted '*sorry*' to George. He picks his food up and takes a large bite.

'What about a sorry to Mummy for playing with your food and making such a mess when she's made you such a nice dinner?'

Tom looks at his father with saucer-like eyes, chewing what's in his mouth slowly.
He clearly isn't going to apologise unless he's forced to. Grace, anxious to smooth the situation over, scoops the spilt onions into her napkin and uses it to pat the sticky mark.

'It's OK, George. I think he's over-tired. He was so excited to see Esther back. Look, there's no harm done.'

Tom ducks his head towards the table and carries on eating steadily, bread and sausage disappearing bite by bite. George shakes his head at the two of them. He doesn't wait to see if there's cake or fruit but gets up from the table as soon as his own hot dogs have been finished and gets his school things together.

'You going so soon? Grace asks.'

'Meeting about the football team. We've been invited to an inter-schools competition at Iten but Mr. Chegwe doesn't like the idea of paying out petrol money for the school bus to go so far. I've got to try and sweet talk him into it.' He picks up a notebook and sets off through the front door to walk down to the blue house.

'Good luck with that,' Grace says to thin air. Picturing George making his way down the track towards the headmaster's house, she realises there has been no sign of Mrs. Chegwe or her little blue car since they've been back. Perhaps the awful woman has decided to spend more time in Nairobi with her children. Perhaps her job, whatever it is, has called her away. Perhaps she is marooned inside the house because the car has broken down. This last thought gives Grace some vindictive pleasure but really she doesn't care where Mrs. Chegwe is or what she's doing, as long as she doesn't poke her nose into Grace's affairs. She wonders anew how Mrs. Chegwe was so sure that Grace and Isaac were friends. She pictures how horrified she would be if she knew exactly what had happened between them. Grace, now, can't use the word '*lovers*' even to herself. It implies some commitment and she is more uncertain, as each day passes without news of him,

191

that he has made any kind of commitment. She wants so much to be with him, but the longer time goes on, the more their entire relationship seems like a fantasy, a blip in her ordered life. If he has crossed into Uganda, surely he could write, just to let her know he is safe. Would it be asking too much? All the time she doesn't hear, she can only imagine the worst. It has been three weeks, more, since she saw him, and she is beginning to worry that she will never see him again. She doesn't think she could cope if that happened. '*Where are you?*' The silent plea fills her head while she clears plates and puts left over food into Sungu's dish. Tom, with the utter unpredictability of children, drags a chair over to the sink when she starts to wash up and climbs on it. He leans against her, sucking his thumb, making it very clear that he has decided to forgive her maternal lapse. Grace bends her head sideways so it rests on his blond hair; she feels such a surge of relief to have her old Tom back.

'I love you, Tom.' She whispers.

'I know, Mummy.' He strokes her arm. 'I love you back.'

They stand like that, harmony restored, while Grace gets on with the washing-up. They are still standing there in front of the window, Grace with an indulgent smile wreathing her face, when, two heads appear over the top of the hedge, people coming in the direction of the house. One is barely visible and all Grace can tell from the glimpses of bright fabric that bob up and down is that it's a woman. The other head is covered in a twist of faded red *kikoi* that Grace recognises easily. What on earth is Esther doing back so soon?

Chapter Thirty-seven

Esther doesn't let herself in but walks round to the front of the house, knocks and waits for Grace to open the door. She is making it clear she is not here this afternoon as a housegirl, but as a visitor. She and the younger woman with her won't come into the house, though Grace opens it wide and stands back for them. They stand on the grass at the foot of the steps looking up at Grace in the doorway. She feels ridiculous towering over them like this so, in the face of Esther's insistence on staying outside, she walks down the three steps onto the grass and rests her bottom against the low veranda wall beside them.

The young woman, when Grace gets level with her, takes an immediate step back, a reflex, but Esther, with a sharp word in Swahili, puts a hand firmly on her back and pushes her forward, where she stands almost toe to toe with Grace, awkward and embarrassed, obviously reluctant to be there. She stares at the blades of grass at her feet so intently that Grace thinks she must find them utterly absorbing.

'This Akumu.' Esther announces. 'My daughter.'

Though she had no idea a daughter existed, now she looks more closely, Grace can see a family resemblance. Akumu is shorter and lighter-skinned than her mother but there is the same round face, the same well-muscled arms, the same watchful eyes. And, because she is looking at her so closely, Grace can't miss the swelling stomach.

Ah, thinks Grace, that's what's going on; an unwanted pregnancy.

'You should have told me about the baby this morning,' Grace speaks to Esther above Akumu's head. 'Do you want more time off? Or do you need some money for a doctor?' Grace knows medicine and good hospitals, like much else, are beyond the reach of many of the village locals. 'There's meant to be a very good doctor in Eldoret I've heard about, I can take you there in the car if you want.' Esther shakes her head and the red fabric quivers, loosening its grip on her tight curls.

'No doctori,' she emphasises her words with more head shaking. 'She needs husband. Baby's father.'

Grace is amused at first, wondering what she is expected to do. Then she sees, not only the seriousness in Esther's expression, but the flare of hope in Akumu's in the brief second she dares to raise her eyes to Grace's.

'Do you need money for him to marry her? A dowry?' Grace has no idea if they have a dowry system or not; if they do, are she and George expected to buy a cow or a couple of goats?

'He has gone away, the father.' Esther states. 'Akumu needs to find him. His child needs a father. Where can my daughter find him?'

'I don't know,' Grace says, springing away from the wall and looking from the older woman to the younger. They both look back at her now, faces inscrutable.

'I don't understand,' Grace insists, but when she meets Esther's eyes, she has a terrible foreboding, and she thinks she is beginning to understand only too well.

'Kithu. It is Kithu.' Esther removes all shadow of doubt and Grace feels her world fall apart. She collapses back against the wall, clutching her throat, where a large sharp stone seems to have lodged. Eventually, when the Africans neither move nor speak, she lifts her head, wrapping her arms tight round her body to stop her chest from thumping.

'When will the baby come?' she asks. She can hear her voice, dull and lifeless.

Esther barks a few sharp words at her daughter, words Grace can't understand, and in a few rapid sentences Akumu finally whispers answers to the questions being fired at her.

Big rains,' Esther informs Grace when she is satisfied with the answers she's given.

So, November. Grace works the calculation out in her head and takes a crumb of comfort from the fact that whatever went on between Isaac and Akumu was long before she met him. And what did go on? A proper courtship? A passing fling? A one-night stand? This last thought quickly sobers Grace up; after all, what more was she?

'Does Isaac know?' It's important for Grace to establish some facts.

'No,' Esther admits. 'Akumu is at home, far away. I don't know till my son come to Marigoi to tell me. Then I leave. I know Kithu was with her; I find him work here. But he goes away, he doesn't see her.'

Everything falls into place. Grace realises that Esther must have brought Isaac here because she imagined he was going to be her son-in-law. After all, a well- educated manis a prize worth catching in rural Kenya. He'd easily find work and the whole extended family would benefit with a provider like that. Esther must have watched him with Grace, and understood far more than Grace thought when she and Isaac spent time together in the garden talking. Grace remembers the arguments in the kitchen, the sudden silences, and the not-so-veiled warnings. Esther must have seen her chance of an easier life vanishing before her eyes. Her increasing sullenness towards Grace makes complete sense and it is no wonder she treats Isaac with such antipathy. She has reason to dislike him.

'I can't help you,' Grace wants to convince Esther. 'I don't know where he is. I haven't heard from him.'

Esther says something to Akumu, who, never happy to be there in the first place, brushes off her mother's hand and sets off back through the opening in the hedge. Grace, as if she has a need to apologise, dashes indoors and comes back out with her purse, taking out five hundred shillings and pressing the notes into Esther's hand. There is no false show of reluctance to accept the money. Esther tucks it down the front of her blouse and follows her daughter home. She has to trot to catch up with her and the loose red head covering unravels even more from its original knot, floating behind her like a scarlet veil.

'Funny Esther, she used the wrong door.' Tom, forgotten by Grace, is sitting on the top step, where he has listened to everything that was said. 'Why did she use the wrong door?'

'She wanted me to meet her daughter,' Grace tells him. She picks him up and hugs him close, carrying him into the house. 'We had more grown-up stuff to talk about.'

'Where does Esther keep her big girl when she's looking after me?' Tom's question falls on the crook of Grace's neck. 'Does she have a special hiding place?'

'I don't know, darling, perhaps she does. Somewhere very special.'

The blue sky is masked by grey clouds, sudden and unexpected, and very soon large drops of rain splash down, taking Grace completely by surprise. They wash the colour from the garden and flatten leaves against the branches of the trees. If a sudden downpour makes this much of a difference, what will the big rains bring?

Chapter Thirty-eight

Grace doesn't know quite how he's managed it, but George has got Mr. Chegwe to agree to a team entering the football tournament. His powers of persuasion are clearly greater than she gives him credit for. He isn't specific as to which exact arguments he used, but George must have convinced the headmaster there will eventually be something in it to his advantage. He wouldn't be prepared to spend precious school fees on diesel otherwise.

They are setting off in the bus - fifteen boys, George and Jackson Kirui - first thing in the morning. If the team gets through to the final stages, they will be away till the weekend, though George admits to Grace that he's fully resigned to being home again by tomorrow evening. When he first walked in the door and told her, Grace was perversely irritated at the thought of him swanning off, but now she sends up a prayer that his wretched team does brilliantly and stays away as long as possible.

Tom has been surprisingly silent on the topic of Esther and Akumu so far, but it won't be long before this latest nugget of information pops into his head and he blurts it out over the cornflakes or while he's splashing about in the bath.Grace tires him out for the rest of the afternoon, playing endless games of chase up and down the garden, and gets him into bed as early as possible after supper. George is packing an overnight bag, hoping he might need it, and by the time he's finished Tom is fast asleep.

George leaves very early next morning, while Grace keeps her eyes firmly shut, pretending she's asleep. She hears him open Tom's door to look in on him and pictures him tucking the blanket in and stroking Tom's head, then she hears the door creak as it's pulled to and George's firm steps down the corridor. However careful and quiet he tried to be he must have disturbed Tom because, not long after Grace hears the key turn in the lock of the back door, a small sleepy figure appears at the side of her bed, rubbing his eyes. Grace throws back the cover and Tom crawls into the warm space George has left and they both fall back to sleep.

They are still there when Grace hears the lock click again. She looks at her watch; despite everything, Esther is bang on time. Grace huddles in bed. She simply can't face her just yet; she is too emotionally exhausted to cope with Esther's accusatory expression over the pots and pans. It's only when Tom begins to stir, moaning he's hungry, that she forces herself to get up. She dresses slowly; too slowly for Tom, who wanders off to the kitchen. She hears the sounds of cereals being shaken into a bowl, the slam of the fridge door, as Esther gets his breakfast, and above it all, the sound of him chattering away.

Knowing Tom is being taken care of Grace sags onto the edge of the bed, reluctant to move. She doesn't know what to say to Esther. Part of her wants to weasel out every last detail about Isaac and Akumu, the minutiae of every meeting, and part of her wants to close her mind and ears to all of it, and pretend none of it has anything to do with her. She thinks her hardest job will be convincing Esther she really has no idea where Isaac is. Grace stands up, runs a brush through her hair and braces herself . What is she worried about? Esther's only the housegirl, after all. She doesn't call the shots. Tom and Esther are putting packets and bottles away when Grace goes into the kitchen. Esther says '*jambo*', polite but flat, no lilting cadence in her voice as there always used to be.

'Can you clean out all the cupboards in the bedrooms today?' Grace says. 'Wash all the shelves down and put clean paper on them, will you?' Grace reckons that a job like that will keep Esther busy the whole morning, and at a safe enough distance from her to make the chances of an unwelcome conversation as remote as possible. To sway the odds more in her favour, she intends to spend the whole morning in the far end of the garden digging out a new bed, though what she plans to grow there she hasn't decided. Perhaps she'll try the roses that she was considering before Isaac came. Surely they'd survive if she watered them often enough; nurtured them.

She marks out the contours of the flowerbed with twigs snapped from the poinsettia and, when she's satisfied with the shape, cuts a clear line through the grass. She gives Tom a trowel and he 'helps' by digging at one end, though every time Sungu rubs her nose against him and whines, he wanders off to play with her before coming back to poke at a few more tufts. He comes and goes all morning. From the hours of watching Isaac work in the garden, noting the economy of his fluid movements, Grace knows how to wield a *jembe* to best effect and works smoothly and efficiently. She has to use some effort when she meets stubborn roots or stones but eventually she has a large patch cleared.

She stands up to admire her work, stretching and rubbing the small of her back. She sees Esther closing the back door and turning for home, without a '*kwaheri'*, and is surprised to find it's already midday. She holds her face up to the noon sun, enjoying its heat on her face, and she is standing like that, still and relaxed, when she hears a sound behind her. She turns, expecting to see Tom or the dog coming back, but there's nothing there. She expects there might have been a rat moving through hedge, scenting the rubbish pit, and gets on with collecting up the tools. When she stoops to pick up the trowel from where Tom has dropped it, right at the foot of the hedge, she hears something again, faint but clear. From her crouched position Grace sees the lower leaves in the bushes move as if shaken by a breeze, on this still, airless day.

Grace pushes her way into the field. She doesn't see him at first, he is so well hidden by small branches, in the way his forebears covered themselves during the insurrection. She finds him only when he moves a hand to disturb the leaves and catches a feeble hold of her ankle.

'Isaac, what in God's name have they done to you?' She brushes the leaves away from his face.

The last time she saw him, he was changed by weariness and defeat. Now it is by brutality. The left side of his face is destroyed, the result of a savage *panga* attack. The lower half of his ear is missing, gristle and cartilage showing along the clean cut. The same cut has laid open the cheek as far as his mouth, blooded gums marking where teeth used to be. A separate swing of the weapon has sliced across his forehead, scalping a small section of hair and leaving the eye so black and swollen it is shut tight.

The effort of crawling here has put Isaac beyond talking but, as Grace brushes aside the branches as gently as she can, he watches her steadily with his one open eye. Grace can see that, as well as the lacerations, bruises cover every inch of his body; along with the *panga* cuts, he has been systematically beaten. His shirt is ribboned by cuts and stained brown by old blood. There is a particularly livid purple bruise across his ribcage but the single wound that worries Grace most is a deep cut on his arm. From the way it drops useless by Isaac's side she guesses the tendon has been severed, perhaps the muscle. But most worrying is the greenish-black pus oozing from its gaping mouth and the foul stench that rises from it. How he managed to get here in this state shocks her more than seeing him at all.

'Mummy? Mummy!' Tom's shouts remind her he is only feet away, too near for her to risk him seeing this.

'Stay still. Be quiet for a bit longer.' Grace whispers and Isaac touches her hand to show he understands. Hating doing it, she piles leaves over him again. She makes sure no-one is watching from the fields and slips back into the garden. Tom is sitting in the middle of the new flowerbed, his arms round Sungu, and looking woebegone.

'Where were you? I thought you'd left me.' Tom throws himself at her. He knows how to tug her heartstrings.

'Silly. I'd just gone to fetch your trowel. It had wiggled right under the hedge.' Grace waves the trowel at him. Sungu, let loose, bounds up, nose twitching , and begins to sniff her way back over Grace's footprints. Grace grabs her by the scruff of the neck, hooking a finger under the dog's collar so she can't escape. While Grace drags her away, Sungu tries to twist her head, yelping behind her, inquisitive about the exciting smells emanating from the field.

'Oh, Mummy, you're holding her too tight.' Tom complains.

'You come and take her then. I saw a big snake just now and we don't want her to get bitten, do we?' Grace improvises.
'No.' Tom is frightened at the thought and clutches the dog collar tight with both hands. The effort of holding on to her shows in his face. 'I'm putting her indoors,' he tells Grace. 'I'll only be a little while.'
'Good boy. Then you can help me carry the other things back to the shed. We won't do any more this afternoon.' Grace raises her voice so it carries over the garden. 'We can do some more later on, when it's cooler.'

Chapter Thirty-nine

There is nothing else she can think of to do. Isaac would no more be able to crawl as far as the house as crawl to Nairobi, and Grace certainly couldn't lift him. She waits for the lights to go out in the boys' dormitories and for the banging and shouting that signifies a normal evening at the Chebeles' house to stop. She carries a sleeping Tom out to the car and puts him on the front passenger seat, cocooned in blankets. She drops things she will need in the well at his feet. As she slips behind the steering wheel a light flickers nearby and heavy footsteps sound by the eucalyptus. Grace sits there in the dark until Hezekiah crosses the football pitch on his first round of the evening.

When the pale beam from his torch veers away to the Wambuis', Grace turns the key in the ignition and drives the car straight across her lovely garden towards the field, ploughing up everything in her path. Maize and marigolds are flattened, the passion fruit vine is ripped up by its roots and she clips the trunk of the lemon tree, showering hard green fruits down like small grenades. She manoeuvres the back of the car as close as she can to the hedge, more a five point turn than a three, bumping over the lip of grass. The freshly dug flowerbed bed, sweated over only hours before, is churned to nothingness by the car wheels. Grace doesn't care.

She opens the rear door and lays the back seat flat. She takes the axe from the front well and uses it to cut down a wide section of the hedge, enough for her and Isaac to get through. When she's satisfied the gap is big enough, Grace feels gently with her foot for the mound that is Isaac. He hasn't moved, she didn't expect him to. For a moment he is so still that she is terrified she might be too late but, when she bends low, she can see the slight rise and fall of his chest, though his breathing is so shallow as to be imperceptible.

'Isaac.' She rubs his good arm gently. 'Isaac, do you think you can move? Just a bit?'

She waits for what seems like minutes, but perhaps is only seconds. His right eye opens, half-focused, and he nods, one movement of his head. He doesn't speak.

'I'm going to try and get you into the car. Can you move at all?'

Isaac nods again, but his eye stays shut this time. Grace half drags him from the ditch and he makes an effort to push the heel of one leg into the ground to ease himself along, but their progress is slow and tortuous. Every jolt over the uneven ground causes a grimace of fresh pain to fleet across his face but Isaac clamps his teeth to stifle any cry and pushes again till they are at the car. Grace is sure, if it were her, she'd be screaming in agony by now. They wait, gaining their strength, before, withGrace's arms around his chest and one final push on his foot, he is heaved into the back of the car. Grace covers him with more blankets, hiding him completely. When she is back in the driver's seat Grace reaches down for one of the bottles of water she put by Tom and passes it back to Isaac.

'Drink this. There's more if you want.'

For the first time since she found him in the field Isaac manages to speak. 'Juma,' is all he manages.

'Yes,' Grace reassures him. 'That's where I'm taking you.'

There is no traffic out at this time of night and the drive to Kakamega is swift and uneventful. Grace finds the same part of the forest that they parked in before but, after that, she is lost. She stands by the car, hoping its headlamps will pick up something she recognises, but every track looks the same as the next in the dark, a bewildering mix of brush and trees, and, beyond the reach of the car lights, utter blackness. Grace is in despair. She hears Tom cry out and takes him out of the car and hugs him. He is still half asleep and she wraps the blanket tight and stands and rocks him like the baby he will never be again, her own eyes shut. In the silence Grace realises sounds are penetrating the darkness where light can't. An owl is hooting somewhere far off, some small animal is rustling through the carpet of fallen leaves and a more human sound reaches her, the sound of voices. Grace follows her ears, shielding Tom from overhanging branches, and the voices become clearer. The nearer she comes to them, the more she notices another sound, the crackling of wood, and she can see pale grey smoke rising against the black sky, as good as an Apache signal. The charcoal burners have lit their pits and are watching over them day and night as Isaac told her they had to.

They are sitting on log stumps, passing the night watch with cigarettes and *changa,* when she stumbles out from the trees into the clearing. They must think her a ghost, they jump up in such alarm, and one goes so far as to run away, but his friends laugh after him and wave their hands at her to come closer to the heat from the pits.

'Juma,' she says. 'Juma.' Grace knows it is pointless saying more, they won't understand he r. She repeats his name over and over till one of the men finally nods.   '*Mzee, mzee.,*' He points over his shoulder. '*Mzee Juma.*' Grace's relief is palpable.

Juma organises the men to carry Isaac from the car and put him on the old table in his hut. Grace is surprised it can take his weight, it looks so rickety. Juma touches and prods every mark on Isaac's body, exploring wounds and feeling for breaks. The bag is taken from its nail behind the door and pots are placed on the *jikko*to warm. Grace is mesmerised by the old man, his fingers so quick and sure, but despite her worry, the heat from the stove in the tiny room full of people sends her to sleep.

'Mummy, why are we in the forest man's house?' Tom is blinking in the smoky environment. 'Why am I in my jamas?'

'We had to come for a little ride. Isaac came after you'd gone to bed and I said I'd bring him to see his friend. We were so tired we fell asleep, that's all.'

They are the only two people in the hut. Nothing simmers on the stove, a row of cleaned pots stands on one side of the door and a pile of dirty rags on the other. The table is empty and has been newly washed down. Pools of bloody water are collecting in its dips and crevices and dripping through the cracks in the old planks into puddles on the floor. Grace panics when she sees its bareness, terrified all her efforts have been for nothing.

Isaac has been moved outside onto a rough mattress made of grass and rags. Grace holds Tom's hand and they stand by the makeshift bed looking at him. He is still, his eyes closed, but he looks less ravaged. The smell of infection, so strong yesterday, is alleviated by the smell of herbs, and the strange mixture is somehow reassuring.

'Boy, come.' Juma holds out his hand to Tom. '*Kasuku.* Come.'

Tom looks at Grace, bewildered, but she's no help.

'*Kasuku, kasuku.*' Juma encourages Tom again.

'I don't know, Tom.' Grace apologises. 'Juma, I'm sorry I don't understand.' She wishes for the hundredth time she'd bothered to learn more Swahili.

'Parrot.' Isaac's voice is weak, but clear. 'He wants to show Tom the parrots.'

Grace shooes Tom off with Juma. *Parrot.* It's the loveliest word she's ever heard.

'Hello, you,' she says. 'Uganda didn't want you then? Do they treat all visitors this way?'

'Not Uganda. Kisumu.' The effort of speaking even so few words exhausts Isaac and his head falls back. Grace stands and watches him, praying

Juma can work one of his miracles. There is so much she planned to confront Isaac about, to challenge him with, but it fades into insignificance at the sight of his battered body. She pushes the memory of the piles of bodies she saw in Nairobi to the back of her mind; she forgets all the things Helen told her. She can't bring herself to care about Akumu; whatever went on there is nothing to do with her. Everything out in the world can wait. All Grace is concerned about is Isaac, here on the ground in the forest, struggling to live, and where they will go if he survives. What will become of them?

'I saw a baby parrot in its nest.' Tom rushes up full of excitement and snaps Grace back to the present. There is nothing more she can do here; she would be in the way. Juma will take care of Isaac. She has to focus on Tom. She needs to get him back to Marigoi as soon as she can. For all she knows George might well be there already, if his team has done as badly as he feared. That alone would put him in a bad enough mood, without coming home and finding his family disappeared in the middle of the night. He might be waiting and worrying, imagining who-knows-what, and when he learns the truth, which Grace knows, this time, he is bound to, he will never forgive her. It is a step too far.

'I'll come back in two days,' she tells Isaac while Juma hovers on the track, impatient to see her to the car. Remembering how she let him go without a word last time Grace crouches close to

210

Isaac's ear and adds, 'I love you.' She doesn't know if he hears her.'

Chapter Forty

Grace runs her hand over the white scar sliced into the trunk of the lemon tree in the middle of what used to be her garden. In the daylight, it looks every bit as bad as she feared, if not worse. Any hope she had of explaining it away to George as some sort of freak accident flies out the window. Her headlong plunge over the lawn has left a set of deep parallel tramlines gouged through the grass, and crisping flower petals, once vibrant yellow and pink and purple, are bleaching in the sun. The scale of the destruction she wreaked in so short a time is impressive. Someone has been quick enough off the mark to slip through the hedge and help themselves to the sour lemons and heads of corn she felled. Grace suspects that, very probably, it was the Chebele children. She hopes they enjoyed them.

The way Grace feels, it seems right somehow for the garden to be in such a state. What good would it do her if the grass were smooth or the beds blooming if Isaac weren't here to take care of it with her, talking about planting and harvesting and life. What was she doing in the first place, trying to recreate a patch of England here? Why would she want roses and summer borders in Africa? She could have stayed at home for that. She should have stayed at home; then, at least, she would have avoided this mess. This heartache.

Grace knows, in one respect, she's been lucky because, when she and Tom drove home, there was no sign of George; Marigoi first team – only team

–must have exceeded his dire expectations. His absence gives her room to think, to come up with something plausible to say to him. There's not only the garden. Grace, when she's being rational, accepts that George is going to have to know about Isaac. She can't go on with this never-ending turmoil that churns her stomach whenever she thinks of him, which is all the time. She wants to find a way to explain and has spent every minute, from leaving Kakamega to now, going round and round in circles, and getting no closer to finding a clear way forward.

Grace's over-riding problem – not problem, concern - is that she knows her options are limited by Tom. She always comes back to him. Sometimes, when she remembers the day at the elephant caves or the night she went to Isaac in the shed, when there seemed nothing else in the world but the two of them, she thinks she will just pack a bag, up sticks and go. She would be happy to take her chances with Isaac. She wouldn't mind dodging from place to place until he was out of danger, but how could she expose Tom to the kind of life that would be?

At other times she tries to be more pragmatic. She half persuades herself that, if she makes up some sort of story about the garden and keeps quiet about everything else, she can survive. George, desperate for his life to resume its natural rhythm, would pretend to accept what she said at face value. They could both live a lie, covert collaborators. Grace, though, if she considers it for a moment, can just imagine what would happen if they tried. Tom's little voice would soon pipe up to tell his daddy about all the exciting things he's seen and done. He only has to say '*kazuku*' and the whole story will tumble out, a tap that can't be turned off. And, once it's been said out loud, George won't be able to pretend any more.

Grace wonders what Esther thought of the chaos when she saw the garden this morning. She hopes she thought that Grace had simply had a fit of madness, piqued by the news of Akumu. Her other neighbours around the compound are bound to notice, if they haven't already. Hezekiah must have seen the state of the place almost as soon as she'd driven off to the forest when he made his next round. He would have told Glory when he got home and Glory would have told whoever popped into the office this morning. While Grace was watching Isaac, the smoke from the charcoal pit swirling around them, and Tom was looking at parrots with Juma, Anne Negu and Primrose and Sammy might have been listening agog to the latest gossip about the strange expats. If Prudence Wambui knows, the world will know. But, please, Grace hopes, not Mrs. Chegwe.
Mrs. Chegwehas made it abundantly clear that she's unhappy about Isaac's comings and goings, but Grace's instinct tells her such antipathy comes from more than disapproval of any relationship there is between a gardener and the wife of one of the white teachers. Mrs. Chegwe is a clever woman, by all accounts, who seems to see far more than she ought. Grace doesn't want to give her an excuse for another lecture. She's determined

214

that the headmaster's wife stays ignorant about what happened here last night. It's important that nothing gives her the slightest cause for suspicion.

Grace moves away from the lemon tree and follows the car tracks down the garden. The rectangle of earth by the hedge is criss-crossed by tyre marks, clods of soil thrown in every direction. Two deep ruts pinpoint where the car ended up. Behind them a gaping hole through the shrubs shows where she hacked her way through to the field. She remembers what an effort it was to get Isaac into the car and, like a freeze frame from a roll of film, she can see herself dropping the axe to get a tighter grip of him. She didn't pick it up again.

Grace searches for it, ranging up and down the hedge looking for a glint of the axe head in the leaves. She scours left and right, yards further than anything could possibly land from where she dropped it. She retraces her steps and, when she can't see it, kneels down and gropes around the place where Isaac was burrowed with outstretched hands. The axe is not there. Perhaps Hezekiah found it, or one of the workers from the maize field, and took it home. An almost new axe is a good find, after all.

She gathers up some of the cuttings and props them into the gap in the hedge as best she can to disguise the hole. From a distance no-one will notice its clumsy pruning. The hedge will look the same as it always does until the dismembered branches exhaust their dregs of sap. Then the green leaves will brown and shrivel, withering away one by one.

Grace uses another branch to sweep over the flowerbed, obliterating the tyre marks, and finishes by stamping soil down into the ruts with her sandalled foot. The garden may still look awful, as if a cyclone has hit parts of it, but the damage is now limited within the compound. What went on beyond its boundaries is invisible..

Grace walks back to the house. As she passes the lemon tree she sees a strip of bark hanging loose and tries to peel it away from the trunk in one long strip, for luck, like peeling an orange in one. It splits and breaks off halfway down and when Grace bends to finish the job, a swarm of red ants rushes from the fresh tear, alert to danger. They are quick to defend their nest from an intruder and Grace jumps back fast, smacking her palms together to knock off the tiny bodies already biting her and stinging. Within seconds the insects vanish back under the remaining bark, having seen off the threat to their home and colony.

Grace sits on the top step of the porch, debating whether there's any chance she can persuade Tom to keep another secret. He's playing happily in the living room, all his cars emptied on the floor. He drives them in turn round the patterned border of the rug, parking them bumper to bumper along the edge of the hearth. When he sees her, he scoots the length of the room on his knees, pushing a blue plastic tanker steadily at Grace. When he bumps into her he doesn't miss a beat, running the tanker up her back, over her shoulder and down into her

216

lap, 'vroom, vrooming' in the deepest voice he can manage.

'Watch it, mister,' Grace smiles. 'I'm not a road.'

'I'm being you in the garden,' he says, driving the tanker down the steps.

'What do you mean?' Grace's smile is wiped clean.

'When we went to find Isaac when he was playing hide and seek in the field.' He turns and looks backwards at her. 'You made so many bumps, Mummy. It was funny.'

Grace was so sure Tom was asleep the whole time, convinced of it. It must have been the bumping that woke him up. She sighs at the futility of thinking she has any choice. Tom can, apparently, keep secrets when he wants to, but she doubts she will be able to persuade him to keep hers. Her decision has been made for her. It's time to tell George everything. Nearly everything.

Chapter Forty-one

It is dreadful. Telling the man she once loved so much that she is in now love with someone else is harder than Grace imagined. Grace thinks, '*people do this to each other every day of the week, the world over; how can they bear it?*' George doesn't make it easy for her, why should he? He makes it only too clear that everything she says cuts him deeper. Every time she opens her mouth it's like slicing into him with a razor, each little word a fresh nick, as if she were dissecting his heart on a slab. Pain rips across his face as plainly as if she were physically assaulting him, nipping at his cheeks and eyes.

He listens to her at first as she stumbles along, trying to find a way of explaining, but after that he seems to switch off, a light going out, as if he's listened to as much as he can stand. He doubles up, winded, like a wounded animal. Grace had no idea it would be so painful. She stretches out to touch his shoulder, a touch of empathy, but he rears up, knocking her hand away before it has a chance to make contact.

George's hurt gives way to sheer rage. There's an engorged vein in his neck that starts to throbs and pumps a red mask up to his hairline like mercury rising. The pulsating is so visible that Grace wouldn't be surprised if the vein burst and sprayed them both with hot blood. George is so angry she's frightened he's going to hit her. She flinches, as she did when the red ants bit, expecting him, too, to lash out to save what's his.

'I'm sorry, I'm sorry. I didn't plan any of this. I couldn't help it.' Grace is crying.

'Don't be so fucking feeble, Grace, of course you could. You could've stopped at any time and thought, *'Oh, perhaps this isn't a good idea, perhaps I ought to remember I'm a married woman with a little boy and screwing the local help isn't clever'.* You knew exactly what you were doing.'

'Don't make it sound so sordid. Once I slept with him, that's all, when he turned up one night before we went to Nairobi.'

'Christ, Grace, did you think I didn't know? Did you think I couldn't smell him on you when you crept back into bed? How thick do you think I am?'

'Why didn't you say something then? How could you not say anything? All the time we were at the coast and in the city, you never said a word. Why start yelling and shouting now if you knew anyway?'

'All the time you didn't talk about it, it was easier to pretend it wasn't happening. I thought if I kept my mouth shut and didn't rock the boat everything would go back to the way it was, because I thought you would wake up come to your senses. Because I hoped he'd gone; a bloody African savage who was going to do us a favour and get himself killed. Because I was scared.'

'He wasn't gone, George. Not where it matters.'

'No. Well, I know that now, don't I?'

Grace and George are drained. They sit, her on the sofa, him at the table on one of the hard wooden chairs. Grace stares at the photo of Tom above the fire, forever three months old, while George traces the whorls in the wood in the table. They sit in their own worlds, their own thoughts, the only sound the clock on the mantelpiece ticking off the minutes; five, ten.

'I had to take him to his friend, George, when he turned up in such a state. He would have died otherwise. I had no choice, surely you can see that.' Grace breaks the silence.

'Of course I don't see. All I see is, a few months ago I had a wife I trusted and a good life. I was happy. As soon as he arrived, everything changed. You changed. You were bloody obsessed, hanging on his every word; '*Isaac says this, Isaac says that*' till I was sick of him. You were like a schoolgirl with a crush, but I never, not for a moment, thought you'd crawl into bed with him.'

'Just because you were happy, it doesn't mean we all were. And don't you dare write off my feelings as a 'crush'. Could you have chosen a more pathetic, infantile word than that? Who's acting like the child now?'

'You're not turning the blame on me, Grace. I'm not the one fluttering my eyelashes. I'm not out chasing a nice village girl.' George spits the words at her. 'I wonder how you'd like that.' Their amnesty was short-lived.

Grace crosses her arms in front of her, digging her nails into the soft skin over her ribs to distract her from doing what she wants to, which is jump up from the sofa and take two steps across the room and slap him, whether or not he's or hurting. She's hurting too; he doesn't have a monopoly. 'Apart from anything else, he was a human being in trouble so I helped him. I will again, if he needs me to. I've told you about him, about us, because I don't think we can carry on the way we have been, it's not fair. I would have helped anyone we knew in the same situation.'

'You've told me because you had to. And don't kid yourself; you would no more have gone to that much trouble, put yourself in so much danger, for Primrose or Hezekiah or any number of people. I hope you don't expect me to save his skin.' 'I'm not asking you to. I'm just trying to be honest with you. I've had enough of it, George, this running around and skulking in corners, trying to remember what I've said from one day to the next. And all this secrecy can't be good for Tom.'

'Don't you dare mention Tom. No, wait, do mention Tom. Did you ever think about him, even once, and what you're doing to him?' George wheels round from the table, as if just remembering his son.

Grace stands and thumps the cushions back into shape, to keep from thumping George. 'I think of nothing else, George, nothing at all. Why do you think I'm still here?For you?'When she's delivered this final wound, Grace goes to bed. She leaves George alone. He must decide where he goes from here.

He is sitting in the same place when she gets up the next morning, though he has washed and shaved and found a clean shirt. He didn't come into the bedroom for it; she slept so lightly she would have heard, so he must have got Esther to iron a fresh one as soon as she arrived for work. Tom is sitting opposite him, making a tower of toast. Neither of them seems to be actually eating much. Grace pours juice and sits at the far end of the table.

'Are you going to eat some of that toast Daddy's made? Or is it just for building?'

'It's horrible. Daddy burnt it.' Tom holds out a slice for Grace's inspection and it is very crisp and dark at the edges.

'Go and ask Esther to do you some more. I think there's a new tin of pineapple jam in the larder, if you look.'

Tom wrinkles his nose. 'Don't like pineapple,' he says. 'I'll ask Esther for red jam.'

Grace closes the kitchen door after him and sits in his chair, nearer George.

'What are we going to do?' she asks him, crumbling the slice of burnt toast Tom left onto his plate, making black crumbs like charcoal.

George is calm, no shouting, no temper this morning, but there is steel in his voice.

'What we're going to do is this. I'm not going to tell the authorities that a wanted man was here only three days ago and is now lying injured somewhere in the Kakamega forest. I'm not going to tell the world what you've done, divorce you and make damned sure I get custody of Tom. I'm prepared to leave Marigoi and find a job somewhere else in Kenya, even before this

222

contract's up, and we can start again, perhaps have another baby. We can put all this behind us, forget it.'

Grace squashes the charcoaly crumbs against the blue china with her thumb, till they are reduced to dust.

'And me? What am I meant to do?' She lifts her thumb and looks at it. It is ingrained with grey.

'You are going to forget all about Kithu. God, Grace, you were just infatuated. You were bored, I can see that. That's why I think a baby's a good idea. Or a job, if you want, like I said before. We can move to any big town in the country that has a good school for me to work at, you can choose. And, when we start again, don't try and cross the divide. You will never understand these people, however much you try.'

Grace can't but marvel at how deluded George is. He thinks he understands her so well, despite giving every indication that he hasn't a clue. It may as well be a stranger sitting there sharing the table with her. She doesn't know what more she can do to shake him into reality. She pushes the dirty plate away, suddenly disgusted, while she struggles to find a way.

They both look up, out of the window, at the sound of wheels turning into their compound. An army jeep drives past the canna lilies at the corner and crunches over the furrows grace made down the side out of the house. It travels out sight of the window and they hear its brakes being applied, too sharp, by the back door. Grace and George stand together, pushing their chairs back so roughly that

George's topples over. They don't say anything. There is, despite everything, a lingering understanding between them, the ghost of long unity. Unity is what they will need to see them through; it's important not to let the cracks show.

Chapter Forty-two

Something is striking the door with such violence that it shakes in its frame and a screw works lose from the bottom hinge and pings onto the floor and rolls under the fridge. Esther hovers in the kitchen doorway, uncertain what to do. Tom tries to push by her, keen to see what's happening, but she blocks his way with her body.

'Alright! Give me a chance, for Christ's sake.' George shouts, exasperated at the continuous hammering. Taking the offensive helps hide his nervousness.

Three people are standing there when he pulls the door open with a sharp tug. One of them – dark, burly, not a local - is dressed in the uniform of the GSU and isusing the butt of his rifle as a battering ram on the door.He has it raised mid-air, ready to launch another hammering, when George surprises him by flinging the door open. Another soldier, the driver, waits in the jeep, picking at his fingernails like a bored bystander. Between them, standing on one of the few strips of flat grass left, is Mrs. Chegwe.

'Mrs. Chegwe,' George asks her, pushing the rifle butt from his face before he ends up with a broken nose. 'What's happening? Why are you doing here?' He is genuinely surprised to see her. 'We have come to search. We believe a terrorist is here, that you are helping him. You or Mrs. McIntyre, I mean.' She looks at Grace.

'What on earth are you talking about? Who are these men?' Grace stands next to George, blocking the doorway. Her surprise isn't as great as George's.

'Mrs. McIntyre, I'm sure you recognise the uniform perfectly well.'

'I don't see you wearing one,' Grace snaps back.

'I am with the department for Internal Affairs. It is my misfortune to be posted here, to keep an eye on these troublesome Luo. Do you think any self-respecting Kikuyu would leave Nairobi for a place like this unless they had to?'

Grace feels George's fingers find hers. He steps forward, toes over the threshold, so the soldier is forced to back away, tripping down the steps. Angry at this loss of dignity, he starts to adjust the rifle to a better firing position but Mrs. Chegwe's voice barks out a single word in Swahili and he lowers it. It is clear who is in command.

'Mrs. McIntyre, I've warned you many times to be careful. You should have listened. Listen now; tell me where the rebel Kithu is and we will go away. He is of no concern to you and Mr. McIntyre, just a treasonous Luo who threatens Kenya. Why should a wicked man like that be allowed to upset a nice white family?'

'We haven't seen Isaac Kithu for weeks,' George insists. 'I sacked him before the school holidays. You're wasting your time here.'

'Mrs. McIntyre, we have been watching Kithu, and many others like him, for a long time. These students, they are lucky to get a chance of a good education, and what do they do? Instead of listening to their teachers at the university to learn,

226

make themselves useful to Kenya, they listen for the wrong reasons. They let themselves be brainwashed by Communists telling them to destroy Kenya. Don't feel sorry for him; feel sorry he has involved you. Tell me where he is.' Mrs. Chegwe waits as if she has all the time in the world.

'My husband told you, he hasn't been here for a month. We've been away ourselves, the whole holiday, so we haven't seen anyone.' Grace holds George's hand so tight her fingers are numb. Mrs. Chegwe doesn't budge. 'Where else would he come than to the nice *muzungu* lady who is always helping him so much?' She looks at George for an answer.

'Helping him? Helping him how? We barely know him, he's only a gardener.' He puts on a convincing show of indignation. He grips Grace's hand tighter.
'Ask your wife, Mr. McIntyre. Ask her about where they go driving day and night. Ask your wife why she was in Nairobi at the very time we know Kithu was there, planning to destabilise the country. For that matter, I might ask you, Mr. McIntyre, what you were both doing in Nakuru when everyone was under curfew. Did you know he'd been there, or just your wife?''

Grace untangles her fingers from George's, stretching them to get some feeling back. She wraps them round the door instead, pulling it as wide as it will go and pushes herself in front of George.

'And how do you know when we were in Nakuru? If you have such an important job to do, I can't believe you waste your time following me up and down the country. You must be mad.' Grace doesn't feel half as assured as she hopes she sounds.

'Luck, Mrs. McIntyre. I was liaising with my colleagues there on another matter. I just left a driver sitting in the car when I went to buy oranges and he saw you, walking in the street.'

So, Grace thinks, *I wasn't being paranoid. It was Mrs. Chegwe's blue car I saw in Kenyatta Avenue, waiting to tuck into the tail of the official convoy before it swept down the rift to Nairobi.* She begins to feel very afraid.

'We've been following these scum for weeks. They thought they could infiltrate SONU with no-one noticing. They thought they could fly air force planes to Kisumu and take protection from Kisumu politicians and we wouldn't find out. They must be more stupid than they look.'

'I'm a teacher; I've only been here five minutes.' George insists. 'Why do I know about things like that? I don't care. I've only been to Kisumu once, for God's sake.'

'Do not blaspheme, Mr. McIntyre.' Mrs. Chegwe reproves him. 'These men were in Kisumu again last week; we thought we had sorted the problem out then, once and for all. But this Kithu is a clever man, cunning. He survived our meeting. Tell me where he is, or you will have to bear the consequences.' Mrs. Chegwe is growing impatient.

Grace and George remain defiantly silent. When she sees they will not co-operate Mrs. Chegwe shouts, loud enough to be heard in the kitchen. 'Mama Esther.'

Esther comes out of the kitchen and peers between Grace and George, keeping Tom well back.

'Mama Esther, *ambaponi Kithu?* 'Mrs. Chegwe shouts again, perhaps hoping to scare Esther into an answer.

Grace catches Isaac's name and guesses the question. *Where is he?* If only Mrs. Chegwe knew how much Esther would give to know the answer to that herself.

'*Wamekwenda,* ' Esther calls back. 'Gone. Far away.'

Mrs. Chegwe's patience has been tried long enough. She nods to the soldier beside her and he rushes back up the steps, only too keen for a chance of retaliation for his recent humiliation. Using the rifle as a shield to force his way in, he scatters Grace and George and Esther out of his way. He takes special delight in hitting George hard in the chest as he barges into the house. This soldier is as intent on showing them his power over them as he is on rooting out Isaac. He doesn't notice the small figure hiding behind Esther, trying to absorb what's going on, and he knocks Tom flying. He lands on his bottom and is sent spinning across the concrete floor, knocking into the wall with a thud. The three adults in the doorway all rush to pick him up but it is Esther who reaches him first, and Esther he clings to, screaming; high-pitched one note shrieks that fill the house.

His shrieks don't cover the noise of the soldier ransacking the house. Grace can hear books being swept from shelves, cupboards and drawers being opened and the beds being overturned. She guesses from the sounds that the soldier finds it vital to his search to smash glass and china and pull down curtains. After wreaking havoc for ten minutes he comes back, gun slung over his shoulder. He shakes his head at Mrs. Chegwe. For the first time she loses her composure, kicking out at divot of grass and swearing.

'We will find him, Mrs. McIntyre. If we have to come back and ask you again, imagine how upset your boy will be then.'

She snaps an order to the soldier and he clambers into the back of the jeep and sits hunched on an old oil drum, his rifle propped between his legs. When the driver leaps down from his seat to hurry round and open the passenger door for Mrs. Chegwe Grace catches sight of something stuffed into the back of his belt. It's an axe; a gleaming, new-looking axe.

Chapter Forty-three

The drawers have been pulled right out of the chests in the bedroom and left, upended, on the floor. Grace thinks that even the GSU can't believe a grown man could squeeze into such a tiny space. No, she realises, the soldier who in came here was intent on trouble, just for the satisfaction of it. She picks her way through the mess, gathering up bits of costume jewellery; nothing worth anything. She isn't surprised to find odd pieces missing; a little signet ring that used to be her father's, a few glittery chains.

Her heart skips when she sees the silver photo frame is missing from the side of the bed, but not for long. The soldier must have been so intent on only looting what he thought he'd be able to sell that he's ripped the photo from the frame and tossed it to the floor like rubbish. For the sake of putting a few extra shillings in his pocket, he's missed an opportunity to make Mrs. Chegwe a very happy woman. Poking out from under the photo is a corner of creased white paper. Isaac's note is still protected by her parents. She picks it up and puts it, with the other personal things she's found, in a handbag at the back of the wardrobe. Esther left as soon as the jeep drove off, a combination of fear and fury at being caught up in this situation sending her scuttling. Grace can't blame her. It will be far worse for her if she gets on the wrong side of GSU than it will be for expats. George isn't here either. Tom was so frightened that George took him out to help him get over the upset. Grace thinks it will take a lot more than a walk to the river to watch the butterflies emerging from their cocoons to pacify him, but George is, at least, trying. Sungu went bouncing out the door with them, always ready to go exploring.

There is more smashed glass in the bathroom. When Grace bends to pick shards of mirror from the floor and basin she sees her face reflecting back to her. She is appalled at how tired and worn out she looks. Her hair is lank around the nape of her neck and her eyes are pink with constant rubbing. She isn't thirty yet and she looks like an old woman. She is fed up with it, all this worry and subterfuge and living every day with fear and guilt gnawing at her insides.

Mrs. Chegwe's visit has proved one thing. Grace can't put Tom through that again. George, for all he has every right to hate her, didn't give her or Isaac away. There's no escaping the fact that he lied for her though he must have been itching to say, 'He's hiding in Kakamega forest with the charcoal burners.' George has kept his side of the bargain. Grace didn't give him an answer when they sat at the breakfast table this morning, but she knows she must, and she knows what it must be.

If she doesn't act now, while the memory of armed soldiers at her door and Tom's petrified face is still raw, she will find an excuse to put the decision off forever. She leaves the broken mirror, tiny splinters twinkling at her from the bath, and goes. She doesn't brush her hair or change her shirt

or pick up her purse. She takes her keys from the
hook and sets off for the forest.

Monkeys screech from the tree tops When Grace
traces the track to the bivouac of huts she disturbs
a small group of monkeys that screech in alarm
and run up to the tree tops, swinging from one to
another till they're out of sight. Small green
parrots are sitting on a low branch squawking,
hopping from foot to foot and stretching their
heads forward to watch her. She supposes she must
look terrifying to them.

Forty eight hours have seen a transformation in
Isaac. He is on his makeshift mattress, but propped
up today, talking to Juma and one of the other
men. Juma has stitched the ugly gash in Isaac's
cheek with thick thread and, though he will carry a
livid scar, it looks clean and dry. His broken arm is
splinted, clean rags wrapped round and round a
piece of rough wood. Grace is so relieved she
could cry. It makes it easier for her, that she's not
abandoning a dying man.

Juma and the charcoal burner take their cigarettes
and beers further into the forest and Grace makes
herself as comfortable as she can on the ground by
the mattress. Grace recognises the smell of wet
embers from her first visit; the fires in the pits have
had their three days burning and have been
dampened, waiting to be cleaned out. How long
ago it seems.

'You saved me,' Isaac says. 'I knew you
would.'

'I don't know about that. Juma did the saving. I
was just the private ambulance.' Neither of them

laughs. 'How are you, really?' Grace looks at his good hand, lying so close to hers, but she won't hold it. If she did, she might not be able to let go. 'Juma says I have broken ribs as well as the wounds that show, but he says my liver is fine, and my kidneys. I am a very lucky man.'

Grace looks at him, to see if he is teasing her the way he used to, but he seems perfectly serious. She wonders what it would take for him to think himself unlucky.

'Grace, I must tell you what happened.' He eases into a better position.

'You don't need to. I had a visit from a member of the Internal Affairs ministry this morning; Mrs. Chegwe, the headmaster's wife, accompanied by a pair of GSU goons. She gave a pretty good summary of what happened in Kisumu.'
'I didn't expect them to come calling on you. I thought they were finished with me after Kisumu.' He shakes his head. 'They will never give up, these devils.'

'They will at some point. Eventually they'll lose interest.' Grace wants what she says to be true.

'No, I think the authorities let this happen, to give them an excuse to stamp out dissention. They had their informers; they knew our plans for August 1st. They could have stopped us long before we got near to the radio station but it suited them to let us have a long leash.'

'I read that Ochuka and the other ringleaders took planes from Nairobi and flew them over the border,' Grace says, hoping to encourage him. 'Won't they be safe now they're out of the country? You could join them when you're well.' 'Even those who did get over the border won't taste freedom for long,' Isaac says. 'Countries like Tanzania will make a show of giving them sanctuary but international politics is a slippery thing. They will come to an agreement sooner or later, a mutually agreeable compromise, and Ochuka and the others will be deported back here. And when they have them they will hang them. They will hang anyone they can. My only chance is to leave Kenya for good.'

Grace has put off saying what she has to say for long enough. The time has come. The late afternoon sun is already weak in the middle of the forest and she's conscious of needing to get home while it's daylight. She has that house to tidy up before Tom goes to bed; the tiny fragments of glass to collect, the beds to make. She takes deep breath.

'I met Akumu last week, Esther's daughter.'

Isaac doesn't look at all perturbed. He nods at Grace as if recalling a slight acquaintance. 'Yes, I knew her at their place, at Esther's *shamba.* How is she? Has she come to work in Marigoi with her mother?'

'She has come to be with her mother because she's pregnant, Isaac, and she says you're the father.' Grace looks at Isaac carefully, half hoping, even now, to see shock or hear a denial, but instead he smiles, a broad grin that his ravaged features make grotesque.

'So, I will be a father,' he says. 'It is good for a man to have a son.'

Grace is so surprised to hear the pride in his voice that she doesn't bother pointing out that it is just as likely to be a daughter that Akumu carries. She is unreasonably hurt by his happiness; so easily side-lined.

'Will you marry her?' she asks.

Isaac lifts his head clear of the mattress and turns to face her fully. Now it's his turn to look surprised.

'Of course not. She's a Kalenjin. I could never marry a Kalenjin. Have you learnt nothing about us? It would be like you and me being together, impossible.' He sees the sadness in Grace's eyes, how wounded she is. 'Grace, I always told you, there is no future for people like us in Africa yet.'

'It's the 1980s, Isaac, not the 1880s. Others have managed it.'

'Not others like me,' he says simply. He waits, deciding, before he goes on. 'I think it will be good if you did not come here again. It is better if we do not see each other. I must try and leave this place. When I am far away, you will be out of danger. Go home to Mr. McIntyre. The authorities won't bother you anymore.'

For all the times she's been going over this scene in her head, picking and choosing the right words, he's made it easy for her. Grace's planned script isn't needed; she has no need of it. She doesn't have to tell him she realises even loving him can't surpass loving Tom. Loving him can't excuse

236

brutality and cruelty, or shattering fear. Perhaps it never could.

Grace stands up ready to leave. She wants to pour her heart out to Isaac before she leaves, but she can't think of a single thing she could say that would let him know quite how much he has touched her life and changed it. That their parting is a kind of grief, as sharp as death. She looks up at one of the nearby trees where dozens of noisy yellow birds are fluttering upside down, threading strappy leaves into a newly constructed nest. Weaver birds making sure they're cut off from predators.

'Do you remember when I showed you them at Elgon?' Isaac asks. 'That was a good day. I felt free there.'

Grace hears his despair, a fear of impending betrayal. He is as hunted as the animals in the game parks. Not those pursued by tourists with cameras but those who stumble into poachers' traps and die struggling in their efforts to escape the tightening noose.

Chapter Forty-four

The house is pristine. George has not only cleaned up every last inch of glass and broken china but he's rehung the curtains in the living room and put fresh towels on the rail next to the bath. He's been busy in the kitchen, too, because Grace can smell onions and garlic floating from the oven.

'We saw lots of butterflies,' Tom tells her as soon as she's through the door. 'Yellow ones with little brown spots. Daddy says you'll help me find them.' He's dragged his *Book of Creepy-crawlies* off the shelf, ready and waiting. Grace kicks off her sandals and collapses onto the sofa and he climbs on her lap and snuggles close. They turn the pages together.

'You didn't say you were going out,' George says when he comes through, holding a bowl of something hot. He's keeping his fingers from burning with a pair of pale pink, floral oven gloves, that a friend once gave Grace, and looks faintly ridiculous. 'I thought you'd scarpered again.' He tries for light and bantering but misses the right tone and sounds peevish and accusatory.

Grace flashes a look at him. If he'd made a remark like that in the past, she'd have taken it for the joshing, throwaway comment it was. She suspects now that he will never fully trust her and that her guilt will always keep her attuned to the fact.

'When Tom's in bed, I'll tell you about it. It's no secret.' Grace has made up her mind that there won't be secrets from now on. She bobs her head back to the book and turns the page to a shiny picture of a yellow butterfly.

'That's what me and Daddy saw,' Tom shouts, jabbing his finger at the page. 'They were coming out of poo!'He giggles and watches her face in the hope he's shocked her.

Grace makes a suitable moue of revulsion and raises an eyebrow at George.

'They lay their eggs in dung,' he explains. 'They all hatch at once, hundreds of them, and these delicate yellow things emerge from the cow pats and fly out to the water. It makes you wonder how something so lovely can come from muck.' 'I had to go and see Isaac. I had to let him know GSU were on the hunt.' Grace is making firelighters out of twists of old paper and placing them in a grid pattern in the grate. George is kneeling on the rug making a wigwam of wood over the twists. It's a cool evening tonight and they need the heat. Besides, it will be nice to curl up in front of a log fire.

'I thought you'd have the sense not to see him again. I thought that was our deal.' George puts a match to the paper twists and blows gently to get the fire going. 'Are you ever going to let him go?'

'George, don't be ridiculous. That's why I went, to finish it for good; say goodbye.'

'He would've soon got the message if you hadn't.' The fire catches with a whoosh and George kneels back and watches the flames lick up the chimney. In profile, Grace can see his hair has grown too long, curling over his shirt at the back. If she is going to stay, she has to make some sort of effort. She reaches out and runs her finger under his collar.

George grips her hand and twists on his knees and buries his face in her lap.

'If you do this to me again, I'll never forgive you.' He begins to cry, holding her tighter and tighter. 'No second chances, none.' He lifts his head to hers and begins to kiss her. Wet kisses land on her neck and face, searching for her mouth.

Grace battles down the wave of revulsion that threatens to swamp her. George is rushing her into intimacy too fast. Despite him talking about babies, Grace has put any thoughts about what her commitment to stay means on hold. She doesn't want this, not yet; it's too soon to play happy families. She quells her distaste because she can't let George see how desperately she doesn't want him to touch her, when he could expose Isaac to Mrs. Chegwe with a word. She cries silent tears onto his blond hair while he paws and gropes. She thinks all the time of Isaac and the little shed.

Over the next two days, they build a carapace of harmony between them. It's the weekend and, for once, George isn't on duty. He spends most of his time in the shambles of the garden, doing his best to restore order, which isn't made any easier by Tom racing all over the place on his bike and the dog digging holes in the turned over soil. George saws the broken lemon tree down to a stump in the hope new growth will restore its symmetry and Grace harvests the fruits still clinging to the fallen branches. She is making bitter marmalade, using extra sugar to make it edible. She puts a tray of jars in the oven to warm and cuts circles of waxy paper to seal them. She wishes she could stay in the kitchen forever.

'Mummy, Mummy, look.' Tom comes into the kitchenwith something cupped in both hands. He is walking very slowly, keeping his eyes fixed on what he's holding. 'It was in the hedge.'

It's a shallow, bowl-shaped bird's nest, with a clutch of three speckled eggs nestling inside. Tom places it carefully on the table. It tilts on its side and one of the eggs rolls over the edge and across the table. It bumps into the preserving pan with a tap.

'Shrike's nest.' George follows Tom through the door, wiping his hands on his trousers. He bends over the nest with Tom, turning the two remaining eggs with a gentle finger. 'I think it's been abandoned, though, there was no sign of the hen. It was in the dead bit down by the boundary.'

Grace shudders when she thinks of where he must mean. She wants to forget all about what went on there so few nights ago.

'Butcher birds, that's what they're called, aren't they? Vicious things.' Grace picks the stray egg up, seeing a hairline crack running down the shell. It's cold.

'Are they? I didn't know that.' George looks doubtful. 'You know the oddest things; shows what a wealth of information is opened up to you being a librarian.' When she doesn't answer, he looks at Grace for long seconds. He says, very quietly, 'It wasn't the library, was it? I'm guessing we have Isaac to thank for that as well.'

Grace swallows and nods her head. Tom looks up from the nest and nods his head at George too, all seriousness, and says,

'At the mountain when we saw the big caves. He says they use all the thorns on the bushes like little hooks for their food.'

Grace steels herself for the expected outburst from George; either that, or for him to turn on his heel and storm back to the garden. He disarms her by ruffling Tom's hair and saying, 'I don't know, Tom, trust you to remember something like that; the more gory the better, eh?' He moves the nest to the sunlit windowsill. 'We'll leave this in the warm for a day or two to see if anything happens, but I expect the baby birds are dead, with no mummy to look after them.'

Grace goes back to stirring the marmalade. From time to time she lifts the wooden spoon clear of the boiling mixture and watches the syrup drop back into the pan, judging for a set. Slivers of softened peel burst the jammy bubbles swirling in the pan before sinking to the bottom. Grace blames the hot, sugary steam for her red cheeks and clammy hands.

Chapter Forty-five

Akumu comes to work with her mother next day, her belly swathed in green and yellow *kikoi.* She sits in the kitchen while Esther scrubs and rinses but, if Grace so much as walks past the door, jumps to her feet and lowers her head, as if she's been caught doing something she shouldn't. When Esther takes brushes and dusters to the rest of the house, Akumu follows, nervous of letting her mother out of her sight, like a dog scared to be left alone. The only time she relaxes is when Esther sends her into the garden to peg out the laundry and she drags that simple job out to half an hour. Grace gets so irritated by seeing the girl's frightened face every time they cross paths, and as the house is so tidy from all George's hard work on Friday, that she tells Esther to finish work early and take her daughter home. They are gone not long before George gets home for lunch, frustrated by another of Mr. Chwgwe's plans.

'He's cancelled lessons this afternoon. The vice-president's due to ride through on his way to Kisumu and he wants the boys to line the route. Can you believe it?'

Grace can. 'Staff too? Have you got a three line whip?'
The day is humid and overcast. George's shirt is clinging to him and damp patches show under his arms. Clouds hang low in the sky, threatening to burst.

'He hopes. Look at it; it's bound to rain. We'll be standing out there getting wet for hours because the vice-president'll be running to his own clock, if he comes at all, and when he does all we'll see is a flash of black Mercedes with darkened windows. The only way the boys'll know he's been is seeing the national flag on the bonnet.'

'Well, you know Mr. Chegwe. The vice-president holds the purse strings, so he'll be looking to wheedle some extra funding out of him, Kikuyu to Kikuyu.'

'Probably, but it won't do him any good. Sammy was just saying, in the staffroom, the VP's not at Finance anymore, he's been moved to Home Affairs.'

To Grace, it is too much of a coincidence that the man who is now, to all intents and purposes, Mrs. Chegwe's boss is on his way to Kisumu, That he chooses to divert his cavalcade off the main tarmac road and bump over the pot-holes through an insignificant town like Marigoi, seems perverse. Grace wonders if this display of favours might be a thank you to the headmaster's wife, a reward for loyalty. Or could it be a reminder that he's keeping a close eye on events here and she can't relax her efforts for a moment.

'I'm going to bunk off,' George says. 'Act African.'

'What are you planning to do? Hide under the bedclothes?' Grace laughs, despite herself. Tom giggles with her, nearly choking on his sandwich.

'No, I'll have to get right off site. The trouble with being white here is you stand out like a sore thumb. When the head notices I'm missing, he'll send out a search party. Do you need to go to

Eldoret? Shopping or anything? Only we need to be quick, the boys are being walked down the drive at one.' George taps Tom on the back till he stops coughing.

Grace is at a loss. There's nothing she needs, in Eldoret or anywhere else. The last thing she feels like doing is dragging herself out for the sake of it.

'The forest,' Tom says, now he's recovered his breath. 'I want Daddy to see the parrots.' He's saved the dark crusts of his bread till last and finishes them off now, nibbling with his small white teeth. 'The man with the medicines can show him.'

'I don't think that's a good idea,' Grace tells him, struggling to keep her voice neutral. 'It looks like rain.'

'I'll wear my welly boots,' Tom says, pragmatic. 'It's lovely in the forest; it's fun.' He turns his appeal to George. You'd like it Daddy.'

'No, Tom, not today.' Grace insists. 'No forest.'

Tom ignores her. He fixes his attention on his father, his eyes seeming to grow rounder than ever. Grace thinks he's actually managing to make his chin wobble.

'Please, Daddy, pleeese! You can find feathers and all sorts. We might find another nest. Please let's go.' He slides off his chair and goes right up to George, holding him round the waist while George is swallowing hot coffee. He has to hold the cup in the air to stop it spilling. 'Mummy can take her brella.'

245

Grace and George both know from experience that Tom can keep this up forever. As Grace suspected, George is the one to capitulate first.

'We can't go and see your friend, the charcoal man, he'll be busy. He must have lots of work to do for all the poorly people who go to see him. But Mummy told me the forest is huge, so perhaps we can go to another bit of it, just so you can show me. How about that?'

'But we won't see the baby parrots.' Tom is adamant.

'They'll be tucked up if it's raining, won't they, Mummy?' George tries to include her in his decision.

'Mm, definitely,' Grace agrees, glad for any excuse not to go. Tom looks doubtful. 'The poor baby parrots haven't got any nice wellies like you to keep them dry, have they?' He doesn't have an answer to that.

Grace knows something is wrong as soon as they twist off the tarmac into the forest; something she can't, at first, put her finger on. Much looks the same. The combined effects of cars and wagons passing up and down and tree trunks being hauled from where the charcoal burners have felled them to the pits further in, make the track resemble corrugated iron. The surviving Meru oak stand tall and the bamboo is lush, barely swaying. Smaller tracks still disappear in all directions, criss-crossing the forest floor.

But everywhere is silent, and it is the silence that makes Grace alert, wary. There are no monkeys swinging through the branches, no

246

flashes of black and white as colobus play and chatter. The large grey parrots that usually swoop in and out of the trees are not only silent, they are invisible, as is any sign of every other bird Grace is used to seeing here in such numbers. No finches, no glossy starlings, no great blue turaco with its impressive crest. No small creatures scurry through the leaves. Even here the patter of rain drops is missing because the clouds still hang heavy, swollen, the expected downpour refusing to fall.

'George, it's too quiet. There should be birds everywhere. Even when you can't see them, you can hear them.' Grace turns from side to side in her seat, hoping to catch sight of some living thing.

'They can probably sense a deluge is on its way. It'll be their natural instincts kicking in.' George hits a deep pit and the exhaust pipe scrapes along the ground.

Grace twists round to the back seat and encourages Tom to keep looking out the rear window in case he spots something she misses.

'You shouldn't make sarcastic jokes about being followed,' George says quietly. 'Either that, or we've got very bad luck.' He stops the car and Grace swivels back the right way.

The track is guarded by armed police. They don't display the ferocious efficiency of the GSU who turned up at their door but look more like the regular police who they've grown used to seeing on patrol in Eldoret and the other major towns. One of them holds a hand up to them and walks over to the car.

'Forest is closed off,' he says. 'You must go back.'

'What's going on?' George wants to know.

'Local trouble,' the policeman says. 'Local fighting, nothing for you to see. Nandi on the warpath.' He laughs. 'Forest is closed till we finish clearing; perhaps two days.'

The situation can't be too serious if the policeman's in such a good mood. Grace's nervousness starts to subside, the pounding under her ribs ratcheted down to a fluttering sensation at the base of her throat. But the tics of concern don't dissipate entirely; they still nag at the pit of her stomach and she wants to see for herself that the people she has got to know are safe.

'How about if we stick to the main track? Carry on till Kakamega?' Grace leans right over George and pokes her head out his side window so the policeman can hear her. He is about to refuse when she adds, 'I've got an appointment at the hospital.' She prays Kakamega has a hospital.

The young man goes off to confer with his colleague and after much hand waving and head shaking, no doubt debating the sanity of crazy *muzungu,* he beckons George forward with his finger. George drives slowly in case the guard has a sudden change of mind, but the man encourages them on their way with an extravagant wave of his arm. When they draw level he stops them again.

'Do not go into the forest, there are still *shifta* there. Bandits. Drive to Kakamega fast, my friend,' he reminds them. He proffers his hand for George to slap, and the two men exchange

248

goodbyes; '*kwaheri*', '*kwaheri, brother.*' As the car passes, the policeman sees Tom looking out the back window. He grins at him, his broad mouth stretched wide over large, white teeth, and cocks his thumb and forefinger and pretends to shoot. Tom, happy to play the game, clutches his chest and rolls onto the car seat.

Chapter Forty-six

Grace can't quite leave the nagging worries behind with the policemen. The car bends a curve in the track, near the clearing she's parked at before and from where the myriad of smaller footpaths diverge. Today these little paths are all cut off from the main track on both sides by makeshift fencing. An untidy assortment of pallets, wire and boxes is roughly piled up with one intention; to keep people out. The barrier serves its purpose in that it's giving fair warning to the villagers to stay away, but it's so ramshackle that Grace realises anyone who wanted to could easily find a way in.

'Look, smoke.' George points ahead. 'Your charcoal burners are obviously safe enough; they've not been put off working.'

'They shouldn't be burning again yet; they only opened the last pits a couple of days ago. They'll still be cooling.' Grace follows the trail of smutty smoke as it drifts low among the trees. She breathes deeply. The smell of fresh, damp embers is missing. Instead, Grace can almost taste the acrid tang of very dry foliage underlined with some other odour, a hint of roasted meat.

'Pull up, George. I want to get out.' Grace has already turned the handle and holds the car door half open.

'Watch out, you'll be flat on the ground at this rate.' George warns her. 'Let me at least stop.'

'I'm just going to look over the fence, see if I can see anything.' Grace is out of the car before it

250

fully stops, rushing over to the fence and climbing up on one of the stronger boxes.

'For Christ's sake, Grace, get down. You're bloody mad.' George revs up the engine to encourage her back to the car.

'Turn it off. Come here.' Grace tries to climb higher.

George realises the only way to get her to leave is to see what she wants to show him. He leaves the engine idling, tells Tom to wait in the car and joins her on the barricade.

When his eyes follow where Grace is pointing he can make out the remains of a small collection of huts in a clearing. What little is left of the walls and roofs are smouldering and the doors hang askew, blackened by fire. Every hut has been burnt out. There is no living sign of the community who built them and worked near them but, as they watch, Grace and George see two more policemen come out of the furthest hut carrying a body. They swing their arms once, twice, till they have the momentum to send the body forwards in the air. Grace is too far away to hear the soft thud as it lands on a pile of other corpses but she watches as it slithers down the pyramid till it finds its own resting place.

George grabs Grace's arm, rough, and pulls her away from the fence, pushing her down the heaped up scraps. She gashes her leg on a piece of jagged wood and barbed wire tears at her skirt. George shoves her back in the car, slamming the door against her knees. He speeds away from the desolate scene. Grace is shaking and sobbing, at a loss to make sense of what they witnessed. Why would anyone do that? What harm were charcoal burners to anyone?

George doesn't touch his foot to the brake till he sees the traffic on the main Kakamega road. He stops at the edge of the forest and roots in the cool box for cold Sprites. He gives one to Tom, but Grace shakes her head when he holds one out for her.

'Wish this was a beer,' he says. 'Wish it was a G and T.' He drains his bottle of soda in long gulps. 'Talk about 'a bit of tribal trouble' or whatever that policeman said. They're mad, these Kenyans, I tell you. Bloody barbarians.'

'Not all of them.' Grace is defensive. 'There's bad everywhere.'

Tom suddenly jumps up, splashing Sprite over the back seat, and bangs on the car window.

'It's the man with the medicine,' he screeches in Grace's ear. 'He can show Daddy the baby birds.'

Juma is crouching at the side of the road by the exit from the forest. Over his shoulder is the sack Grace recognises from the back of his door and under his arm is a thin mattress, rolled and tied up with the same thread he used to sew Isaac's cheek. Another man slumps beside him and Grace's hopes flare, but it is not Isaac. It is the youngest of the charcoal burners, the one who ran away from her the other night.

George puts out his hand to stop Grace when she moves but she shakes it off.

'I must talk to him. I must find out.'

252

'Two minutes, then I'm going.' George threatens.

Juma is grey with tiredness and smoke. His ragged trousers are singed at the hems and he has a livid red burn on his left hand. He hasn't had time to use his own ointments. The younger man doesn't seem burnt, but one hunched shoulder is bleeding profusely and he is feverish, almost unconscious. Juma holds a slim cylinder of shaped wood in his hand, the shaft of an arrow. One bloodied end shows where he has pulled it from the charcoal burner's back.

'What happened, Juma?' Grace hopes he can understand. 'Where are the others?'

Juma raises his arms and mimes firing arrows. 'Burn houses,' he says. 'Nandi.'

'And the people?' Grace urges.

The old man shoots his imaginary arrows again, this time aiming at the young man next to him. He takes Grace's hand and makes her touch the wound. 'Bad, bad,' he says.

Grace can feel the arrow head embedded under the skin. She has no doubt the man who made it took great satisfaction in imagining the extra suffering he would cause by applying a liberal layer of poison to its tip.

She goes back to the car and opens the rear door. 'The huts were fired, by flaming arrows I think, and when the villagers ran they got more of the same. Some of them must've got trapped inside, though, which is why we smelt…' She realises Tom is listening to every word and keeps the final thought unsaid. 'Jump in the front, poppet,' she tells him. 'We're going to give Juma and the boy a ride to the hospital.' She starts to move the cool box and Tom's toys off the back seat.

'No, we're not,' George says. 'Not on your life.' He glares at Grace, daring her to argue. She doesn't disappoint him.

'Don't be ridiculous. The boy has a poisoned wound, he could die.'

'What's one more?' George asks with callous indifference.' It's not our fight. I mean it; I'm going.' He switches on the engine. 'Let them all kill each other and be done with it.'

A wave of pity breaks over Grace when she understands that George is not going to budge this time; pity for the boy, surely as good as sentenced to death, and pity, too, for George, and what a petty, spiteful man he has become. She takes the last of the cans of sodas and goes back to Juma and squats beside him. She hands him the cold bottles. She can't leave without finding out for certain what has become of the man who is so much more to her than George.

'Isaac?' she asks. 'Did he go? Escape?'
Juma recognises the name, but no more. He shakes his head.
'Elgon? Uganda? Where is he?' She is desperate for a way to make him understand.

'Shifta,' Juma tells her. ;Nandi. Kill, kill.'

He's mistaken; it can't be true. She won't let it be true. She shakes Juma, shouting at him. 'Isaac, where is he?'

254

The old man picks up the arrow shaft again and stabs at his own chest with it, five or six thrusts around the heart; too much poison to survive. 'Bad, bad,' he tells her again. 'Nandi find him.'

Grace stumbles back to George and Tom. She is so distraught she is dry-eyed. She has heard people say they were 'turned to ice' and laughed at their over-exaggeration, but now she knows what they mean. Her insides are numb, feeling nothing. George shows better sense than to ply her with questions. He avoids looking at Juma and the charcoal burner as he pulls out of the forest and turns the car to Kakamega town. They will have to go home the long way round.

The sun hurts Grace's eyes but, every time she closes them, she sees the policemen in the forest hurling another nameless body onto the pile and can't help but wonder.

Chapter Forty-seven

Esther arrives on Tuesday with no Akumu in sight. She seems in a much happier frame of mind, more the Esther of old. When she sees Tom is still in his pyjamas she bustles him off to the bathroom and Grace hears a lot of giggling and splashing. After she's dressed him -bright green shorts and an orange T-shirt, very Kenyan -   she sets to making fresh flatbreads for breakfast, flour scattering the table as she kneads the dough with strong hands. Grace likes to look after Tom and fix the meals herself, but she's so relieved at the change in Esther and that the stony silences have come to a sudden end that she lets her get on with it.

 They are all sitting at the table, waiting for the bread to arrive hot from the griddle. Neither Grace nor George has mentioned Isaac by name since they left Kakamega forest. Grace has the wit not to share her memories with George, who would hardly appreciate them, and, more than that, she wants to hugevery one to her, keep a private space that George can't invade. But something niggles away at the back of her mind; a phrase ofJuma's that grows in significance whenever she thinks of it.

'He said, *'the Nandi found him.'* Why would he say that? I can understand GSU and the army being after him but not tribesmen. Perhaps Mrs. Chegwe has local help.' She speaks to herself as much as George; she barely realises she's said the words out loud.

'Grace, you went out of your way to make sure Mrs. Chegwe's little gang didn't know where he was.' He waits while Esther puts the first tray of bread down. 'Anyway, if they found out, I'm sure they'd be only too happy to take the credit themselves. The president would be highly appreciative.' George talks through a mouthful of flatbread.

Grace looks at him, sitting so contentedly at his breakfast. Her own food is empty. 'It just seems so convenient that the raid happened when it did, and that Isaac happened to be one of the ones killed. It's too much of a coincidence.'

'Coincidences do happen, you know.' George reminds her. 'And if Isaac was in as bad a state as you say, he'd hardly be able to charge off into the night, would he?'

'Exactly. He was a sitting target.' Grace can't let it go. 'Someone knew he was there.'

'For Christ's sake, Grace, drop it.' George grips Grace's wrist, jolting her elbow off the table, and shakes her into silence. 'Personally, I'm enjoying the irony of him wasting all his time and energy on his grandstanding politics and changing the world just to end up getting himself killed by a common or garden tribal skirmish that could have happened any day of the week. That's divine retribution.' He lets go of her arm, his point made.

His fingers have left a bracelet of pale, rosy stripes in the thin skin below Grace's elbow and she rubs at them till her arm tingles. 'There's nothing divine about it, George; nothing.'

257

George opens his mouth to say something, but stops. He shakes his head at her, weary of the argument, and throws the last of his flatbread, now cold, onto his plate. He scrapes back the chair and slams through the door into the garden.

'Daddy shouted,' Tom says. 'Daddy hurt you.' He scrambles up from his chair and crawls over the table and kneels on the edge of it in front of Grace. He puts his hands on her cheeks and kisses her with his little rosebud mouth. 'All better now.'

'Yes, poppet.' Grace wraps her arms around him and hugs him tight. 'All better.' She is squeezing so tight, Tom starts to wriggle to escape. Grace lets him go and lifts him to the floor. She has to do something to take her mind of this obsessive replaying of Juma's words. 'Come on, why don't we take that dog of yours for a long walk, just the two of us?'

The little dog keeps at Tom's heel as he trots along next to his mother, one hand in hers and one firmly on the lead. Sungu walks well on her lead now, all George's patience has paid off, but when they get as far down the drive as the headmaster's house, she sniffs and whines, pulling until the *askari* comes out from the gateway to fuss her. Her tail wags so wildly that it thumps against her rump in a steady beat.

'Ah, my friend,' the old man says to her, scratching her ears. '*Jambo.*'

Grace is confused. She's certainly never brought the dog this way. It must be on George and Tom's route.

'Do you say hello to the caretaker when you're with Daddy?' she asks. 'Sungu seems to know him very well.'

'No,' Tom shakes his head. 'She's just friendly.' Grace isn't convinced.

They walk up the long road towards the market, following the cows to the butchery.
The murram is dry and dusty, red clouds puffing up from their footsteps, and Sungu begins to sneeze, which makes Tom laugh. Grace usually drives to the market and is surprised today by the uphill slope, hardly noticeable in the car. She feels sweaty and uncomfortable before they are halfway, though Tom and the dog don't seem to notice.

When they get to the church, Grace persuades Tom to have a rest. Through the gateless space in the wooden fence a path leads straight to the church and a narrow track winds off to one side to the breeze block building where the priest lives. She collapses against a shady tree at the side of this house while Tom sits on the ground. He's bored within seconds and bounces up, still holding the dog.

'We're going to run right round the church,' he tells Grace. 'Count how long it takes us.'

She is quite alone and hidden by the shadows when Mrs. Chegwe comes out of the church, head covered by a black lace mantilla. *Where did you get that?* Grace wonders. Before she can answer her own question there is another movement at the church door and Mrs. Chegwe turns back to talk to someone who's still loitering inside. Grace can't quite picture Mrs. Chegwe as a devout Catholic so

259

she waits and watches, curious to find out whom she's been meeting, that she needs to find such a quiet spot. She watches until the other person emerges from the doorway and steps out next to Mrs. Chegwe on the path. It is Esther. The two women talk some more, urgent, whispered words, then set off down the path, heads close, black mantilla and brilliant scarlet *kikoi* touching. At the road they shake hands in the exuberant two handed grasp the Africans favour before they go their separate ways. Esther pushes something small down her ample cleavage and turns back to the village, retracing the path Grace and Tom have made, and the headmaster's wife crosses the road to where a driver waits with her blue car. She snatches the black lace from her head and tosses onto the back seat. She leans back in the passenger seat and closes her eyes as the driver pulls away towards the tarmac road. Mrs. Chegwe has a smile on her lips.

'Mummy, Mummy! How many was I? I was quick, wasn't I?' Tom, a streak of vivid green and orange, races up to Grace, the dog at his heels. They are both panting. Globules of drool hang from Sungu's mouth and, when she shakes her head, they fly out; dark, damp speckles spotting Tom's shirt.

'Sixty-one,' says Grace, plucking a random number out of the air. She hasn't been counting seconds, she's been too caught up in the little scene she's just witnessed; too preoccupied by the questions it poses and those it may well answer.

Chapter Forty-eight

Grace and George are in the kitchen cooking supper while Tom counts knives and forks onto the table. Grace is stirring the ingredients of a meat sauce, ready to fill the pancakes George is expertly tossing one after another, everyone perfect. Every time he flicks his wrist and sends one sailing up into the air Tom looks, hoping for disaster, but every time the pale golden disc lands flat in the middle of the pan, and his attention goes back to the cutlery.

'Did you know Esther and Mrs.Chegwe knew each other?' Grace says, squirting more puree into the mix.

'I'd be surprised if they didn't, place like this.' George pours more batter from a jug into the smoking fat, his eyes watching as it froths and bubbles. 'Doesn't everyone know everyone?'

'No, I mean *know* each other; close acquaintances know, not just recognise by sight know. Tom and I saw them together at the Catholic church this morning.' Grace tastes the sauce and turns the heat low.

'I didn't saw them,' Tom tells George. 'I didn't.'

'Well, I did. And when I thought Esther was still here, working.'

'Perhaps she wants her to go and work for her,' George suggests, not really interested.

'Why go to the church? Why not call at the house? What if Esther told Mrs. Chegwe about

261

Isaac, or the other way round? They'd both be happy to see him dead.'

'Don't be ridiculous. Esther was probably still hoping for money for Akumu.' George turns the last pancake onto the warm plate and passes it to Grace. She puts a generous spoonful of mixture in the middle of each and rolls it carefully.

'You're probably right. Besides, she didn't know where Isaac was.'

'She did.' George is quite matter-of-fact. 'I talked about it with her.'

Grace is cutting one of the savoury pancakes into small pieces for Tom and the knife slips from her fingers. It clatters onto the plate, chipping the rim.

'You did what?' Grace busies her shaking hands with finding another plate for Tom and transferring the small squares of pancake onto it. She doesn't risk looking at George. 'When, exactly?'

'I don't know, one day. She said she was going to send him a message. I didn't know you'd kept it from her as well; she sounded as if she knew already.'

Grace looks at him now, calmly sprinkling cheese over his supper, and could hit him.   Instead she says, 'Have you any idea what you've done? We agreed we wouldn't tell anyone. You promised.'

'I tell you, Grace she made out she knew. I don't think I told her anything she didn't know already. They were friends, her and Isaac, always drinking *chai* together in the kitchen, and then there was the thing with the daughter. How was I meant to know she was on your list? Telepathy?'

262

'You bastard, you bloody bastard. Of course she was nice to him when she thought she was in with a chance of being his mother-in-law; it's something else altogether when she's in a fury that her daughter's been discarded. Discarded, what's more, because of the tribal thing; the disgrace.'

'Don't be so paranoid, Grace, going on like some conspiracy theorist. At this rate you'll soon find yourself a prime candidate for the loony farm. Esther and Mrs. Chegwe were probably in church for some perfectly harmless reason; arranging the flowers or polishing the floors.' He's mocking her; she can hear it.

'It's not Canterbury Cathedral; they don't have ladies doing flowers. And you don't believe Mrs. Chegwe would polish a floor any more than I do.'

'I don't like Mrs. Cheggie,' Tom pipes up, his face solemn. 'She frighted me when she came with the soldiers.' He looks from one to the other. 'She's not nice. Esther's nice. I love Esther.' He forces more pancake into his already full mouth, cheeks bulging like a hamster.

'No, she's not nice.' George agrees. 'But she was doing her job. She was looking for bad men.'

'How can you say that? How can you?' Grace slams her hand down on the table so hard the glasses rattle and jump. 'Don't you care you've helped them murder a man? You may as well have stuck the knife in yourself.'

'Didn't think it was a knife. Thought we'd established it was an arrow.' George steadies the glasses before they topple. 'And it was nothing to do with me.' He reaches for another pancake. 'Get

263

a grip on yourself, Grace. Stop the wondering this and wondering that and just accept this kind of thing happens in Kenya; you can't turn back the clock. Drop it, or you'll destroy us forever.'

'Drop it?' Grace gets up from the table, her meal abandoned. Tom and George watch her, the one steadily chewing, wide-eyed, and the other shaking his head, a sigh escaping him. 'How do you propose I do that?'

She walks out into the dusk of the garden. There's barely a flower left and the parts George hasn't been able to clear yet look like a battlefield, but, even in this poor light, Grace can see signs of regeneration. Tiny shoots, so pale a green they're almost white, are growing from the base of the passion flower and a clump of cannas that somehow survived are fat with buds. Where she hacked at the hedge new leaves are sprouting on the bare brown branches, like emeralds strung on a necklace.

It seems obvious to her now; despite what he says, that George must have told Esther where Isaac was. She was a fool to believe he'd just forgive her and be done with it. She expects Esther already had some kind of agreement with Mrs. Chegwe, it would explain a lot. Grace pictures Esther taking the dog for her walks when they were on holiday and calling in at the big house; no wonder Sungu recognised the *askari.* She remembers how cheerful Esther was this morning, how unexpectedly polite and helpful after the frosty atmosphere of the past week.

Grace finds it odd that the headmaster's wife hasn't been back to harass her and George, after her threats; there must be a reason for it. If she knew her problem was solved, why would she bother with them? She sees Esther this morning, pushing something into the fold of her breast, and knows it must have been money. A fat roll of shillings for services rendered. Shillings that Akumu was owed, one way or another.

Grace is convinced she is right. George is as much to blame as the Nandi who sharpened his arrow head and dipped it in poison before setting out for the forest. None of it -no pact, no understanding, no death – would have been worth a jot if George hadn't opened his mouth.

How can she be expected to stay with a man like that? If she did, she would be no better than him.

Chapter Forty-nine

George sleeps, fitful and restless, and the first time Grace tries to get up in the middle of the night, he stirs and mumbles. She pulls the foot that has just touched the cold floor back under the covers, quick, before he wakes up fully, and waits. Ten minutes later she tries again and this time he rolls away, silent, and she can escape the covers.

She turns the handle of the door, checks he is still asleep, and goes out into the chilly corridor. She wishes she had a sweater on, or some socks. She opens the cupboard in the passage, making every movement quiet, and begins to sort clothes from the shelves, hers and Tom's. She takes them into the spare room and starts to fill a case, rolling them tight, not bothering about creases, so she can fit as much into one bag as possible.

Tom's door is open and Grace can go in like a silent ghost. She picks his favourite toys and books, takes a few more T-shirts and some pyjamas from the little chest of drawers under the window and remembers to pick up his good trainers. She doesn't bother with the green wellies. She goes back across the corridor and adds the meagre pile to the case, squashing everything down and checking it will shut.

When she has done as much as she practically can while in the dark hours of the night, Grace slides back under the covers, glad of the warmth thawing her frozen body. George rolls back towards her, this time half awake. 'Grace?' His voice is bleary.

'Sh,' she quietens him. 'I thought I heard Tom, that's all. It's OK; you go back to sleep.'

By the time George arrives into the kitchen in the morning, Grace is up, has made tea and toast, and is encouraging Tom to finish his cereals without splashing his spoon in the bowl to make milky waves. If George notices she's dressed rather better than usual, he doesn't say. He sits in the kitchen by Tom, munching toast and drinking two cups of strong green tea, the start of another ordinary day.

Grace wishes he would move a bit faster. If only it were staff meeting day and he had to go early. She wants him to pick up his bag, ruffle Tom's hair, say '*See you lunchtime,*' and leave them alone. She still has a lot to do.

'Shall we go swimming at the weekend?' George says, out of the blue. 'Not Kisumu; there's a new club in Eldoret, a sports club up by the roundabout. You'd like that, eh, Tom.'

'Yes, please, Daddy. I want to swim under the water, like a fish.' He demonstrates by pushing his finger into his breakfast bowl and wiggling it along. Milk goes everywhere.

Grace shouts at him, 'Stop it!'

'There's no need for that.' George reaches for the sponge from the draining board and dabs at the spill. 'It's only milk.' He pulls a face at Tom, who giggles.

'No, I'm sorry. I didn't sleep too well, I'm exhausted.' Grace makes her lame excuses but, really, she's thinking, '*What does a bit of mess*

267

matter? We'll be gone soon and Esther can get on with it.'

The minute George has finally torn himself away from the house Grace finishes her packing. The little box, minus its stolen jewellery but with Isaac's note folded inside, is sitting on her dressing table and she puts that in her handbag with her parents' photo. She rummages in the drawer till her hand finds what it's looking for; her passport, with Tom's name added, and slips it next to the box. She turns to the wardrobe. Tucked away, right at the back, where she expected them to hang, unneeded, for a long time, are their winter coats. Looking at it now she worries that Tom's won't fit him, though it was big on him last year; and she hasn't worn hers since she got on a plane at Heathrow all those months ago. Deep in the pocket, undisturbed since the day they arrived here and she hung the coats up, is a leather wallet holding the last of her English cash, less than fifty pounds, and her keys. She clutches them to her, thinking of the house at home and the tenants who will have to be evicted.

The last thing she does before she closes the door on this room for good is to go and stand by the window. The Chebeles' jacaranda has faded, its fallen blossoms carpeting the ground, and, across the hedge tops, the Nandi flame trees carry none of the flowers that stand up like crimson Christmas candles when they're in bloom. Today only leaves dress their branches. As she watches, a tall figure pushes through the hedge from the field and her heart surges with hope but, of course it isn't Isaac, just Hezekiah doing his rounds.

She finds Tom playing with Sungu and a pang of guilt assuages her. She'll buy him another dog in England; he'll soon get over it. She hears Esther in the kitchen, banging pots and pans.

'Come on Tom, we're going for a drive. Get your sandals on.'

'Is Sungu coming? Are we going to walk her somewhere?'

'No, not today. Leave her here with Esther.' Grace fastens his buckles and shoos him off to the kitchen with the dog. She makes sure he's safely out of the way before she collects the case and their coats from the back bedroom and loads them into the boot of the car. When Tom does come out to her, skipping down the steps, she sits him in the back seat and gives him one of his books to look at.

'I've just got to go and let Esther know something,' she tells him, straightening up.

Grace climbs the few steps to the back door, noticing for the first time how the paint is peeling, blistered by the sun. She runs her hand over the dent where the GSU rifle hammered at it, and hears the small squeak as she turns the handle and the door swings open. If ever she hears doors creaking in the future, she will think of this house.

'Esther,' she calls. She can see her through the open kitchen door, humming while she dries dishes. Grace has never heard her hum before and the woman's clear happiness enrages her. 'Esther, we won't need you any more, we're going to

269

manage without you. Mr. McIntyre will pay what we owe, but you can leave. Now.'

Esther drops the tea towel in surprise. Grace is expecting her to protest, to plead for her job and the money to feed her family, but, when Esther looks at Grace, she must recognise the steel in her eyes because she says nothing. The two women, their lives very different, look at each other for many seconds and each knows the other understands what is happening in this little Kenyan kitchen. Esther unties her apron and hangs it on the hook by the fridge. She picks the towel from the floor, draping it over the rim of the sink, and pours the dirty water from the bowl down the drain.

Grace stands back and holds the door open but, as Esther passes, she thrusts out her hand, palm upwards. Esther hesitates then reaches into the waistband of her skirt and hands her door key back to Grace. Grace's fingers close round it as Esther walks out the door, too proud to beg.

'Esther's going early,' Tom says when Grace is climbing back into the car. 'Who'll look after Sungu?'

'Daddy will be home for lunch; he'll make sure she's alright.' Grace reassures him. 'Daddy will look after her; they'll look after each other.'

The car skirts the football pitch and bumps down the school drive as so often before. Through the windows of the classrooms she can see ranks of dark heads bent over books and two boys are running as fast as they can to join them. Grace pities them; it doesn't do to be late for lessons here. Outside the office Glory and Prudence are standing at the office door, Glory with a pen stuck through her tight curls and holding a sheaf of papers. Prudence is carrying a basket of eggs, off to find customers. Grace slows as she passes, ready to wave, but they are deep in conversation and don't so much as notice her.

Chapter Fifty

'What's got into you? You can't just bugger off back to England.' Helen is incredulous.
It's lunchtime and she and Grace are sitting in the Norfolk drinking beer, much like the first time Grace ran off to Nairobi, and yet so different. James is with them, morose and watchful, but Ravi is long gone; fled with his family before the regime cracks down even more on the Asian community.

'Had plans to settle in Toronto and find a job on a paper there but we haven't heard from him.' Helen told Grace when she asked. 'I expect he'll end up running a corner shop with his cousins.'

Now she says, 'I warned you what would happen if you got involved with that man, never mind him being a terrorist. It was never going to end happily.'

'Helen, I don't want to go over it again; it's done. But I can't carry on with George; living in that place where everything reminds me of Isaac and having to wake up every morning knowing he might well still be alive if my husband hadn't betrayed him.'

'If he were alive, he still wouldn't be with you.' Helen sips more beer. 'He'd still be on the run.'

'I don't care. It wouldn't matter. At least he'd be alive.' Grace watches Tom, who has gone to play with his cars, driving them along the low wall around the terrace. 'I don't want Tom growing up here, being a little colonial boy who thinks he's better than everyone else.'

James shuffles in his seat, sitting more upright. 'Grace, if you don't mind my saying so, you're talking bollocks. How Tom grows up will be due to who he's with, not where he is.' Opinion given, he slouches back against the cane seat and cradles his half empty glass.

'You can both say what you like. I'm going home and that's that. I don't want your advice, just your help.' Grace takes her eyes off Tom to look at her two companions directly. 'Please.'

James stands up, glass in hand. 'Count me out,' he tells Grace. 'You're here on an expat contract and you should stick it out. I pity your poor bloody husband.' He swallows the last of his beer and waves the glass in the direction of the bar. 'I'm going to get another Tusker.'

Tom comes back to the table and climbs on Helen's knee. She hugs him and says to Grace, over the top of his head, 'If you're absolutely determined to be such a martyr, I won't say another word. What can I do to help?'

'Money,' Grace tells her. 'Can you lend me the money for a ticket, I don't have enough.'
As it is, Helen decides Grace's visit to the morgue with her can be construed as work and the plane fare home is fair recompense. They drive the roads Grace remembers so well to *The Standard's* offices and Helen marches off to a small cubicle, Grace and Tom in tow, and presents the accountant with a chit for two air tickets to London. The man looks at it, and looks at Grace above his glasses, but when Helen leans on his desk and says,

273

'Today, preferably,' he scratches his signature along the bottom and hands it back.

Grace and Tom have a long afternoon to fill. There isn't time for another visit to the game reserve, but Helen takes them to Giraffe Manor to see the animals there. One of the giraffes, Betty June, is so tame she eats from Tom's hand, like a domestic pet, though Grace has to will herself not to snatch him away when she comes close.

Once they are back at Helen's house, and while she tries to conjure what little there is in her fridge into a meal, Grace persuades Tom to sleep for an hour, something he hasn't done since before his birthday, and she has a long bath. She relaxes in the warm water, and lets her mind wander. George will be home from school by now, wondering where she is. She's left enough behind her for him not to suspect she's left for good and, when she thinks of him worrying, has a moment of savage glee. He deserves it. She will send him a telegram when she lands in London, or perhaps get her father to ring the school. Grace pictures the phone ringing in the big house at the end of the drive and the headmaster having to let George use it. Surely, even Mr. Chegwe would have to agree an absconding wife counts as an emergency.

The British Airways flight is due to leave a few minutes after midnight. Grace waits her turn, the queue crawling to the check-in desk, as passengers of all ages and races wait to be allocated their seats. A young Asian girl, perhaps eighteen or nineteen, stands in front of Grace as they filter through. She reaches the desk and passes her papers over, a radiant smile on her face. The clerk reads the ticket, once, twice, and taps it with her pencil. She passes it back to the girl and says something Grace can't hear. The girl takes the ticket from her, scanning every word on it, and thrusts it back across the desk. The clerk has no time for her; she's already calling her next customer, Grace, to come forward.

'What's the matter?' Grace asks while her bag is being weighed.

'She's missed her flight.' The woman wraps a sticky label round the handle of Grace's bag. 'These Asian people think they're so clever and she can't even tell the time.' She grins at Grace. As she and Tom walk towards their gate, the girl is slumped on one of her bulging suitcases in the middle of the concourse, sobbing as if her heart would break.

'Are you alright? Don't cry, please don't cry.' Grace bends over and touches the girl on the shoulder. Tom hugs Grace's knee.

'The ticket said twelve, I thought it meant midnight. I don't know about this twenty-four hour clock. I didn't understand.' The girl looks at Grace. 'My plane went while I was eating my lunch. That woman said there is no more room; the plane is full. I will have to wait till tomorrow or the next day. Surely they can't punish me for a mistake?'

We're all punished for our mistakes, Grace thinks. She prays she and Tom really were lucky enough to get the last two free seats, and that the Asian girl, though she was careless, hasn't been the

275

victim of deliberate malice, but she suspects she has. How the tables turn in this country.

'Why are we going on a plane, Mummy?' Tom pulls at Grace's skirt. 'Where are we going?'

'We're going a long way, darling, so we need the plane. It's too far for Mummy to drive.'

'Are we going to the beach again? Will I be able to see the boatmen?' Tom stares up at Grace, his neck straining.

'No, not the beach. Not that beach, anyway.' Grace imagines Tom, next summer, hobbling over the pebbles at Whitstable, shivering in an English summer. 'You'll be able to see Nanna and Grandpa. You'll like that, won't you?'

Tom nods, but Grace can tell he hasn't any idea who she's talking about. She picks him up and carries him up the escalator, through the gate and onto the Boeing.

Their seats are near the back and Grace can look forward and see row upon row of empty seats; the plane is barely half full. Her heart sinks at the mindless nastiness of some of these people. Tom clambers into a window seat and kneels up, staring out as the engines are fired up and the plane readies for take-off. Even buckled in he manages to twist and keep his eyes on what's going on outside.

Grace watches over the top of his head as the plane cruises forward and begins to rise into the night sky. She can pick out the stream of cars on the tarmac road below by the glow of their headlights. As the plane climbs higher and higher the cars shrink to black dots, and Grace thinks of the safari ants marching through her compound, destroying everything that stood in their way.

Tom squirms in his seat and Grace unbuckles his belt now the light has gone off. She takes him onto her lap.

'Why didn't Daddy come?' he asks, sleepy, his thumb in his mouth.

'I told you, he's going to look after your dog for you. Besides, he's busy at work. He can't have holidays when he wants.' Grace rocks him, waiting for his eyelids to droop.

'Esther could have looked after Sungu, like last time. I want Daddy.'

'Daddy and Mummy are a bit cross with each other.' Grace strokes his silky hair. 'So Mummy thought she's take her favourite boy on an adventure.'

'Why are you cross? Did Daddy hurt you again?' Tom can barely talk, he's so close to sleep.

'No, but he told Esther something he shouldn't. He didn't keep a secret like he promised and that's made me very sad.' Grace moves along the row of empty seats so Tom can stretch out. She covers him with the thin blanket from the overhead locker. 'Daddy told Esther where Isaac was hiding.'

Tom eyes flicker open, their beautiful blue shining at Grace.

'No he didn't.' His small head shakes, blond hair flopping from side to side. 'I told her. I told her after Mrs. Cheggie was mean to us. Esther said Isaac was in lots of trouble and she had to help him so I said about the forest and the

277

medicine man and the charcoal men and the baby parrots.' He puts his thumb back in his mouth. 'Where's Isaac now, Mummy? I 'spect Esther will be kind to him.' He drifts off, a smile curving his mouth.

Grace sits upright in her seat throughout the flight; nine long hours to fill with memories and regrets and worry. She thinks of Isaac working in her garden for the first time, sun dancing off the *panga.* She remembers the touch of his hand, the sound of his voice, the fire in his eyes when he talked. If there had been no coup, would there have been a future for them? Probably not; he was right in that. If he wouldn't marry Akumu, what chance did she have?

Tom's confession has chilled her; not so much what he revealed but the fact it makes Grace realise how badly she has misjudged George. He had kept his word after all, and she doubted him to the end. She will write to him tomorrow, a long honest letter. Perhaps if he leaves Kenya and comes home they might yet rekindle some of the love they once had. It produced Tom, after all.

She lets her own eyes close, like Tom a smile hinting at her lips. Along with memory and regret and worry the hours are filled with one further emotion. Hope.

279

280

Bibliography

Adiga, Aravind, *Between the Assassinations,* Atlantic Books, London, 2010

Badejo, Babafemi A., *Raila Odinga;an Enigma in Kenyan Politics,* Yintab Books, Nairobi, 2006

Barnes, Julian, *The Sense of an Ending,* Jonathan Cape, London, 2011

Biddlecombe, Peter, *French Lessons in Africa,* Abacus, London, 1995

Booker, Christopher, *The Seven Basic Plots: why we need to tell stories,* Continuum, London, 2009

Bwakali, D.J., *The Birds and People of Kakamega Forest, Western Kenya,* www.environmentalafrica.com, retr. March 2012

Drayson, Nicholas, *A Guide to the Birds of East Africa,* Penguin, London, 2009

Gachuhi, Roy, *The Untold Story of the 1982 Coup Attempt in Kenya,* www.afroarticles.com, retr. March 2012

Hanif, Mohammed, *The Case of Exploding Mangoes,* Vintage, London, 2009

Jones, Norah (ed.), *Liquorice Ice Cream and Other Just Desserts,* Hird Publications, Hull, 2005

Kelman, Stephen, *Pigeon English*, Bloomsbury, London, 2011

Kumekucha, *The Chaos that was the 1982 Coup,* www.kumekucha.blogspot.com, ret. April 2012

Leon, Donna, *Drawing Conclusions,* Arrow, London, 2012

Levy, Andrea, *The Long Song,* Headline, London, 2011

Lodge, David, *A Man of Parts*, Vintage, London, 2012

Miller, Andrew, *Pure*, Sceptre, London, 2012

Moore, Peter, *Swahili for the Broken-Hearted*, Bantam, London, 2003

Morgenstern, Erin, *The Night Circus*, Harvill Secker, London, 2011

Shreve, Anita, *Rescue*, Abacus, London, 2012

Vogler, Christopher, *The Writer's Journey*, Michael Wiese Productions, USA, 2007

Waheed, Mirza, *The Collaborator*, Penguin, London, 2012

Young, Louisa, *My Dear, I Wanted to Tell You*, Harper Collins, London, 2011

Printed in Great Britain
by Amazon